BLIND SPIRIT

SCOURGE SURVIVOR SERIES – BOOK FOUR

JL MADORE

To those who love the Haven gang, so much has happened yet there is so much more still to come. I hope you come along with us.
To my Writers' Community of Durham Region family: You are without question, the greatest and most talented community of writers ever assembled. You energize me. I'm honored every day to be your President, your peer and part of the group. Rock on WCDR!

To my editors, Ruth and Gwynn of Writescape: The journey is nearing its end. Thank you for being there for every word and every sentence.

To my writing circles/guides, Critical Realm, BookEnds and the gang at 20Books: your critiques are invaluable, your support immeasurable, and your friendships irreplaceable. Much love.

PROLOGUE

*E*merging from the Portal Mirror, Galan nodded to the Talon soldiers awaiting the arrival of his family. He both admired and trusted Cowboy and Kobi, but his pregnant mate and his sister were the breath which filled his lungs. If there was any chance of danger, he wanted it taken care of before their arrival. "Are you certain the village is secure?"

Cowboy stepped toward him, his southern moniker accented by his loose-hipped swagger and the black cowboy hat he wore. "S'all clear, Highborne. No sign of trouble. No scent of Scourge. We posted men around the village and Aust has the wolves patrolling the trees. You're good to go."

Nausea swirled inside him, likely from the magical mode of travel but he feared the turmoil to be more.

When Galan nodded, Cowboy tapped the communicator at his ear. "All is well, Julian. Send them through."

If not for the spirit ceremony, Galan would never bring Lia back to the Highborne Village. It was, however, the last opportunity to do right for their beloved Tham. Dearest friend. Brother in all but blood. It was also precisely the type of event the Scourge would exploit to recapture his sister.

It was the first time he allowed Lia to leave Haven since her rescue eight months earlier. Given any choice, she would be there still.

CHAPTER ONE

The two Elves standing before me were dead—the first I understood, the second I did not.

Verily, I knew Cameron was dead, Aust's father had been killed when Scourge raiders attacked the village. But dressed in suede pants and a fine ivory tunic with his quiver stocked and slung across his back, the male looked as vital and solid standing at the crux of the rivers as he had my entire sixty years of life.

Shifting my gaze past our intimate group, I tried to discern if anyone else saw him. Aust? Elora? At the very least my brother should, Galan being the Sentinel of Souls, after all. But though the eight of us had been granted the ability to see Tham's spirit during his Veil ceremony, Tham seemed to be the only spirit the others saw.

"Lia, it is your turn, little one." Galan gestured to the water's edge.

Oh, yes. I stepped down the slight slope to the water's edge, the green leaf-pod I crafted that morning cupped in my palms. After choosing the brightest mallow leaves and the most succulently scented flowers in the rainforest, I wove them as tightly as I could, to honor our fallen brother.

May Tham's spirit sail on e'ermore.

As the little leaf-shaped vessel bobbed in the shallows, I recited the wish penned on the parchment sealed in its belly. "My wish for you, Thamior, is that your heart remains as full of life and love in the next phase of your *Ambar Lenn* as it has in this one. Blessings and abundance, brother-mine."

"Blessings and abundance," the group repeated.

I nudged my offering, sending it past the lazy ripples lapping the bank, to where the pull of the current snatched it up and swirled it down the river to join the others.

Brushing my damp fingers against the fabric of my gown, I straightened and stepped to stand before Tham, the male who—whether born of my blood or not, deceased or not—was my brother in every sense of the word.

He stood before me as all males in our Elven race: handsome, proud, lithe, lean, flaxen haired and fair of skin. But Tham held a mischievous light in his Highborne-blue eyes no other ever had and I doubted ever would again.

He was the purest joy, the truest love.

Stepping close, I whispered his soul name for our last goodbye. "*Amin melalle, Quynn.* You were taken from us far too soon."

He winked and raised his fingers to my cheek. I could not feel his ghostly touch, though I knew the warmth he exuded.

Amin mela lle, my sweet Ryanne. I love you as well.

Tham's speaking of my soul name was, as always, the most intimate sensation. It kindled warmth beneath my skin and brought my most private, guarded emotions to awakening. Soul names triggered a joining of souls. A merging of love. And now, with him having lived a mere century and one, he would never speak it again.

Galan handed me a handkerchief and after the others launched their wishes, we followed the sounds of celebration and headed to the ceremonial ruin site above the village.

The musicians filled the velvet night sky, their ballads gliding from the glittering crowd to the stars far above the ancient platform.

Though absent from the village since my capture, things remained as I remembered: the silk covered altar-stone buried beneath an endless bounty of refreshments, the torch-lighted mantel stones encircling the plateau clearing, their burning light raining down an ethereal glow from twenty feet above, and the couples linked together, swirling and swaying as one in gossamer and suede perfection.

The females' gowns and hair flowed behind them as males floated them around the dance floor in tailored slacks and velvet embroidered jackets.

The lonely longing of my absence evaporated in an instant.

I was home.

I inhaled the rainforest breeze and the scents of orchid and hyacinth greeted me. Tropical heat crept deep into my body and warmed my chilled soul. So much had happened since Galan, Aust and Tham ventured off on their *Ambar Lenn*.

So much would never be the same.

Life's Journey. I sighed at the painful naivety of life before their quest began. In the past eight months, Galan mated, was expecting twins and now served the God of gods. Aust lost his father, Cameron, had been stricken by the gods at Dragon's Peak and exiled from the village.

And Tham was dead.

No matter how many times I repeated those words to myself, I failed to believe them. On a morning no different than any other, he set off on a jog through the Haven forests. Set upon by Rheagan's minions, the most joyous male of our race was taken to a lost city of Fae and beaten to death for no reason other than to prove it could be done.

"Why aren't you dancing, sweetheart?" Cowboy asked, gesturing to the life celebration in progress before us.

My escort for the evening—Talon bodyguard in truth—the southern Were shifter, tilted the brim of his ebony hat toward the crowd. "You're pretty as a prize pony and a dozen young studs have already checked you out. Go on. Have some fun."

As much as I appreciated his kindness, the truth was, I could never ask a male to dance. That honor was of the male's choosing and, thus far, no male had been so inclined.

I twirled the end of the new ribbon woven into my hair and forced a smile. "My adventures outside the village have left me something of a pariah within the village, and those who would ask me as family are elsewhere."

Iadon had taken Nyssa and Ella to his cousin's cottage for a visit. Aust and his mother Elora were spending time at Cameron's pyre site while he was permitted entrance to the village. And after I promised Galan I wouldn't leave Cowboy's side, my brother took Jade for a forest tryst.

Cowboy frowned, the torchlight catching the gold reflection of his inner animal in his eyes. "It's a damn shame. If I wasn't on duty, I'd take you out on the floor for a spin."

I reached to my tiptoes and kissed his bristled cheek. "Fash not—I tire anyway. It has been quite a day."

"Hold that thought, sweetheart. I think you're up."

As a group of my peers made their way around the inside edge of the circle of stones, Cowboy retreated two steps in what I assumed to be an effort to appear less assuming.

Impossible. All Weres possessed an unavoidable draw. Strength. Power. When coupled with his southern drawl, warrior's build, and dressed in black leather battle gear, the Wolf drew the attention of all —male and female alike.

Durian led the trio striding toward us, dapper as ever in a long navy coat embellished with silver leaves sewn along the lapel. I smoothed my hands down my dress and ordered my quickened heart to settle. Many flowers had lost their petals while I daydreamed about that male in the south meadow.

He glanced over his shoulder at Kaya and Ava, as if he too was nervous. They proceeded until the three of them stood before me. "Lia," he said, "I wish . . . *we* wish to ask after you. Are you well?"

I inhaled his scent and the wings of butterflies fluttered against my insides. "I am well, though saddened for the reason of my return. Tham was a remarkable male."

Durian nodded. His hair had grown to midway down his chest while I was away, but still, it failed to hide how his ears flushed an adorable pink right to their gentle tips. "We heard . . . well, your *eda* told the council . . ."

He hesitated and I braced myself. I could only imagine what *Eda* told the council. My sire detested me from birth. In fact, today he had failed to acknowledge my existence at all. Galan and Jade ranked a loathing sneer from across the party. I seemed unworthy of even that.

Kaya crossed her arms over her now ample breasts. "Is it true you died and passed Behind the Veil?"

I adjusted the velvet mourning choker banding my throat. "Uh no, well, . . . in a fashion."

"And yet you returned? Were you turned away from the After?" The cool mockery in Kaya's tone caught me by surprise. We were friends. Or I thought we were.

"I did not die . . . exactly. Galan and Jade rescued me from my state and brought me back."

Kaya's gaze narrowed as she scowled. "How fortunate for you. Dozens of loved ones *did* die during your capture—Ava's father, Durian's brother—and yet your brother and his magic-wielding mate brought you back to live on?"

Ava stepped forward and flicked a lock of my hair. "To think, we admired the silver of your hair. So different. So beautiful. But it symbolizes you being the abhorrent offspring of a maniacal Queen and heir to Rheagan's throne."

Durian frowned. "Shall we bow to you, Lia? Now that you destroyed our lives and moved on to rule a realm which hates our very race?"

The party fell silent. My eyes shot around the ruin site. It skipped over the glimmering perfection, bounced off the accusing glares of strangers I had known and loved my entire life. "I am *not* the heir to the throne."

Kaya yanked the fist clenched at my side. Pulling it forward, she pried my fingers open. Hidden in the palm of my hand, gleamed a blue-diamond large enough the entire gathering could see it from any distance. "You wear the Queen's ring."

Vomit bit the back of my throat. Tears blurred my vision as I struggled for what to say. "I . . . the ring cannot be removed. If it could I would—"

Cowboy's snarl ripped through the night. The long rumbling timbre of his wolf vibrated in my chest. When his muscled frame shifted to stand at my side, my three friends stumbled back. In a blur, he pulled me tight to his side and Flashed me to Tham's cottage in the center of the village.

When he released me, I breathed through the sensations of magical travel: the flutter of my stomach, the airy lightness in my head and the squeezing of breath from my lungs.

They hated me. They blamed me. They thought I . . .

I turned and tried to . . . what? Where could I go? I had no home. Not in this pocketed village. Not in the Realm of the Fair. Gasping shallow breaths, I yanked the mourning band from my neck. "I cannot breathe."

"S'all good, sweetheart. That was bullshit up there. A few deep breaths and you'll be finer than frog hair."

The dead silence of the celebration above, echoed in my head. "I ruined their lives. I ruined Tham's celebration. I ruined my own family. I killed my mother simply by being born. Did you know?"

Cowboy grabbed at my flailing arms but I lurched free and headed for the river.

With trembling hands, I tugged the ribbons from my hair and threw them to the ground. Guilt and loathing crushed my lungs. I wished I was strong like Jade and Lexi. I wished . . . a lot of things. I wished I had a place . . . a purpose . . . a male to love me. The truth glowed in the eyes of my friends.

I had nothing.

I waded into the water, deeper and deeper still. I dragged my legs against the resistance until the current swept my skirt and soaked my bodice. My tears fell in earnest and the day overtook me. One more step and I could collapse into the inviting warmth of the river mouth and be lost. I would let myself sink. The weight of my grief would pull me down. Down until my boots touched the pebbled bottom. Down until the world disappeared and the hurt washed away.

My lungs would burn with the urgent need to draw breath, but I would hold fast until oblivion claimed me.

Durian is wrong, sweeting. Cameron stood on the river bank opposite me, his wide, callused palms open. *The village attack was the act of a madman and his quest to rule the realm. You are no more responsible for your ancestry than Aust for being born with his gift to speak to animals. Naught of this is your doing. I do not blame you.*

I pounded my fist against the unrelenting pressure which had compressed my chest for months. "They came for *me*. You and the others were killed because of *me*."

And you carry that with you always.

I rubbed my forehead. It felt like someone cleaved my skull in two and my body failed to recognize I was dying. In the throbbing haze of one of my worst headaches yet, I glanced around. "Oh, gods, what do I do?"

Your best, neelan. Is all you can do.

Lost in the impossibility of my life, the current tugged on my sopping gown, inviting me into the depths. I looked back to the riverbank. It was empty. Had Cameron truly been there or was my mind so far off that insanity conjured him?

Strong arms wrapped around my shoulders as Cowboy hugged me from behind. He rested his chin on top of my head and exhaled. "You're scaring the stuffing out of me, sweetheart, just so you know. Yelling at the riverbank is one thing, but I don't like you pondering a midnight swim. And FYI, Weres can't swim. We sink. So, if it's all the same to you, how's about we get our feet back on dry ground?"

Without waiting for an answer, he turned my shoulders and led me back toward the bank.

"Apologies," I said, my voice thick with tears. "I am so embarrassed ... weary ... and ..."

"Lost." He stopped us in the shallows and set my hair behind my shoulder. "You're a little lost right now, Lia, but other than your pretty dress getting waterlogged, there's no damage done. Just you and me taking an unexpected stroll in the river."

I looked down at the two of us standing drenched in our clothes and would have laughed had my heart not been breaking. "They hate me, Cowboy. Everyone I ever loved despises me."

A shadow fell over Cowboy's gaze as if he felt the ache of my pain himself. "That's their loss."

"And simply not true, sweeting." Standing on the bank with his mother, Aust offered me a hand out of the water. His ice-blue cat's eyes held so much compassion, I wondered how anyone could miss the gentle soul he was. "We heard about what Durian and the others said to you. If anyone knows the cut of Highborne judgment, it is me. The attack was not your fault. Anyone with an ounce of Elven logic will agree."

Elora wrapped an arm around my shoulder. "It seems we have all outgrown this village. Let us leave this narrow-minded aristocracy behind once and for always."

CHAPTER TWO

*O*ver the next weeks, I put things behind me and sought a
productive place in Haven society. Easier planned than
executed, considering Galan's obsession to ensure my safety. He felt
too many unsavory characters frequented the Hearthstone. I was not
qualified to work at The Academy of Affinities. And no matter how I
tried, I could not convince him to let me work in the market square in
one of the merchant shops. Helping in Jade's clinic was deemed the
only suitable place for me.

"Pretty sure those herbs have learned their lesson," Jade said.

I glanced at the dried mixture within the pestle and released my
steel grip on the marble mortar. "Apologies, I fell to distraction. I'll
clean this up."

Before I could take my first step, a bloodied trio Flashed into the
center of the room.

"A werewolf, a demon and a mute walk into a bar." Cowboy
coughed. "Gods, I wish this was a bar."

Cowboy's joke fell flat as his fellow warriors staggered under his
weight and headed toward the stainless-steel operating table. All three
Talon Enforcers looked in need of medical care, but it was Cowboy
who wore his innards across the front of his blood-drenched leathers.

"Yeah, buddy," Kobi said, easing Cowboy's battle vest off his broad shoulders, "we'll hit the Hearthstone as soon as Blaze can Humpty Dumpty you together again. Promise."

Jade tied her long, burgundy curls away from her face and surveyed the group. "Shit boys, take a drink now and it would likely leak out the holes. Here. Get him up so I can see what I'm dealing with."

Savage, the largest and most fearsome of the Enforcers, bled heavily from his arm. Still, he shifted support under Cowboy's shoulder while Kobi struggled under the other.

"Shit, Wolf," Kobi grunted, "ever hear of Jenny Craig? You're a walking hernia."

"Pussy." Cowboy's ashen complexion drained further as they moved him. Brow tight and slick with perspiration, the male's bloody hands covered his abdomen in an effort to hold his organs in place.

As his brothers-in-arms shifted him to the surgical table, an inhuman snarl echoed off the pale green walls of the clinic. Weres were temperamental, violent creatures at the best of times. Injured Weres, well, they were downright dangerous when their animals felt vulnerable.

I stiffened as Cowboy bared his teeth.

Jade grabbed his jaw and held his half-lidded gaze. "Don't you shift on me. With this jumbled mess, there's no telling where your insides will end up. I mean it, Wolf. Stand down."

As Cowboy fought for control of his wolf, Jade massaged her nails through his hair and sang to him. Her voice, mesmerizing in its magical tone, rose in rich, seductive notes. My heart beat slower and my body grew heavy.

Cowboy's eyes returned to their usual caramel gold and he nodded. "S'all good, Blaze. I got this."

The acrid tang of blood burned my sinuses and churned my stomach. I crossed the room and fetched the stainless-steel rolling cart of surgical supplies.

A healer by birth, Jade was a true force. A female accustomed to such scenes, she studied the wound as she snapped on gloves. Her smile remained genuine and her scent confident and calm. "Wow, you really got sliced and diced. Did you at least get the guy who did this?"

Cowboy rolled his head on the table, his focus weak. "Bet your ass . . . lit the fucker up like a Christmas tree."

Jade nodded in approval, drew the knife sheathed to her thigh and slid it up each pant leg of Cowboy's leathers. In a graceful series of motions, the male's pants were removed and a cotton drape covered his bare hips.

Swallowing hard, I forced down the retch building in the back of my throat and breathed through my mouth. Jade prepared a syringe and I turned away. Mayhap I should excuse myself and go out to the corridor—

"Lia, breathe past it, I need you."

I swallowed. "Of course, how can I be of aid?"

Jade leaned close to the wound and gently shifted the mound of pale intestines as they coiled and flopped loose. "Okay, it doesn't smell like the bowel or anything's been perforated, but I can't see what I'm dealing with. Glove up and give me a hand while I look under this mess?"

It took me a moment to realize she literally wanted me to give her my hands. After pulling on a pair of latex gloves, I fixed my gaze on her emerald green eyes across the table. Holding my arms out, I let her place them where she needed.

"Perfect, don't move." Jade's song filled the space once more and I let my mind drift. When involved in extensive healings, her bard powers helped her connect with her healing powers. The song she sang now was an Elven ballad I knew well. I sang along to distract myself.

With my eyes closed and lost in the entrancing cadence of Jade's healing voice, I startled when she spoke next. "Got it, Lia, you can step away and help the others."

Loose limbed, I peeled off the gloves and went to the sink to wash up. In the time I aided Jade with Cowboy, Kobi had removed his battle vest, his grime-covered muscle shirt, and stapled the curved knife wound across his hip.

Most of the demon's visible skin was either mottled with purple and blue, or smeared with blood. Finished with his own injuries, Kobi regarded the gash running the length of Savage's forearm. "Extra points for exposed bone, Sav. That's nasty. Staple or stitch?"

Savage signaled a response with his hands and blood squirted in a streaming spray.

"Stitch it is." Kobi propped himself on a stool opposite Savage and worked for some time with his fingers inside Savage's arm. The stench of burning flesh suggested he called upon something in his demon nature to cauterize the wound. Withdrawing his fingers, he closed the flaps of skin beneath his grip and began stitching.

I gripped the counter. "Jade shall heal you if you wait."

The stark overhead light of clinic reflected off the line of platinum piercings puncturing Kobi's brow. He also had one through his left nipple. Kobi caught me staring and smiled. "Jade has her hands full with our boy over there. Besides, I've become quite a little seamstress over the years. Not to the level of Iadon, mind you, but I can Martha Stewart a leak."

The demon unwound a length of black suture thread and returned his attention to Savage's wound. He pulled the thread taut and tightened the black loop of the stitch until it pinched his fellow warrior's skin together. Each time it gathered more flesh, another trickle of scarlet pulsed from the cavity of the gaping wound. Blood ran off Savage's tattooed forearm and dripped a steady stream to the surface of the supply counter.

I thought again about retreating to the corridor. Given the quiver in my legs and the slow spin of the room, mayhap it was best not to move. Closing my eyes, I absorbed the muffled laughter and chatter beyond the closed door of the clinic. The bustle beyond the clinic accompanied the sea of students flowing from one course of study to another.

The Academy of Affinities amazed me, from the language and informality of the students, to the emboldened interactions, to the enlightened notion of males regarding females as strong and equal.

"Lia?" Kobi said, his nostrils flared. "You all right?"

Could demons smell emotions like Elves and Weres? I pressed my shoulders back. "Of course. May I assist you?"

Kobi's charcoal eyes narrowed and studied me for a long, awkward moment. He tilted his head. "You could snag me a couple more rolls of gauze and some medical tape from the tall cabinet by the window."

I whirled away from his macabre ministrations and strode across the clinic. The cabinet in question was arranged in orderly rows of all manner of supplies: bandages, burn ointment, unguents, disinfectant swabs and remedies. Rolls and packets of gauze sat piled in a woven wicker basket on the second shelf from the top. I took out a couple large rolls, retrieved the bottle of antiseptic Jade used to flush wounds, and picked up the white medical tape and cutters.

As I passed by the surgical table, I cast a quick glance to the surgery table. Jade had managed to return Cowboy's insides back *in* which was no small feat. I returned to Kobi and Savage and tore the gauze free from its paper wrapping.

"Verily, you males are brave beyond good sense. With the Scourge rising, you must needs take better care. There are those of us who worry about your welfare."

Kobi threaded the loop and tugged the thread into a knot. "You don't hear Sav complaining, do you?"

Savage, who had been left mute after a blade severed his voice box as a teen, raised his middle finger.

Kobi laughed. "There's nothing like a little pain to remind you that you're alive. Besides, it looks worse than it is. Just caught a bleeder, nothing vital."

When he gestured to the cutters, I snipped the thread and handed Savage the bottle of liquid.

The ink-skulled warrior took what I offered, stalked to the sink and rinsed the blood away before opening the antiseptic and pouring it over his wound. Though the students often reeled from the sting of the cleanser, Savage appeared to take no notice as it hissed and bubbled across his decorated forearm. When he turned back, our gaze met.

The male exuded a haunting anger: dark features, dark scent, dark soul. What horrors must a male endure to grow so hardened and utterly violent?

Reaching above the sink, I fetched a towel and put my fear out of my mind. After he blotted the wound dry, I laid the gauze over the long, puckered gash. Despite my body's urge to step away, I taped it in place. With his arm repaired, my attention turned to the blood dripping off the table and pooling on the ivory clinic tiles.

Kobi brushed past me on his way to the utility closet. "Don't worry about the mess, Lia. We're fully housebroken. I'll clean this up."

Ashamed as I was that Kobi had to mop up after battling evil, it was either that or revisit my morning repast.

"Lia?" Jade's asked, "Could you bring me a damp cloth and a towel. We're done here." Jade gently wiped Cowboy's belly and patted his upper chest. "Right as rain, Wolf. Now shift and go curl up on one of the recovery beds for a few hours of healing sleep. If you're good, you'll get to the main house before Elora rings the dinner bell."

Cowboy accepted Jade's help sitting up and nuzzled his face into her neck and against her cheek. I had seen Weres do this before with her. It was the animal's way of showing affection. His usually golden skin remained far too pale for my liking, but with what seemed like the sheer force of his will, he eased his naked self from the table, staggered down the hall, and ducked into the first recovery room.

"He'll be fine," Jade said, setting a hand on my shoulder. "The recovery of any Were in a healing sleep is remarkable. Cowboy is a Beta wolf and a survivor. It'll take him no time."

"Yeah," Kobi said, "by dinner, he'll be cranky, horny, and starving. Good as new."

Jade yawned, her hand rubbing a gentle circle over her belly. The bulge of my brother's twins forced her smock shirt away from her rounding figure. She pulled the elastic binding her deep red curls and shook her hair free. The richness of the color was contrasted by the shining silver of Galan's mating braid hanging to the side of her face.

I was about to suggest she go lie down for a few hours herself when Kobi's phone rang. He tugged it from the back pocket of his tight black jeans. "Yeah? Sure. On our way."

He strode across to where he'd set his belongings, regarded his tattered shirt and tossed it in the garbage bin. "Sorry, ladies, duty calls. You ready, Sav?" After pulling his battle-vest over his bare chest, Kobi checked his knives, patted his pockets, and shrugged his heavy duster over his shoulders.

"What's doing?" Jade asked.

Setting a cigarette between his lips, he patted his pockets. "Not sure. Julian caught a spike of unsanctioned magical energy along the perimeter of the north forest. Could be Scourge opening a bolt-hole."

"Or it could be a couple Lightning Sprights getting busy in the woods," Jade said.

Kobi nodded. "Take care of our canine. We'll be back to take him for that drink in a few hours." He shrugged his lean, muscled shoulders into his jacket and checked that Savage was ready.

"But," I said, raising my hand, "you just sewed yourselves up. Surely, there are others who could—"

Kobi exhaled a cloud of sweet-smelling smoke. "No rest for the wicked, babycakes. Talon is working double time these days."

After a quick nod, the two Flashed and were gone.

When Jade turned to the mess of her operating table I drew a deep breath and retrieved the cleaning supplies. "Jade, you are exhausted. Go lie down. Allow me to clean this up."

Jade chuckled and arched an elegant brow. "No offense hon, but if you start cleaning the blood, we'll have vomit to clean up too. Clinic gore isn't your strong suit."

My ears warmed. Jade grasped her purpose better than any female I knew and I knew nothing of mine. "Yes, well, until we discover what my strong suit is, Galan has tasked me to assist you as I am able. I mean to. Please. Go rest."

Jade raised a hand to her neck and absently swept her bridal pendant along its silver chain. After studying my resolve, she conceded. "Maybe just for a little while. I have things to do later."

❧

For the remainder of the morning, I tidied the surgical area, inventoried the stockroom for herbs, medicinals, and unctions, and readied for the next barrage of wounded. With the rise in Scourge activity, it seemed the endless threat of wounded hovered without end.

Verily, Jade needed help, and though Lexi's mate Rowan—a gifted surgeon—came when needed, and I admired the work they did with all my heart, I was not the female for the job. I would have to find a way to convince Galan that this was not my place.

Since my kidnapping, I had imagined this madness ending. I dreamed of returning to the village, being courted and mated by a gentlemale, and living a productive life. In my dream, Galan and Jade visited often and their young, who would grow up playing and laughing with my own.

The picture had been so clear in my mind, I believed I could will it into reality. My return to the Highborne village shattered that dream. Now, I wondered where the Fates and my future would take me.

As Cowboy said—I was lost.

"Jade? Are ye here, Luv?" The cadence of Samuel's voice was recognizable even before I came out of the stockroom and saw the raven-haired male. My heart went out to him. The unfortunate soul, was seven months into his recovery from a magical explosion and no matter what attempts Jade and the other doctors, healers, and wizards made, he remained blind as a star-nosed mole.

Meticulous in his appearance, he wore slacks, a silk shirt and a worn leather slicker. As much as I wished to support my brother's hatred of Jade's previous suitor and despise him on principle, Samuel risked his life to save me from the Scourge and then lost his sight while rescuing Bruin's mate, Mika, from her captivity with the same vile group.

Friend or foe, the male was undeniably heroic.

"Apologies, Samuel," I said, sliding the stockroom door closed behind me and joining him by the examination table. "Jade is sleeping in one of the recovery beds. Was she expecting you?"

Samuel retrieved his tinted glasses from his pocket and covered his sightless, diamond-white eyes. "Aye, she was, but if she's resting, let her be. My exam will keep."

The scent of his concern filled the air as strongly as his affection. And though I knew Jade would never love another to the depths she loved my brother, she held a special warmth and gentleness for her ex-suitor as well.

"It is thoughtful of you to let her rest. She exhausted herself healing Cowboy this morning and with the pregnancy—" I winced as his frame stiffened. "Apologies, that was insensitive of me."

He scrubbed his palm over his darkened jaw and exhaled. "Cowboy was hurt, ye say. Is the Wolf all right?"

"Perfection in every way," Cowboy said, stepping out of his recovery room. He stretched, naked in the hall and as he strode forward to join us, he accessed his powers and clothes appeared magically upon him. "Hey Merlin, we missed you this morning. Your blue bolts zinging through the air would have been a welcome addition while we cracked Scourge heads in Deleran."

Samuel frowned. "Deleran? Abaddon's army started a mangle with the Centaurs? What would possess them?"

"He's crazier than a shit-house rat?"

Samuel glanced down the corridor and stepped toward his friend. "Does Jade know the Centaurs were attacked? Chiron wasn't hurt, was he? The old man was her tutor for years and the two of them are still tight."

Cowboy shook his head, his tri-colored flaxen hair still matted with sweat and filth. "A few guards along the wall got messed up, but not too bad. Chiron called Reign in as soon as the scouts detected Scourge movement in the forest. The bastards hadn't even had the chance to make a run at the gate by the time we got there. Score one for the good guys."

Samuel raised an ebony brow. "The Centaurs called for help?"

"Times, they are a'changing, Merlin. Reign's made it clear to all races we can't let Abaddon's army gain ground with Rheagan floating around. The Talon is on call 24/7 to ensure we keep those fuckers at bay. Even still, it's an uphill climb."

Samuel rubbed his eyes under his mirrored glasses. "Ye won't be able to keep it up forever. What happens then?"

Cowboy shrugged. "No idea, but I gotta skedaddle. Lia, where'd you hide my weapons, sweetheart?"

I opened the cupboard by the door and handed him his leather vest, weapons, and his bolo-necktie. "Jade wants to assess your condition before you leave, Cowboy."

He winked and lifted the hem of his shirt to show me the long pink line across his tight, rippled belly. "As much as I'd love a sponge bath and some extra-special TLC, I'm ready to saddle up. Don't you worry. I'll roll over and let Jade rub my belly at dinner."

I laughed and retrieved his black hat. "I swear you say the craziest thing that pops into your head."

Cowboy slung his necktie and vest on and checked his phone. "Damn, Reign called a debrief an hour ago and I slept through half of it. Gotta dash. See y'all later."

The moment Cowboy Flashed out to join his fellow warriors, Samuel's expression went blank. To look at him, one could see only a devilishly handsome wizard with black hair and mirrored sunglasses. I smelled the ache of his loss. The male was a warrior—a hero likely ne'er to battle again.

To give him a moment, I hung my apron on the hook by the door and gathered my wrap. "Fash not, Samuel, I am certain Jade will figure out your sight—"

When I touched his arm, he recoiled and caught the corner of the exam table. He toppled back in a windmill of hands, cursing wildly. Fearing he would fall, I grabbed his arm. In the next instant, my head buzzed.

We had Flashed.

The moment my feet fell on solid ground, I released his arm and waited for my skin to stop tingling. We stood at the edge of a tree line, the bank of a stream winding across a rolling countryside. "Where have you brought us?"

Samuel lowered a glare on me, the solid glow of his white eyes as eerie as it was beautiful. Even without sight, the male seemed to direct his anger with quite a degree of accuracy.

His lifted his chin and barked a laugh. "I dinnae bring us anywhere. Why would ye touch a man about to Flash? Are ye not right in the head? Ye know how dangerous it is, aye? If ye let go during our travels—"

The ringing in my ears persisted. "You caught your hip on the table. I meant to stabilize you, not intrude."

"Weel, ye have." He crossed his arms over his chest and gave me the muscled span of his back. Though he was not banded with brute strength as Bruin, Reign, or some of the other Talon, Samuel was built with sleek power. The rigid tension in those shoulders all too evident. "Ye have no business bein' here."

"Yet here we are." I pulled my wrap tighter around my shoulders. The sky hung a solid gray, overcast with a cold drizzle misting in the breeze. "You did this. I simply wanted to tell you I am saddened—"

His finger thrust in the air between as he whirled on me. "Dinnae speak of my life, Elf. Ye have no right."

My skirts rustled and frozen grass crunched beneath my feet as I moved to edge of the wide stream.

Winter's ice had all but melted off the surface of the water. The last few patches and clumps clung to the edges of the bank, while a steady trickle of water danced over the stones breaking the sparkling surface. Where the flow was interrupted, the current spun and detoured this way around the rocks, meandering toward a bend down the way.

Samuel leaned his shoulder against an aged oak and reached to capture the rope of an old plank swing. His fingers closed around the worn gray fibers and he swung the seat in a slow arc staring unseeingly over the water.

The landscape struck me. The foliage grew thinner than any I had seen since living in my valley. I searched the sky for the purple peaks of the Haven mountains. The sky and ceiling above spanned in a vast gray sea of nothing, save a few birds passing. I spun a full circle.

"Have we left the sanctuary of the mountain?" Samuel ignored me and my chest tightened. "Please, warrior, where have you brought me?"

If we were not on Haven grounds the Scourge could come. Galan told me Abaddon needed me for his plan to reinstate the power of the exiled Queen. And here I was. Unprotected. I fumbled with the collar of my dress, tugging at my mourning band. Where had the air gone from this clearing? My pulse rushed through my ears like a thundering waterfall.

"Lia?" Samuel's voice registered distant and faint.

My face grew wet. Tears dripped off my chin.

"Lia, what's wrong? What is it?"

Strong hands manacled my wrists as I struggled with my collar.

"I cannot breathe." A dark, unbearable weight pressed on my chest, forcing the air from my lungs.

"Settle, lass, and I'll help ye." He pushed away my trembling fingers, unsnapped the mourning band and pressed his hand flat against my skin. "*Pax vobiscum.*"

At his command, a rush of warm serenity washed through me. It tingled from the tips of my ears to the tips of my toes. My lungs opened. My hands steadied. And the splotches clouding my vision cleared. I closed my eyes and inhaled, grateful for the crisp forest air filling my lungs.

Once I regained some composure, I opened my eyes.

His hand still rested warmly on my flesh, his magic tingling through my body. Close as he was, and momentarily distracted from his hatred of me, my family and my race in general, I was struck by the male. Dark for my light, in hair and skin, he stood taller than I, yet only enough for me to tilt my chin upward to meet his blind gaze.

"Gratitude, Samuel. I am well enough now."

He withdrew. "How long have ye suffered panic attacks?"

I straightened my hair and ran my hands down my skirts before remembering there was no need. Grateful for a few moments of unseen impropriety I breathed deep once more. "Since the Scourge caverns."

A manly spice overpowered the bitter scent of his usual hostility. "I'm sorry ye suffer, truly."

"Apologies, it occurs to me that I never properly thanked you for my recovery."

Samuel waved his hand in the air between us. "Don't—"

"No, I must. If not for you and all you sacrificed, I—"

"—I was duty bound—nothing more." Samuel drew his wand from the pocket of his slicker and ran his fingers along the polished wood. "So, what set ye off, just now?"

I brushed firm hands down the front of my skirt and stared at the toes of my boots peeking beneath the hem. Verily, if he could refuse to listen to my thoughts, I could do the same.

"Ye haven't left Haven since we got you back, is that it?"

"I went to my village a few weeks ago."

"But other than then."

"Galan warned that I must never leave Haven for I shall live the rest of my days hunted by the Scourge."

"He dinnae say it like that?" Samuel barked a laugh. He screwed up his expression as if something were distasteful to him. "Yer brother actually said the Scourge will hunt ye for the rest of yer life, so dinnae think about leaving Haven?"

"Is it not the truth?"

"It may be, but after all ye went through, I'm sure there was a nicer way to phrase it so ye weren't quite so frightened? No wonder ye panic."

I searched the surrounding trees for movement or sound beyond the scurry of woodland creatures waking from winter slumber. The breeze was crisp, the only scent in the air remained the clean scent of male and a subtle hint of what the males of the house called cologne.

"Truth is truth," I said. "There is no need to soften words to make them more palatable. Does it ease you when people avoid the fact you are blind and can no longer fight with the Talon? Does it make the loss any less of a reality for you?"

"No," he said, his jaw twitching. "It cheeses me off."

"So, you prefer when people are direct with you."

"I do."

"As do I." I stepped toward the embankment, running my fingers up the column of my throat, thankful to breathe easy. "I would rather meet what comes than be caught unaware."

"Really? Ye strike me more as a bottle-it-up and pretend-it-didn't-happen type." He moved back to the swing and sat on the plank seat. With his feet firmly on the packed earth, he moved the swing in a slow pendulum.

"You know naught of me," I said. "I was taken, held as a prisoner, and rescued by you, my brother, and the others. Frightening as it was, I acknowledge what happened."

When no reply came, I turned. Samuel stared at me, tracking me as if by the sound of my movement. I paced a small circuit along the bank.

"If we're being direct, that's not all that happened. Is it?"

No. My heart beat faster. Abaddon captured my soul and meant to force me into his service. I remained suspended in the nether realm, Behind the Veil, for weeks, neither dead nor alive. "It was more complicated, yes."

Samuel's blind stare held, his brow arched as if he waited for more.

"I refuse to dwell on it any further."

"Fair enough." He shrugged and stood. "Look, we're nae friends, so ye needn't tell me shit, but you touted the virtues of brutal honesty a moment ago. Stick to yer story and I'll never say a word, but remember, Lia, I was there."

"What is that supposed to mean? You think I lie?"

His mouth curved up in a sly smile. "Just what I said, lass. As far as I'm concerned people can spill it, bury it, or drink themselves into the ground. If ye want to smile and spread feckin sunshine and rainbows, have at it."

No wonder Galan and Lexi detested this man to the extent they did. I propped my hands on my hips. "And this lesson on virtue comes from the male who threw away and then stabbed the woman he loved, yet continues to pretend he is merely one of her closest friends? You may be able to fool Jade into believing your sunshine and rainbows,

Samuel, but I smell your wanton anguish when you near my brother's mate and there is nothing frank or honest about it."

Samuel stiffened and a vicious rambling curse about Highbornes filled the damp air.

I clenched my fists to my sides and fought the impulse to speak my mind. How I wished I was less of a female of worth. Never had I uttered an oath but those living in Jade's home cursed so freely I knew what I would say. Pressing my palms against my thighs, I calmed my thoughts. "I shall not force my Highborne presence upon you any longer, Samuel. If you would return me to Haven, we need never speak again."

"Suits me fine, Elf." Stepping forward, he reached out. When I offered him my hand, he clamped hard around my wrist and in the next moment, we Flashed.

CHAPTER THREE

$\mathcal{M}$y fingers tingled hot with the sensation of nettles after Samuel released his grip. I rubbed my wrist and sighed as I made a slow turn, scanning my surroundings. The turrets and peaks of the main castle rose beyond the skeletal treetops. In the distance to my left, the patina of Jade's rooftop glistened beneath the afternoon sun.

Samuel Flashed us into the forest off the main path.

"Do ye need me to walk ye back?" His eyes were blank, his face as stark as the air between us.

"I think not." I tipped my head back and cupped my mouth releasing a sharp *eeyloooo* from the back of my throat. A replying howl echoed through the trees and, after a moment, the scrub rustled and swayed with life. "The wolves will see me safely home." Without awaiting a reply, I gathered my skirt and swept off for the main path.

Nightrunner, the Haven pack alpha, padded in beside me. He cocked his wide russet head, his amber eyes taking in my resolute stride. Glancing behind us, the wolf pulled his ears back and released a slow, curious growl.

"Fash not, friend. He may hate Highbornes but, in truth, we are none so fond of him either."

Nightrunner raised his head and pricked his ears back and forth. Several others from the pack filled in around us. Faolan, Aust's closest companion from the village, nudged my thigh and I bent to give her a pat. Her silver coat clumped a little with the need to shed her winter heft but she remained one of the most striking wolves of the pack.

A stiff March wind raced through the tree tops stirring a tumult of dried leaves and detritus upon us. Dismissing the uneasiness of my interlude with Samuel, I squealed and ran. The wolves paced me, nipping at the air.

The cool breeze slapped my cheeks and sent another wave of leaves and scrub upon us. Laughing, I picked several from my hair before moving on.

Tightening my wrap around my shoulders, I looked to the sky. Wherever Samuel Flashed us earlier, it was a good distance away for this skyline held hope and warmth behind Haven's mountainous peaks.

"Samuel was vexed," I said to Faolan beside me. "Is it wrong that a small part of me delighted to see him annoyed?" Yes, it was. The wolves paid no mind to my musings and we plodded in companionable silence.

Lost in the search of what Jade found so endearing about Samuel, I jolted when Nightrunner crossed my path. The russet fur of his hackles raised and his ears pressed back. A low growl rumbled from his chest and the rest of the pack took their cue and closed ranks.

Scanning the shadows and sounds of the forest, I stilled and drew a deep breath. Nothing.

Faolan dropped her head low and bared her sharp, white teeth. "What alarms you, girl?"

I followed her line of sight. A young girl sat well back from the path, perched on the large knotty burl of a red cedar. Shaggy brown hair hung to her chest, hiding her face as she bent forward and wept. Thank the gods, it was just a girl. Not Scourge. No danger. After searching the trees and path, I felt certain we were alone.

"Hello?" As I closed the distance between us, I tugged, freeing the hem of my skirt from the grasp of prickly scrub. Nightrunner blocked my way, shouldering my thigh and impeding my progress. I glanced through the shadows and shapes of the forest. "All is well, boy."

He swung his head from me back to the girl, releasing a throaty growl. The subordinate pack members circled, shoulders raised, heads down and eyes riveted on our sad, forest friend.

I moved to step beyond my protectors. Nightrunner lifted his lips and flashed his canines. *Snap.* He bit the air between us. *Snap.* He threatened me again.

"What possesses you? I appreciate your concern, but this girl poses no danger."

Nightrunner strode no closer, whether he was offended I ignored his warning or too frightened to follow. Having heard how he and his pack tore Scourge warriors to bits in battles past, I doubted his motivation could be fear.

"Hello?" I said again. As I drew close, an icy gust blew up my skirt, raising the fine hairs on my flesh. "Are you well?"

She met my gaze. "Are you speaking to me?"

I gestured to a mossy log adjacent to her. "May I sit?"

The girl studied me with a strange expression, her brows raised behind shaggy brown bangs accenting piercing turquois eyes. "I, uh, people don't speak to me . . . ever." Her mouth opened, closed, and opened again. "Who are you?"

"I am Lia, merry meet, and who are—"

A shrill screech pierced the air and a giant red-tailed hawk swooped at my head. The weighty flap of wings sounded close to my ear as feathers brushed my cheek. Raising my arms, I hunched and scrabbled to my feet. The great bird maneuvered between the leaf-bare trees, pivoted and returned.

Again, its sharp shriek cut the air. Mighty talons extended towards me like hooked daggers. I ducked. The thud of the raptor's claws against my back was painless but brought an icy realization. "You thieving scoundrel."

Amazed, I raced after the rust tailfeathers of the bird making away with my favorite wrap. Pale lavender chenille billowed and flapped where it hung beneath the great bird. The mischievous beast tilted and soared through trees pumping its wings to keep my property beyond reach.

A gleam of silver metal flashed against the cool, gray afternoon. Wherever was she taking me? The scrub thinned, the surrounding trees growing taller and more imposing.

I giggled at the absurdity of the entire escapade.

I leapt from the path. Silky tails of fringe narrowly evaded my grasp, but then, the beast's talons released and my shawl fluttered and fell to the forest floor.

The gleam of silver caught my eye once more and I assessed where I—"Jade!"

My wrap fell a few meters from Jade's motionless form. I bolted to her side and dropped to my knees. She lay face down, half hidden by loose brush pulled to cover her. I flung it away. Dear gods. Her knit sweater-coat was twisted like a noose around her swollen belly, her auburn locks matted with blood. "Jade, wake up. Wake, sister mine."

Faolan barked once and bolted off along the path. The wolves took up position around us.

I eased her limp frame to her back. She made no sound. Her chin was gashed, a deep purple bloom pooling across her jaw. "Please, Jade. Please open your eyes."

I pressed my fingers to her neck as I watched her do many times in the clinic. Her skin was not nearly warm enough and only the faintest rhythm met my touch. "Oh, gods."

Brushing the dirt from her face, I looked her over. Even unconscious, her palm cupped the mound of her belly.

"You need to call for help." It was the girl from the tree. She leaned over my shoulder looking worried, pointing down. "She keeps her phone in her right front pocket."

It was not there. I searched the ground. There. The reflection of light from the phone's surface was the silver flash. I lunged to untangle it from the grass, my fingers fluttering like a moth in wind. After several tries, I managed to flip it open.

"How does it work?" I stared at the contraption as moments ebbed by. What if I could not summon help in time? What if Jade and the young died because I was too daft in this world to call for aid? I shoved the phone at the girl. Her face blurred behind the wall of my tears. "Please. Help me call someone."

She pointed again. "Push the star and then the button that looks like the bird's talon."

I swiped my sleeve across my eyes, pushed the buttons and pressed the phone to my ear.

"Yo, Blaze. Whassup?"

"Julian! Julian, it is Lia. I need help. Hurry. Jade is unconscious and bleeding. Someone has attacked her."

On the other end of our connection there rained a hasty tapping of fingers to keyboard. Jade's adopted brother held an unmatched intellect. He would know what to do. "Okay, Lia, where are you?"

I scanned the forest but my bearings were skewed from chasing the hawk. Where was I? Oh gods, please, where was I? "I cannot say. Oh gods, Julian—"

"Okay. The GPS on the phone is activated. Are you all right? Are the attackers gone?"

I glanced around. "Yes . . . yes, I believe so."

The tapping of keys continued. "Okay, I gotcha. Hang tight." Julian's voice grew distant as he spoke away from the phone. "All call. Campus grounds. We have a hostile. Blaze is down. Sending coordinates to all systems now."

The air surged with energy and Talon Enforcers Flashed in. Daggers, swords, and wands were drawn. First Reign appeared and then Savage, Julian, Cowboy, Sin, Rue . . .

"She will need Galan," I said. "And Bruin's phone fails when he is deep within the Dens."

Julian grabbed the leather cord around his neck and pulled out his skirl pendant. Made from one of Bruin's shed bear claws, the talisman was a powerful tool to call his brother. Putting the satin finish of the claw to his mouth, Julian blew, long and hard.

The response was instant.

"Julian?" Bruin Flashed in at a ready stance.

His gaze flashed first to his brother and then to Jade lying motionless in front of me. He growled, lunging forward and dropped to the ground. "Lia? Who did this?"

"I cannot say. I found her thus."

"Give her a sniff, son," Reign said. "We'll take care of Jade, you and the boys hunt and flay the bastard."

Bruin leaned close to her cheek and drew in long and hard. "I smell that ginger-haired kid who's always with Nash. What the fuck's his name?"

"Clay," Reign said, his obsidian eyes flashing to his other son. "Julian, use that million-dollar surveillance system of yours and find me Clay Wells. Now."

"Get Nash here too." Someone yelled behind me. "He and Clay are joined at the hip. The kid might be innocent and met her for something Academy-related."

"Fine," Reign snapped. "Find first. Flay later."

"Why would one of the students do this?" I asked. "Everyone loves her."

The cold blast of air gusting through our group was cut by another electrical surge.

"Blossom." Galan launched forward and joined Bruin and me on the forest floor.

"Hmmph," Jade mumbled, sliding her hand toward her head. "Wha—"

"Love, are you well?" Galan lifted her hand to his kiss.

Jade's emerald eyes fluttered open and found Galan. "I think. Oh .. . cold."

She struggled a little, but Bruin placed his hand firm on her chest. "How about we call in the big guns to make sure you and the babes are good before you do a jig?" He looked to Reign who nodded and Flashed away.

A huge shudder overtook her and her teeth started to chatter. "C-c-cold."

Bruin ripped opened his shirt and slid beside his sister. He gathered her against his body and wrapped his arms around her. "We'll snuggle for a minute and take the chill off." Jade's eyes were closed, but she smiled and nuzzled closer. Bruin raised a hand and a blanket appeared, suddenly draped over both of them.

I'm always amazed that Weres could do such things.

After a time, her chattering slowed and the crease between her brows eased. "There we go," Bruin said. "See, my inner furnace is handy, eh? Better?"

"Mhmm."

In a flash of golden mist, Reign returned with Castian, God of gods. Both of Jade's fathers looked ready to kill.

Castian stormed forward. "I have Jade, Bruin. You find who did this and bring them to me." Castian's voice, usually liquid velvet, cut like glass shards.

When he laid a gentle hand on her belly the whole forest rumbled and shook. Birds flew from the trees. The wolves howled. I planted my hands on the ground to keep from toppling over.

The next moment the forest fell away in a blur and I found myself with Castian, Jade and my brother in the opulence of the Palace of the Fae.

I stood to find Jade laying on a padded bed. Healers rushed in and without a word of direction from Castian, with both haste and great care, they peeled away her clothing and began examining her.

I stepped out of the way when a member of the house staff rushed to collect Castian's heavy velvet cape. "Galan, you stay with Jade. Lia, you come with me."

Castian's command left no hope of discussion.

Exiting the examination area, my legs trembled and my mind was at once both fully present and numbingly vacant. What could the God of gods want of me? Verily, Castian had always been cordial but, at this moment, his anger consumed the air around us.

As he rushed forward in that authoritative, potent way of his, the hairs on my arms stood erect.

Outside, storm clouds gathered in swirling ferocity. Lightning skittered and streaked through the sky. Thunder cracked and my heart jumped inside my chest.

Castian led me to an elegant parlor with gold velvet couches and a brown tufted ottoman the size of Jade's dining table. The room smelled of parchment from the tomes lining the bookcase and wood smoke from the hearth's smoored fire.

"Tell me, Lia. All of it."

"I discovered her, Sire. I cannot tell you much."

"Start from the moment you first met up with Jade this morning. You were working at the clinic, yes?"

I sat on the edge of one of the sofa cushions and clasped my hands in my lap. Castian sat on the ottoman opposite me. "I was in the clinic, though in truth, I am not much aid. Jade knows how I love the hustle and energy of the students and encourages me to socialize."

Castian nodded, tapping his fingers against his thigh. "What happened today?"

I recalled our day, as best as I could, starting from the two of us opening the clinic, the students tended to and their injuries, Cowboy's surgery, Kobi and Savage, and her napping when Samuel came in for his exam.

"Wait," Castian said, raising his finger. "She said she didn't want to sleep too long because she had things to do. Did she mention meeting anyone?"

I thought hard, trying to recapture every word of the conversation. "Apologies, I am certain she never mentioned anything more."

He scowled. "Okay, then what?"

I continued, skimming over my altercation with Samuel, our return, the wolves and their strange reaction to the girl in the forest.

"And you've never seen this girl before today?" he asked.

I shook my head.

"Yet she seemed familiar enough with Jade to comment on where she kept her phone?"

"Verily it struck me as strange, but I assumed she was a student and noticed Jade's habits in passing."

Castian's lips tightened and he tilted his head. "Did you get her name?"

"I asked it of her—and this is going to sound unreal, but I swear on my honor it is truth—before she responded, a giant red-tailed hawk swooped in and stole my wrap."

Castian's emerald green eyes snapped wide. "Say that again—"

"A huge red-tailed hawk, a massive and majestic creature, snatched my wrap and flew straight to where Jade was buried beneath the cover of loose brush. If it were not for the bird—"

Castian Flashed from the room like a clap of thunder and I was left to myself.

CHAPTER FOUR

The Palace of the Fae twisted in a veritable warren of golden corridors. Stained-glass transoms spilled a kaleidoscope of color over priceless antiquities, breath-catching works of art and into endless nooks, open spaces and withdrawing rooms. Insignificant in the grandeur of it all, I was left to find my way back to Jade and her healers.

Verily, as Castian's daughter, Jade would be well cared for. By the time I found them, I was certain she would be resting peaceably with Galan at her bedside. Or so I prayed.

After an hour's time, I found myself no closer to knowing where I was than where I had been. Several times, Fae goddesses wearing one-shouldered gowns, and elegant chignons, swept past me. It seemed, I was invisible.

Twice I thought to approach one of them but, at the last moment, held my tongue and continued on my own.

At the end of one of the main corridors, the space opened into a vast, vaulted rotunda. Shimmering gold walls reached up five stories and terminated with a domed Oculus. Centered on the marble mosaic beneath the arched ceiling, stood a life-size bronze of Castian battling two evil and hideous beasts. With one foe in front of him and the other behind, he was frozen in a twisted stance, sword raised, blocking a killing blow. As I walked one full rotation, I examined the craftsmanship. Try as I might, I would never be able to describe its majesty to Maryssa, our village sculptress—assuming I ever ventured back to visit the Highborne village.

Pressing on, I ignored the wide, slow arc of the marble staircase. If nothing else, I remained certain that at least I walked the correct floor. As my steps quickened, my chest tightened. What if Galan needed me? What if something unspeakable happened to the unborn twins? Turning the corner, I caught sight of a pale blue gown disappearing through a doorway.

Enough was enough.

Hustling along to the withdrawing room, I peered in. "Hello?" I rapped my knuckles on the door jamb and waited. Strange. The room appeared to be empty.

Three overstuffed plum sofas created a u-shaped seating arrangement before a wide, marble hearth. Though not lit, the faint scent of chestnut lingered from its last burning. Four picture windows covered with sheers and framed with heavy velvet drapes spanned the back wall. It seemed sunlight prevailed over the clouds and the brilliance of the afternoon light filtered in.

"Hello?" I repeated.

One of the drapes rustled and a young woman peeked out of its shadow.

"Sorry," she said, looking over my shoulder. "I'll explain—" As quick footsteps terminated outside the doorway, the woman's eyes grew round and she ducked back behind the drapes.

"Who are you?" a female asked from the hall behind me. Though the iridescent skin of the goddess standing outside the doorway was beyond beauty, her austere glare took me aback. "Why are you wandering around loose in the palace?"

"I am Lia, merry meet."

She brushed past me and scanned the room, hands fisted on her hips. "Have you seen Zophia?"

"Apologies. Who?"

The female turned on me. "Zophia. She was headed this way. Long brown braid, dark blue eyes. . .." She leaned closer. "Have you seen her or not?"

"I cannot say—"

"Who were you talking to?" She stepped forward, staring down the sharp bridge of her nose. "I heard voices."

I buried my hands into the folds of my skirt. My fingers brushed over something hard in my pocket and I held out Jade's phone. "I was speaking into this . . . to someone . . . not in this room. Someone at Haven." I nodded once and exhaled. "Yes. I was speaking to someone at Haven on this telephone."

The female lost interest and paced the room. "If you see her—"

"Apologies. Who?"

"*Zophia!*" An unflattering blush crept up the female's long ivory neck. "Good grief, are you daft? Okay, I'll speak slowly. If you see Zophia, tell her Castian's love-child has gone and gotten herself beaten in the forest somewhere."

"Jade. Yes, I was there." I tucked the phone back into my pocket, lest she somehow make the connection it was not mine own. "Is she well? Are the young—"

The female crossed her arms under her ample bosom and scowled at me. "Do I look like a news reporter?"

I shrugged. "Verily, I cannot say, but if you could direct me back to—"

"Not a tour guide either," she said, holding a hand between us. "Zophia needs to assure Uncle we had nothing to do with this. Some human did it, not us." Message delivered, she swept back toward the door, muttering to herself. "This is why people of the realm don't deserve free will. Look at the trouble they cause us when left to their own."

I stood there dazzled until her voice eventually faded down the hall. Blinking at the empty doorway, I drew a deep breath.

"Sorry about her," the girl in blue said, extracting herself from the draperies. She approached, hand extended. She did indeed have chestnut hair and midnight blue eyes and now that she was in the open, her opal skin shimmered in the sunlight as well. "I am Zophia. You're Lia, right? Galan's sister?"

I shook her hand and nodded. "I am. Merry meet. How did you know?"

"It's the hair." She pointed, her mouth twitching in a shy smile. "I am the Keeper of Lives in Progress in the Realm of the Fair. Right now, Galan and his sister are the only two living descendants of Rheagan."

I stiffened.

Her grip tightened and she shook her head. "No. Please don't be alarmed. We are family, distant, but blood none the less. I am Castian's niece as well."

Her melodic voice emphasized the *as well* and I took pause. "Verily, I never considered myself Castian's niece, but I suppose...."

"You're the great-great-great however many times daughter of his sister, Rheagan." She swept her intricate braid to her front and draped it over her arm like a wrap. The length still dangled halfway down her gown toward the floor. "I'm the daughter of his brother Dane. We're cousins."

"I am quite certain your sister does not feel the same familial tie."

Zophia giggled. "You're better off. I wish I were invisible in the lives of Zana and my half-sisters. Maybe they'd leave me out of their drama. Instead, I'm a modern-day Cinderella. It's exhausting."

As she spoke, she fluttered toward the open door and peeked out, looking up the hallway and down. "Coast is clear. Would you like me to take you back to Jade and Galan?"

"Oh, I would be in your debt."

Zophia waved her hand. "After saving me from Zana, it's me who owes you. Now, let's go see what's happening with Jade, shall we?"

The fear when discovering Jade in the forest was naught to the panic which gripped me when Galan greeted me in her recovery suite. His hair hung loose of its usual leather thong and looked as though he fingered through it like a madman. His essence bled agony and when he embraced me, his trembling squeeze sucked the breath from my lungs.

I glanced to the recovery bed and my hand went to my throat. Sweet Shalana, Jade was dying. It was plain.

Though the physical signs of her assault were gone, so too was her vitality. She appeared to be naught but a child, a frail form lost and absorbed in a cradle of pillows and a frenetic weave of tubes. Her rich copper skin, which usually shone as if kissed by the sun god himself, was the putrid color of old tea and her gemstone emerald eyes were dull and heavy.

"That good, huh?" She whispered as she beckoned me closer. "Galan said I was radiant, as always, but I knew he was full of shit."

"Apologies." I caught myself and moved to her bedside. "Galan is correct, you are resplendent as always, sister mine."

Her eyes pinched closed and a groan ripped from deep in her throat. As she twisted on the bed, energy crackled through the air and sparks ignited from her fingertips.

Galan collapsed at her bedside. "Castian, I beg of you, make it stop."

Jade placed her hand on his bowed head and stroked his hair. "It's all right, Galan. Even gods have tenets to live by." She shifted slightly and exhaled. "I'll be fine."

Galan scrubbed his palm over his face. "Of course, you will. You are the strongest female alive and will accept nothing less."

"And don't you forget it." Jade's smile relaxed as she looked to me. "Thanks for the rescue, girly. I heard you found me in the nick of time."

I eased down on the bed's edge opposite Galan. "It was terrifying . . . and quite queer."

"Queer? How so?"

I retold the tale of the giant bird leading me straight to where she'd fallen in the brush.

Her deep-red brow knitted. "A hawk?"

"Yes. One moment it was there and the next, it dropped my wrap and flew off."

Jade looked bewildered, but the distraction of the conversation seemed to lift her spirits. It all seemed so surreal. "Why would one of your students harm you like this?"

Her fingers drifted to her bare neck. "Clay stole my pendant. Said he needed to return it to its rightful owner."

Galan cursed, shaking his disheveled hair.

"Rightful owner?" I said. "You are Galan's mate, by our ancestral traditions you are its rightful owner."

Jade covered my hand with hers and cried out as another wave of electricity snapped in the air. The attack set off alarms and as she stiffened beneath the sheets, a rush of attendants flooded the room.

Galan and I were swept out to the patio.

"Jade is strong, like you said," I reminded him.

While the caregivers hustled on the other side of the decorative glass doors, my brother drew me further across the patio. "It is the young who are in the greatest peril, not their *naneth*."

Though, knowing Jade, the loss of the twins would kill her spirit even if she survived physically.

"Sire," a voice called from the now open door, "she's asking for you."

Galan kissed my head and rushed back inside.

Left with naught for me to do, I stared out upon the palace grounds. Despite the warmth of the surroundings, a shiver ran up the length of my spine.

The manicured lawns Behind the Veil rolled out and away from the palace in a plush emerald carpet. The sky, a perfect cerulean blue, swirled with a soft breeze carrying the scents of mint and bergamot across the property. The beauty of the palace paled when held against Jade's suffering.

Since the moment Galan left for his *Ambar Lenn*, our lives had spiraled in a constant state of turmoil: the Scourge attack, my kidnapping, his struggles finding his footing with Jade, my struggles adapting to an entirely new life. How was I to adapt after what happened. No one spoke of it but—

An agonizing darkness exploded inside my skull. Staggering forward, I rested my elbows on the rail and leaned forward. I breathed deeply as Jade had shown me.

After a long moment, my world righted itself.

A glance over my shoulder assured me Galan had not seen my episode. Good. He had enough to deal with. Deciding to take a moment to gather myself, I trudged off the patio and onto Castian's grounds.

I untied the lacings of my suede boots and slipped them off. I tucked them under a boxwood and strode barefoot across the lawn. Somehow, prancing on the lawn of the Fae Palace barefoot seem wickedly indecent.

However, as the stress of the day continued to bombard, and with no stream in sight, social propriety took second place to making the world melt away. Scrunching my toes into the cool pile of the velvet grass, I raised my face to the warmth of the late afternoon sun and tried to focus.

How could things go so horribly awry in such a short period? This morning, Jade and I sipped tea and discussed the mural to be painted on the nursery walls.

Now? Oh, gods, what now?

I was jostled out of my commiseration, inundated by nuzzling noses and inquiring glances. The wide round eyes of Castian's deer assess me. Dozens of the inquisitive beasts had gathered and surrounded me. I stopped strolling and scanned the lawn again.

"Who keeps your grass so pristine, little ones?" Ears flickered and tails twitched as if in answer. "Is there a Brownie dedicated to the removal of skat from godly grounds?"

An assertive doe with one droopy ear seemed intent on searching my palms and pockets. Huge round eyes blinked as she nudged her insistence.

I widened my stance to keep from being toppled over. "Apologies. I have nothing for you, milady."

Her fellow grazers joined the prodding, their curiosity transforming to insistence. Recognizing my time to leave, I slipped through an iron gate dividing the threshold between lawns and rose garden, and left the herd behind.

Rows of rosebushes and elaborate wooden arbors laden heavy with multicolored blooms stretched before me. It seemed impossible that eight months had passed since I'd last been here, when Galan and Jade had rescued me from the netherworld. Rescued was a deceiving term.

They escorted my spirit back to my body lying vacant and uninhabited, but even yet, I never felt whole.

Fighting the wave of emotions about to overwhelm me, I drew deep breaths in through my nose and out through my mouth. Again. And once more. I called on the strength of Mika's Earth Spirits and focused on the power of her Earth Mother as healing breaths filled my lungs. Better.

"Miss?"

I screeched and spun.

One of the Palace help, a stableman by the look of him, froze upon the garden path behind me. A brawny male, squat in stature, stood a fair distance off, holding his hands open.

"I didn't mean to frighten you, Miss. You have a visitor."

I looked around. "Me? You mistake me, sir, I—"

He raised a beefy finger along the path from whence he came and pointed. "No, mistake. The gentleman asked for you by name, Miss Lia. Described your silver locks. Paid me five copper to fetch you."

He shrugged his broad shoulders, dropping his gaze. "I would've done it for nothing when my work was done, but he insisted it be now. Seems distraught, the poor fellow, more than usual."

"I see. So, who is it?"

"Master Murray."

I shook my head.

"A Celt. Had a string of bad luck last year and stayed here for a while for safekeeping. Didn't seem to want to talk much, but spent quite a lot of time walking the grounds. Can't do much of that now, though, blind as he is."

"Ah, yes, Samuel." I glanced back to the palace. I was still barefoot. What did it matter? There were more important things happening after all. "Very well, where is he?"

"In the arbor, up a'ways. I'll walk you. It's on my way back to the paddock."

I drew in a slow breath. Though testing the air for any hint of fetid musk or deceit, there was none. The stableman gave off the richest scents of horse, hay and the pungent aroma of a male who had worked hard on a sunny day.

I missed that.

As hard as the people of Haven worked, few males knew the blessings of filling their days tending stock. Their hands rarely felt callused, their banded muscles not earned from physical labor but from exercise machines in a training center.

"Very well, sir. Lead the way." We walked side by side, he on the stone walk and me on its grassy edge. "Queer how the weather rebounded after the violent skies earlier."

He glanced at the cerulean sky. "It happens that way at times. When the sky blackens, it's best to keep your head down and wait for the storm to pass."

We walked on, speaking cordially about the grounds and his duties. He had a lovely manner and I decided his sturdy frame would be an asset when handling horses.

"Here we are, Miss. The end of our journey."

I curtsied, then stepped under the arched entrance to an iron gazebo grown over with creeping vines and brilliant blooms of violet, fuchsia and ivory. Before entering fully, I peeked inside. Samuel sat on a marble reflection bench, looking pale as pastry dough.

"Samuel?"

His head snapped to my voice. "You came. Thank you." He stood, hesitated, scrubbing his palms on the thighs of his slacks. "Especially after this morning."

Ah yes. "When you swore you never need speak to me again?" I stepped further inside the arbor and clasped my hands. "Yet here you are."

He sighed. "Aye. Here I am."

"What is it you want?"

"Jade." His voice broke and he swallowed. "I need to know . . . how is she?"

I took a step back. "That is private. A family matter. You have no right to—"

He raised his hand in the air between us. "Nobody at Haven knows a damn thing and I couldna wait around. I thought, maybe you'd know more."

I laughed and stepped further into the shade of the arbor. "And you thought me so genteel I would ease your suffering after you cursed me and the entire Highborne race? Or mayhap you think me as addled from capture as the rest? I assure you, Samuel Murray, I have the good sense to know—"

Both his hands rose. "I'm sorry I offended you."

"And yet you offend me further by asking me to betray my brother's confidence. Have you no propriety?"

He scowled. "Fuck propriety. I'm outta me head here."

"Is that my burden? Galan is my brother. Jade is his life."

"She was my life *first!*" The echo of his voice died off, followed by a tormented silence. He took a tentative step forward and cursed under his breath. "I canna turn off my feelings like a switch just because the Fates say I'm no the one to love her. I would if I could."

He scrubbed his hands roughly over his face and through his hair, leaving black tufts standing on end. "It would be a shit-load simpler not to die more every time I'm reminded she's his now."

"And yet you—"

"Life is messy," he said. "I'm no enjoying any of this."

"Then let her go."

He barked a laugh and shook his head. "Ye've obviously never been in love, because ye dinnae get it. I pictured a future with Jade. In my mind, I bought the lot, built the house and moved us in, bairns, a wee doggy, the whole nine yards. In an instant, it was gone." Staggering back, his leg touched the bench and he sank down and buried his head in his hands.

Though I had no use for the man, the smoky stench of his anguish was more than I could bear. I moved to the bench and sat next to him. "We have a saying in our village, *Lle mela ya llemela*—You love whom you love."

Whether human or elf, suffering was suffering. And Samuel, indeed, suffered. "Verily there is little the mind and body can do when someone captures your soul. And for the loss of your love, my heart goes out to you."

His jaw clenched. "So ye understand why I must know."

"But Galan is my blood—"

"Do ye want me to beg?" He sank to the ground before me, his breath ragged. "Never have I begged for anything, but if ye want it—"

"No. No male should be made to beg and certainly not a warrior of noble character." I pulled him by the elbow until he settled next to me again and sighed. "Jade is resting. The tear on her insides has been mended and her blood level restored."

"And the weens?"

"Weens?"

"The wee bairns. The twins."

"The young are . . . in peril."

"How bad?"

My voice died in my throat as I envisioned Jade thrashing. "When the student attacked Jade, he used a high-powered stunning device. The jolt of current upset the energy balance of her powers. They cannot control the surging. The young are under a great deal of stress. Their survival is doubtful. Castian's caregivers told her to prepare for their loss."

With elbows on his knees, he dropped his head into his hands. After a long moment, he cleared his throat. "Ye may not believe me but, no matter what I wanted for Jade and me, I never wanted anything to happen to her, those babies or yer brother."

Warm tears dripped silently off my jaw. His agony and despair tingled bitter in my nostrils, his pain almost palpable in the air between us but the truth of his words burned sweet. "You love her to that depth?"

His mouth narrowed into a thin line. "When will they know more?"

"They want her to rest undisturbed for several weeks, possibly a full moon cycle. If the young survive until then, well, we must needs wait and see."

He punched the bench, the surface vibrating beneath me. "I hate feeling so feckin' useless. I cannae comfort, Jade. I cannae help with the search to find the bastard who did this. I cannae do a goddamn thing." Samuel stared straight ahead. In the long stretch of quiet, I watched the muscle in his jaw twitch.

I closed my tear-blurred eyes and sent Castian a prayer.

"Here. It's clean." Samuel held out a crumpled, ivory handkerchief with a plaid ribbon embroidered on one corner.

I wiped my eyes, cheeks and nose as delicately as possible. "Gratitude, how did you—"

"I'm blind, lass. My other senses work just fine."

I bit my lip, stifling my urge to respond. We sat there, in sad silence, for a long while. I too felt useless and adrift. "What if there was something we could do?"

His brow creased as he laughed at me. "Are ye a healer, then? Or should the blind man join the search for the Scourge mole, maybe infiltrate Abaddon's compound again?"

I shot him a scathing look and realized my expression was lost on him. "Knowing Jade, she will worry how her recovery time will affect her students so close to their examinations. She has spoken many times to your skills as an instructor of the Academy—"

"Past tense," he muttered. "I'm not that man anymore."

"You could be. The student-filled castle halls would be difficult to maneuver in your current condition, but if—"

"Forget it." Launching to his feet, he raised his palm to the latticed screen covering the arbor wall and stepped away. "If I can't see, I can't teach."

"Why not?"

His shoulders stiffened. "Aside from bumping into the desks, not seeing a raised hand and not being able to write on the feckin' white board, an instructor needs to command the respect of his students to retain control. I cannae do it."

"Pish posh, you are afraid to look a fool. Nothing more."

"Have me figured out, do ye?" His hands clenched in white knuckled fists. "Well, my motivations are none of your goddamn business—"

"But they are."

He glared toward me. "How do ye figure?"

"You wish to help Jade. I do as well. Aust can take up her Herbology classes, but what does he know about Realm History or the Theory of Healing Through Affinities?"

"Those aren't my specialties eith—"

"I realize *that!*" I stretched my fingers and softened my tone. "If I were your aide in the physical aspects of teaching, you could instruct. It is not ideal, but it would be of comfort to Jade to know her classes were taken care of. *And* it would raise her spirits to know you were in a classroom once again."

Samuel's blank stare froze on me while the breeze stirred the scent of his conflict. "Why would ye do it?"

"Why would I not? Jade has been a true and loving sister since the day she and Galan were mated. I can do no other than to be the same for her."

He cocked an ebony brow. "Your brother is going to blow a gasket when he finds out we're working together."

"I should think that fact alone would inspire you to accept."

His mouth twitched up at the corners and after a moment he nodded. "All right. I'll speak to Reign and we'll give it a try. Don't get yer hopes up, though. This is going to blow up in both our faces."

CHAPTER FIVE

"*N*yssa!" Aust's frazzled cry came Ella's nursery at the back of Nyssa and Iadon's suite. With the high pitch of his plea, I could only imagine what calamity he faced this time.

Nyssa and I covered our mouths with wine-stained fingers and tried to muffle our laughter. With the back of my sleeve, I wiped the sweat from my brow and pushed my hair from where it stuck to my face. Dying hide was laborious work, but Iadon needed our aid.

It took mere weeks for his skills as a leatherworker and craftsman to transform the modest tailor shop the males renovated into a roaring Haven mercantile. It seemed everyone wanted a gown, robe or cloak tailored by Iadon.

Myself included.

He and I had discussed, in length, the changeover to my adult wardrobe now that my sixtieth birthing day had passed. I was an adult now. I wanted to reinvent myself, draw an appraising eye, shuck the modesty of youth and embrace my feminine form.

So today, while he manned the workshop and finished sewing the platinum clasps and fur trim on a commissioned velvet cloak, we readied six large skins for the project. We had finished with the midnight blue and had moved on to dye the remaining leather the deepest mulberry we could manipulate. What we achieved was a rich mulberry wine.

The fragrance of crushed berries mixed with bloodroot, smooth sumac, mountain alder and red wine filled the suite with a humid steam and mouthwatering ambrosia.

Nyssa made to put down the wooden paddles we used to lift and stir the steaming caldron, but I stopped her. "Fash not," I said, wiping my hands on my apron. "Mayhap he simply taped his fingers into the diaper again. Let me go."

Nyssa leaned close so our shoulders touched. "Last time he mixed the powder with the cream and Ella's backside was caked with the most awful goop you could imagine."

"Elven hearing," Aust called from the back hall. "Here is a thought —instead of ribbing the male who is changing the young, would it not be kinder to aid him?"

I giggled again and set the rag close enough for Nyssa to grab, if need be. "Coming."

The emergency, though I am not sure it could truly be called one, became apparent the moment I rounded the corner and entered the small pink room smattered with rosebuds.

"By Shalana's grace." I clamped my hand over my mouth and quaked with laughter.

Aust stood covered from waist to eyebrows in a massive splatter of pea-green poop.

I raised my sleeve to my face, my eyes streaming, partly from the ridiculous scene, but more so from the nostril-singeing aroma. Try as I might I was powerless to aid him as he stood, arms extended, covered in excrement. "Oh, Aust, apologies, but you smell like Harilyn's goat pile."

He raised a hand, freeing a chunk of golden hair stuck to the waste pasted to the side of his face. "I was almost to the cream part when the wee little monster made the strangest face. When her cheeks reddened I thought she might cry so I leaned in. I only meant to raspberry her bare belly, but during my approach . . . this occurred."

Another wave of hysteria racked me. "Nyssa," I called, leaning

49

toward the open door, "the praxle juice worked out Ella's little problem."

"Oh, fabulous." Nyssa's voice grew louder as she strode toward us. I stepped aside and let her pass. "I hoped—Oh Aust, love, what did she do to you?"

Ella took that moment to let out an angelic squeal, her chubby little fist wedged deep in her mouth. Stumpy legs kicked and bucked in the air at the sight of her *naneth*.

Nyssa relieved Aust of his duties. With a clean diaper on Ella's bottom, she snatched a fresh jumper from the dresser and eased it over the baby's golden curls. "Aust, take your clothes off and get into the shower."

He hesitated.

Nyssa lifted Ella to her shoulder and frowned. "Do not guard yourself here. We love you, now and always. Now go clean yourself up."

Nyssa pointed to the rabbit clock on the shelf by the crib. "Lia, you need to be going too."

Aust tugged the tie of his soiled tunic, shrugged his shoulders and let the garment fall to the hardwood with a flap. The lacings of his leathers were next. After stripping bare, he stepped over the mound of fouled fabric.

"Where are you off to, sweeting?" he asked and headed up the hall.

I followed him as he sauntered along, hands raised as not to sully Nyssa's walls. Though Aust remained self-conscious of the faint tiger stripes which appeared ankle to shoulder last fall, they were quite exotic.

Reaching around him to get the door, I slid into the bathing-room first and cleared his path. Leaning into the shower stall, I turned on the water and tested the stream until the temperature warmed. "While Jade is Behind the Veil recovering, I volunteered to assist with some of her classroom duties."

"One of the classes I took over? I have nothing scheduled until tomorrow morning." Aust was only half listening as he leaned close to the mirror and examined his splatter-covered face. His chest bounced in amusement.

The sight lightened my heart. It had been months since he had laughed. Before his father was killed. Before he left on his *Ambar Lenn*. Life here at Haven suited him. "I am happy to aid you as well, but today I am in one of the other classes."

The air began to warm and I retrieved two fresh towels from the corner cabinet and set them out. I busied myself washing my hands.

He stepped into the shower and closed the glass door. "Forgive me, little one, but are you up to it? Your headaches—"

I raised a hand. "Please. I am not as delicate as everyone seems to believe."

He narrowed his gaze, his brow rising in a smooth arc. Lathering the soap in his hands, he rubbed his chest clean. "That may be true, but the castle can be loud and chaotic."

"One of the things I love most about it."

Aust's eyes rolled closed as he tipped his head back. Water cascaded over his shoulders and down his body, rinsing the suds toward the drain. After a moment, he laughed again. "Tham would have loved seeing what Ella did to me."

Milling my hands into a sudsy froth under the vanity faucet, I laughed too. "The teasing would never have ended. No one relished a calamity like Tham."

A long silence overtook the conversation and I gave up on ridding my fingers of the dye.

Aust's gaze met mine, filled with compassion and sadness and love. In one moment, with one look, I felt like a child again, weak and unsure. Gods, we all lost so much.

I sent a prayer to the gods to watch over Galan, Jade and the young. How I wished everything was well and they were home and not still at Castian's palace. Reaching for a towel I cleared my throat. "Tell me, how fares your courting of the beautiful Bree?"

Water washed over Aust's back-tilted head as he ran his palms over his forehead and smoothed his hair. He sighed. "Bree is wonderful. Lovely. Warm."

"But?"

"But her coyote self, her animal side, has yet to be won over. After being orphaned as a child, her Were instinct is to claim a dominant, alpha male as her mate."

Aust was many things, intelligent, loyal, brave, and sacrificing but I would never consider him dominant or aggressive. "What will you do to win her coyote over?"

He rinsed the shampoo from the lengths of his wet hair where it stuck to his shoulders. "The Equinox Moon approaches. Weres can already feel their animals growing restless. Bruin is hosting a massive Were run across the mountainside and has given me permission to join them."

"As yourself or in your tiger form?"

He palmed the bar of soap and ran it over his chest and down his torso. "In tiger form. If I can prove myself strong enough, Bree is certain her coyote will relent and accept me."

"I wish you well, brother mine. You deserve every happiness."

"As do you, sweeting." He turned and lifted his face to the water, the suds washing down his thighs under the stream. "Bruin and Mika are coming to the courtyard for evening repast. Will you join us?"

"I should be back in plenty of time." I gauged the light coming in the window and pressed a hand to the glass shower door. "But I must needs run to change my dress. I should hate to be late on my first day."

"No one is staring at you." Linked at the elbows, Samuel and I made our way through the sea of students. Flowing like battling currents, bodies jostled and swept in opposite directions up and down the wide stone hallways of the castle.

I continued my search for the first classroom where we were to instruct this afternoon.

Samuel's night-black brow drew so tight it was a wonder his reflective glasses remained on his face. "Stop your scowling. No one is staring at you."

There was, in fact, a great number of people staring at him as we neared the third-floor classroom where Jade taught Theory of Healing. But, with a lot of eye contact and head shaking, I kept most of the students at bay.

"Merlin, good to see you." Nash broke through the crowd and slapped Samuel on the arm. His smile crinkled the crescent tribal tattoo inked around the orbit of his left eye. The shimmering colors of the ink complimented his russet skin. "I didn't know you were back to teaching, my man."

Samuel's jaw clenched. "Yeah, well, we thought we could help out while Jade is recovering."

Nash ran a palm over the squared peaks of his purple mohawk and frowned. "Fuck, I had no clue Clay was a mole. It makes me sick how close Jade came to—"

"No one blames you, Nash," I said.

The acrid scent of his guilt mixed with the wall of cologne surrounding him was overwhelming. Verily, my sense of smell was far more heightened than the females in his classes, but did they find sprayed-on pheromone appealing?

I rubbed at the tingle in my nose and tried not to inhale too deeply. "If you will excuse us, we are off to shape the minds of youth."

"Or make a complete arse outta myself and destroy what little pride I have left," Samuel said.

I squeezed his elbow. "A little faith would do you well."

Samuel rubbed his eyes behind his glasses. "Lucky me, I'm stuck with Mary-feckin-Poppins as my sidekick."

"Who?"

Nash chuckled. "Well, I'm a TA in Weapons and Warfare down the hall if you need me. Good luck. I'm sure you'll do great." With a wink, the shimmering colors of his tattoo wrinkled then smoothed. Striding down the stone corridor the junior wizard disappeared into the crowd of bodies.

Left unto ourselves, I tugged Samuel back into motion. "Stop expecting the worst."

"Life has taught me well."

"It would do you better to expect greatness while preparing for adversity."

"Could ye tone down the pep rally? I think I might slit my wrists."

I shook my head and with one more turn, found the classroom. "Here we are—"

I misjudged the clearance of the jamb and Samuel's shoulder caught against the frame of the doorway. Hard.

"Jaysus woman."

I winced as he rolled his shoulder, and inhaled the bitter scent of his frustration. "That was my fault."

"No shite." For a moment, Samuel looked like he might dissolve the whole arrangement. "Take me to the podium. Use the desk to lay out Jade's binder. We'll go through the content of the lesson like we discussed."

I led him to the wide chestnut stand in the front corner of the rectangular room and placed his hand on its surface. After gathering the loose papers left by the previous instructor, I tucked them in the shelf below. Samuel slid behind the podium, gripping the sides and drawing a deep breath. Angled in the front corner, opposite the door, he stood in full view of the two dozen students seated.

After witnessing our not-so-elegant arrival, they stared hard at Samuel. I glanced at the man standing at the lectern, wondering what they saw.

There was an edge to Samuel's attractiveness. A sharpness beyond his dark, chic haircut and the way his jaw cut square like a carved statue. He held presence. Behind the pulpit, mirrored glasses in place, he also held the focus of the room.

"Okay, guys." Samuel scanned the rows of seats as if by habit, his cheeks mottled, a slight quaver to his voice. "I suppose ye've all heard about the attack on Jade?"

There was a chorus of affirmation and whispers.

"Some of ye may know, I have nea been in a classroom for a bit, so bear with me. Miss Caleblasse and I will make every effort to fill in until Jade's on her feet again."

Distracted by his use of my proper name, I almost missed when a blond male in the second row raised his pencil.

"A student has a question," I said.

"Okay, shoot." Samuel inclined his head toward the class and we began our day.

"Jade spoke the truth, Samuel. You shine in the classroom." I guided him down the main staircase of the castle and across the congested stone foyer. "You see, all that worrying and you rocked their stockings off."

Samuel smirked. "I think ye mean rock their socks off."

"Is that not what I said?"

"No. No one rocks someone's stockings off. It's socks."

I paused for a group to pass and headed toward for the main entrance. "My point is sound. You did well."

"Better than I thought, actually."

I bowed my head as the blond student from our first class held the oversized wooden door for us to exit. I made certain Samuel's shoulder cleared the frame before we continued through. "Blind or not, you connect with the students. When this is over you should consider staying on. It would give you something productive to contribute again."

Samuel's chest bounced as he laughed.

"What amuses you? Have I said something else you find queer?" I pulled the furred collar of my jacket together and pressed closer to his side. The late afternoon sky hung gray and dreary. Chill-bumps raised on my legs beneath my skirts.

He laughed harder. "First, instead of queer, if ye mean to fit in, maybe ye should use a word like *strange* or *odd*. Second, it doesn't dawn on ye to glaze over the fact I'm blind, does it? Ye throw it out there as if it were no more important than my hair being black or my tie being crooked."

"You are not wearing a tie, Professor Murray." Tightening up on his arm, I borrowed a bit of warmth as we concluded our descent down the stone steps of the castle.

"I'm just sayin' ye surprise me more often than not."

"Tomorrow, we shall be better still—careful, one last step—we have Realm History after morning repast and Theory of Healing with Magic before mid-day."

Samuel's smile faltered. When we stepped onto the path and the crowd thinned, Samuel let his elbows ease from his sides and took a half-step away.

"What is it?" I asked.

"It felt good. Like old times."

"Why does that sadden you?"

"Because if this were then, Jade and I would go to the Hearthstone for a drink after a satisfying day of teaching."

"Well, I have time—"

Samuel stopped and removed his arm from mine. "Look. Lia. Teaming up for the Academy is one thing—I'd suffer through anything for Jade." He scrubbed his fingers over his mouth and exhaled. "Ye see, we're teaching together. That's all. Yer still the sister of the arsehole who stole my future and I'm still the bastard wizard yer entire family despises. This is an arrangement not a friendship."

His words slapped my cheek as cold as the March wind, and by the long silence that grew between us, he knew it.

"Samuel! Lia!" Bruin emerged from the forest on the west path and jogged toward us. His broad chest heaved beneath his leather jacket, a flush on his bronze cheeks. "Did you hear? We found Clay Wells about two hours ago."

Samuel's demeanor darkened further. "Did he confess why he attacked Jade? Did he admit to being Abaddon's pawn?"

"We didn't get that far."

"In two hours? Why the hell not?"

Bruin canted his head to the side. "Cause he's dead. Chopped into shoebox-sized pieces."

"What?"

"Aust's wolves smelled the chunks o' corpse and led us straight to it. Bits of Clay strewn all inside the mechanical shed by Ward 14. Real life Texas Chainsaw Massacre stuff."

I crinkled my nose, but could still imagine the acrid stench burning my nostrils.

"Bits of Clay?" Samuel repeated. "Sooo not funny."

Bruin shrugged, laughing at his own joke. "I was hoping for a go-round with the ginger-haired bastard. Too bad someone beat me to it."

The resonant growl of Bruin's bear filled the air.

As the bass sound echoed in my chest, I shivered. Being drawn and cleaved was a horrific end, but facing Bruin's bear in a fury would be worse. No doubt.

Samuel shook his head, his gaze drifting sightlessly over the landscape. "I dinnae understand why he attacked Jade."

Bruin led the three of us off the path and away from the flow of students ending their afternoon studies. Our boots crunched over the stiff grass near the forest's edge.

"Galan told Reign that after Clay Tasered her, the fucker took her silver bridal pendant."

"Eruanna," I said with a nod. When they both looked blank, I continued. "The pendant is called Eruanna. Jade told me Clay had stolen it when I visited her at the palace."

Samuel scowled. "Ye never mentioned it to me."

"How is Jade's bridal pendant any of your concern?"

"Everything about Jade and her safety is my concern. I made that clear to ye."

"Kids. Hey. Stay on point." Bruin glanced around before leaning in. "Okay, so Clay took the pendant to return it to its original owner. Who is that?"

"Queen Rheagan," I said.

Samuel cursed. "Yer feckin brother gave Jade a necklace belonging to the bat-shit Queen who tried to take over the world? Nice."

I propped my fists on my hips. "Galan only discovered its origin when he visited the Oracles in Toronto. For the past eight thousand years, it has been a treasured family heirloom."

Bruin nodded. "And her Holy Warriors wanted it back. Why?"

My chest constricted at the same moment the white dots popped up behind my eyes. With Rheagan free from exile in a ghostly form, they would try to reinstate her. They believed that being her heir, I was the vessel to make that happen.

I fumbled at my throat, trying to draw air into lead lungs. They had come. They attacked Jade on protected grounds.

There was no place I would ever be safe.

CHAPTER SIX

For the next week, I watched and waited, certain some evil Scourge spy, posing as a student or a diner at the tavern, would grab me. If I was the key to the Scourge plan, the warriors who pledged their lives to her would come. There was no question of *if*, simply when.

With naught to be done about it, I aided Samuel with Jade's classes and refused to surrender what little control I had in my own life. Though, cordial and efficient in our teachings, I never forgot my place after the first afternoon.

We were not friends.

Brittle grass buckled beneath our steps and remained the only sound to break the icy silence as we left the castle and headed across the grounds. Glancing to where Samuel's hand rested on the inside of my elbow, I marveled at the contrast between his chilling demeanor and the warmth of his touch.

Verily we gained a rhythm in our classes. I anticipated his needs, whether in advancing the slides of a presentation or pouring a glass of water when his voice began to dry during a lecture. These, however, were superficial connections allowing him to support his beloved Jade. They meant nothing once the bell rang and the class emptied.

An out of tune squawking stirred me from my musings. The incessant *squawk-honk-squawk* echoed louder, building in fervor. It sounded like a strangled bird, a dozen birds in truth, in a vocal competition to create the loudest ruckus.

"What in the two realms is that?"

Samuel stopped walking. "A flock of Canadian geese." He closed his eyes and raised his face to the gray sky. "Somewhere to the south, there will be a V of birds flying in to feed in the corn fields at the base of the mountain."

Shielding my eyes from the glare of early spring, I pivoted until I did indeed see a string of dark shapes contrasting the gray sky. "They are fashioned more like a lopsided check mark, but yes. Why do they align themselves so?"

"It's streamlining. The lead bird bears the wind resistance as long as it can, while the others ride easier in its stream. When it tires and can take no more, it falls back and another bird assumes the burden."

"Will it be left behind?"

"No, it'll fall to the end of the line and enjoy an easy fly for a bit, until it's time to take the lead again."

"Fascinating." The gracefully awkward creatures flapped and soared over our heads and soon disappeared behind the tops of the forest tree line. "And where do they go from here?"

"After they've filled up in the cornfields they'll scatter until the coming of winter." Samuel tightened his hold my arm and we resumed our walk. "They travel thousands of miles to spend the winter basking in the heat of the tropics. Better to be toasty warm than feel the winter's gale gust up their tail feathers."

"I should think so." As we walked on, I realized why Jade so desperately wanted Samuel back in the classroom. When he taught, he gave of himself. No longer guarded, his anger fell away. And though Jade was now happily mated to my brother, she still adored this male.

"Oh, I have news." I patted his hand and squeezed. "Jade has been given permission to get out of bed and walk the grounds of Castian's Palace."

Samuel's full lips lifted in a warm, genuine smile. "Any word on her coming home?"

I frowned and caught myself. Before I could respond, the energy of the air shifted and my skin erupted in tingles.

We Flashed.

Tightening my grip on Samuel's hand, my stomach rolled with the unexpected transport. I turned to give Samuel a verbal throttle.

Samuel had drawn his wand. Sliding one step in front of me, he pulled me tight to his side. He had not been the one to Flash us. But who—

"At ease, Samuel." Castian's melodic voice brought our attention to where Bruin, Aust, Cowboy, Kobi and a half-dozen other Talon Enforcers stood. Dressed in black leather, they each wore the battle vests Iadon designed which housed a small armory of weapons. Castian motioned for us to join them, his navy cloak and wavy chestnut hair billowing behind him in the breeze.

The churn of my stomach eased and I banished the urge to voice my complaint. Flashing set off my ire but telling the God of gods such a thing would be improper and ungrateful, especially while Galan and Jade remained guests in his home.

Nightrunner and Faolan trotted from where Aust's wolves crouched hidden amongst the brush. They rubbed against my thigh, rustling my skirts. As I scrubbed Faolan's thick, luscious ruff and ebony ears, she regarded Samuel. When her ears pressed back, I took his hand down and held it for her to smell. After an initial pause, Samuel relaxed. The two wolves sniffed him and plodded off.

"If you're ready," Castian said, looking impatient, "I want to go over what happened the afternoon of Jade's attack one more time before we put it to bed. Walking through it might bring back a detail or memory you've overlooked."

The place Castian had chosen as our launch point was the same place Samuel Flashed us when he returned me to Haven grounds. It dazzled me how quickly things could change.

Walking the males through what happened, I showed them where the pack met me, where I discovered the girl crying in the fork of the tree, and an approximate route of where the mischievous hawk led me through the forest to Jade.

Samuel strode silently by my side, Bruin spoke in hushed tones with Castian, and Aust cast worried glances toward me as he carried Cowboy's clothing.

Cowboy had shifted into his wolf form to plod the course nose to the ground. His Were frame was large—much larger than Faolan or any forest wolves I knew—and covered in a thick, tri-colored coat of deep caramel with an undercoat of a lighter gold and silver.

The fast bond of friendship between Aust and Cowboy was endearing. Aust needed that—deserved it—after the decades of forced solitude in our village. I believed Cowboy's animal nature made it easier for Aust to trust him. He was close with all the Weres and most of all their Ursa, Mika.

When our tour of the forest ended, Castian set everyone on task. One by one, the warriors dispersed until only Castian, Samuel and I remained. My heart went out to the male on my arm. His heartache burned like wood smoke in my nostrils. To wish to serve, yet have no task assigned—it would strike a blow to anyone's ego—but to a hero, it was devastating.

Having witnessed the mind-speak of Galan and Castian in the past months, I was aware when Castian and Samuel began a private conversation.

Saying goodbye to the pack seemed the perfect way to give the two of them privacy. My stomach growled as I stepped off the path and I examined the sky. Mid-day repast was long over and soon Elora would set out evening victuals.

Lifting my skirts to step into the brush the soil-stained hem made me sigh. It needed to be soaked and scrubbed as soon as I returned to my suite. Wearing my best skirt for teaching at the castle was one thing. Trudging through the forest was quite another.

With a frown, I glanced around. No sign of the pack. They must have run off with Cowboy and Aust. Cowboy's medallion steadily darkened through the afternoon. He needed physical exertion to regulate his strange condition.

"There's my girl." The smooth, deep voice came from over my shoulder as a pair of male arms secured me from behind. "Wandering through the forest alone are you, baby?"

I froze. Bile rose in my throat. Abaddon. Master of the Scourge, plague of the realm, had come.

For me.

He tightened his hold as I battled to break free of his embrace. My arms were trapped at my sides, his steel frame restricting my movement. Terror made me strong, but Abaddon was much stronger. I screamed.

He chuckled deep and throaty next to my ear. "Now. Now. Don't be like that."

My mind spun to recall Bruin's teachings. Jabbing my elbow did nothing, pinned as I was. I gripped hard under the zipper of his black khakis and twisted. His hiss was gratifying and though he wrenched away from my grip, he failed to release his hold.

"Abaddon." Castian's voice was sweet relief. "Step away from my niece."

Samuel's wand was drawn and aimed, though the impulse was more habit than ability, considering his state.

"Release. Her." Castian's command was low and quiet, the strength of the threat unmistakable.

Abaddon's hold remained, though he did stop groping at my breasts. "I have every right to claim her and you know it."

Castian's expression remained unaffected, his focus locked squarely on the monster behind me. Sensations bombarded: the smell of damp tunnels, the subtle brush of a guard's hand, the lingering stares of wanton when Scourge minions thought no one could see. The forest spun into a green blur as thunder roared in my head.

Lia, focus. Castian's voice caressed my mind and his brilliant emerald eyes drew me into their depths. *Fear not, for I am here.*

His gaze returned to Abaddon. "State your purpose."

The hold on my arms shifted and I was whirled fast and rough so we stood face to face. I stared into the soulless black eyes of my captor. Though most females would consider him handsome, he was

63

my living nightmare. The mere cadence of his voice made my legs tremble.

He pulled me tight against his chest, his arm against my back an iron bar as he lifted me off my feet. "I came to claim my woman. We were separated when she was taken from my compound. It's time wifey and I were reunited."

His words tumbled through my mind but held no meaning. "I am not your mate. I have no mate."

"Come now," Abaddon clucked, arching a cruel brow. "Lying doesn't change fact. Highbornes are bound to their first lover. I was yours. Got the bloody gown to prove it."

I struggled to strike him. "You beast. I am a newling. I have never lain with a male and when I do, it will not be one with a soulless waste of manhood."

A sly smile spread across Castian's face. "She speaks the truth, Abaddon. You can both read her voice and scent a lie. She denies your claim and there is no doubt of her honesty."

Abaddon yanked me by my hair, forcing my face closer. "Look me in the eyes and say that again."

With more bravado than I possessed, I stood as tall as I could manage. I craned my neck to meet him eye-to-eye. "Never have I been sexually intimate with you or any other. You lie."

"Sounds pretty definite to me," Samuel said, his wand still pointed at us. "Let her go before I call in a dozen Enforcers and we beat your ass for holding her against her will on Haven grounds. Or better yet, a brutal beat-down sounds fun."

The release of his hold left me staggering to catch my balance. I stumbled and raced forward. Samuel's arms opened and I collided against his solid chest. Tears streamed. I ignored the ensuing argument and pressed my face into the warmth of his neck. His unique scent did more to settle the tremors racking through me than anything.

"I demand you contact the Fates," Abaddon shouted. "They meddle in every moment of our lives. They'll have proof. I don't know how the fuck she's doing it, but she's lying. When I had her last summer, I fucked her senseless and nothing any of you say changes that. If you want witnesses, I have dozens."

Samuel's arms tightened around me. "You colossal bastard. Ye'd provide witnesses to raping her? Do ye really think that helps yer case?"

"Highborne laws are absolute, asshole. Intercourse is binding and irreversible. I was her first and I put that ring on her finger. Rheagan's heir is mine."

I squeezed the ornate diamond stuck on my finger. No matter how we tried to remove it after my return to the living, nothing worked. To know Abaddon thought of it as a symbol uniting us made me want to sever my finger to be rid of it.

"Enough," Castian said, "I'll notify the Fates of your claim. Ooze yourself back under your rock and when they find time to research your claim, you'll be contacted. I warn you, though, the Fates are fickle ladies. There's no telling when they'll get to it."

"It better be soon. I won't put up with you stalling."

The air snapped and Castian stalked forward. He stopped before Abaddon and pressed a finger to his chest. "Don't piss in my sandbox, little man. As God of gods, I am fair to all members of my realm— even those who make my skin crawl. It would set me off to think you just implied I'm biased."

Abaddon had the good sense to shut his mouth.

Castian turned to me. "Lia, due to your history with Abaddon and his predisposition for violence and treachery, I am assigning you a *garda síochána*. This guardian must be in the service of the Pantheon and will protect you and ensure your rights during the time leading up to the Fates findings."

"I'll do it," Samuel said, his jaw set, his diamond-white gaze staring straight ahead. "Galan would be the logical choice, being the Sentinel of Souls and her brother, but his focus is needed elsewhere. Lia and I are already spending time together and my life was pledged to your service long ago. I offer to guard her, her rights and her safety."

"Ironic. Yet fitting," Castian said, a private look passing between them. "Lia, unless you object, Samuel shall assume his post as your guardian."

I wanted Galan by my side but Samuel was right, Jade needed him. "I, uh, no, I have no objection."

"Then it's settled—"

"The hell it is." Abaddon faced off against us and the air around us crackled. Supercharged. Electric. "I don't want that blind traitor anywhere near what's mine. He's the bastard who stole her away in the first place. She's coming with me."

Samuel stepped in front of me and raised his wand. "You stole her. I freed her. Now, stand down. This is a Haven Sanctuary and no one will force Lia to leave."

"Says the blind man waving his twig. Your wizarding skills are no match for sorcery." Abaddon laughed, the sound hypnotizing. "You're nothing but a pathetic shell of what was once a mediocre wizard."

Samuel whispered something and a blue electrical field enveloped us. Abaddon thrust a bolt of screeching light through the air. The surge hit our protective barrier just as Castian sent Abaddon flying fifty feet into the scrub. With a loud thud, our attacker struck the cold, hard ground and Samuel spun from the force of the blow.

"This matter is settled." Castian's voice echoed through the trees. A violent wind picked up and swirled leaves all around us. We stood in the eye of a hurricane. "Until you are contacted, you shall make no move to speak with, gain access to, or relocate Lia in any way. If you do, I shall strike you down where you stand and declare your claim nullified."

Abaddon staggered to his feet and locked his gaze on me.

Castian matched his movement and blocked his view. "Get the hell off this mountain."

Abaddon cursed, gave in and Flashed out.

I rushed to where Samuel fell and cradled his head in my lap. With the fabric of my skirt, I cleaned the gash bleeding along the line of his jaw. "Samuel, wake up. Are you well?"

I stroked my fingers through his hair, praying his eyes would open.

Though the protective field absorbed most of the energy strike, he took a horrible blast.

"Let me see him," Castian said, easing Samuel flat on the forest floor. He opened Samuel's leather slicker and laid his hands on his fine white shirt. An amber glow built across his chest and as it expanded, a breeze lifted my hair. The succulence of bergamot and mint made my mouth water.

I clasped Samuel's hand and closed my eyes. Sweet Shalana, let him be well.

Castian Flashed us. When I opened my eyes, Samuel lay unconscious on the sofa in my suite and I knelt on the floor, still clutching his hand.

"All is well, Lia," Castian said. "Your guardian will need rest but will recover. Watch over him now and he will return the favor tenfold."

I covered Samuel with the sofa throw and gave Castian a hug. "Gratitude, Sire, you are so good to me."

He brushed a soft finger against my cheek. "You are more than my niece, my dear *Ryanne*. You are Jade's sister now, so in a way, you are another daughter to me."

I stared up at his perfect face. He was ethereal for certain, his eyes the sparkling green of gemstones, his features beautiful, but not feminine. The power emanating from him tickled my skin. How could I ever live up to a father figure like Castian? Strong. Righteous.

His smile widened. Raising his hands over my head he produced a necklace similar to his own. He lifted it until the silver caught the light. "The crescent moon is a powerful talisman for me. When you feel panic overwhelm, as you did in the forest today, touch the medallion and draw on some of my power until you regain control."

He winked, and in a golden shower of mist, he was gone.

CHAPTER SEVEN

*H*ad Castian not assured me Samuel was well, the fact that he had yet to stir by morning would have had me frantic. As it was, I spent hours curled up in the plush club chair thinking and dreaming in a fitful reverie

The events of the previous day haunted me.

It was pointless to try to understand the actions of a madman. Somewhere on Abaddon's journey for dominion, he not only lost his soul but his grasp on reality. I was not, nor would I ever be, his mate. I was a newling and though my age of eligibility recently passed, I had every intention of saving myself for a kind and honorable male.

Galan waited five decades into his eligibility for Jade. I wanted that kind of love for my own.

Whisking around my suite I opened the drapes and welcomed spring sun to wash the room. I enjoyed darkness—though nothing was truly dark with Elven night vision—but loved the golden haze of morning.

The sun wasn't at a place in its seasonal cycle to bring us full heat yet, but the promise of the day to come grew with the champagne sunrise.

Selfish as it was, if Samuel was well, I needed him to wake and be on his way. Despite my personal situation, it was the week's end and I committed to watching over the orphaned Were cubs while Bruin escorted Mika to the Modern Realm to visit her friends in Vancouver.

Looping the drapes into their tiebacks I gazed upon the grounds of Jade's private home. Below, men trimmed hedges and aerated the lawn. As they made their passes from the perimeter wall and back to the courtyard, piles of cuttings marked their path. Sadly, the pool would be covered for months yet, a large black tarp stretched over the waters below.

I missed my late-night dips when headaches kept reverie at bay. Submerging to the silent depths always allowed the chaos of the world to silence.

Several of the men below gathered and bagged pruned branches, making ready for the colorful flowers and leaves to come. I had believed the greens of the rainforest were the most beautiful sight, but the multi-hued reds, yellows, and oranges of this forest a few months ago matched the resplendence of even the most splendid palette.

The hitch of Samuel's breathing caught my attention as he shifted to his back.

What would it be like to be deprived of color? To spend endless hours and days in an empty void of sightlessness? It was near eight months since the explosion. The fact that he lost his vision being heroic would be little consolation.

Samuel's breathing changed as he woke. He fell still.

"Fash not, Samuel. Castian Flashed you to my suite." I poured a glass of juice and made my way to the sofa. He made no move so I perched on the edge of the cushion by his hip. "Are you well?"

A gasp hissed from his chest as he scrubbed his face. With his eyes clenched tight, he shook his head and opened them again. "Sweet Mary, mother of God."

I set the glass on the table. "What is it?"

"I can see." Samuel blinked and spun his glance across the room. I stood as he bounded to his feet, his gaze bouncing from the stained-glass light fixtures, to the area rug and all around the room. "Sort of. Mostly. Shapes and colors come at me. More like auras. Everything's blazing in a mass of jewel tones, streaming from you, the furniture, the windows. It's not sight exactly but I can make things out."

"That's wonderful, but how?"

Samuel walked along the sofa. With his arms extended he brushed his fingers over everything within reach. "Abaddon's sorcery? Castian's intervention? I dinnae care."

He lost himself in the magnificence of the everyday items around my suite, the bouquet in the vase, the painted pattern on a bowl, the books stacked beside the sofa. He strode to the window, raising a hand to shield his eyes. "Jaysus, that hurts like the devil's needles stickin' in my retina."

I grabbed his mirrored sunglasses from the table. "Take things slowly. Mayhap you should ease—"

Samuel stared at me with an intensity which made my ears warm. He raised his fingers, tracing my hair where it brushed my cheek, my collarbone, my shoulders. "Gods, yer just that beautiful."

His eyes, still white, now held the focus they lacked since the accident. Where before they were striking, like an opal in sunlight, now they shone with understanding. He swept my hair behind my shoulder with deliberate slowness. "I forgot, ye see. The last time I laid eyes upon ye was when I brought ye out of those caverns all bloodied and unconscious."

"You saved my life."

He cupped my jaw, his gaze dropping from my eyes, down to my lips.

I swallowed, a queer warmth swirling low in my belly.

When I thought he might kiss me, he wrapped me in an embrace and swung the two of us into a twirling spiral of laughter. "Oh, let's go out and see everything: the grounds, the leaves, the castle—everything. Are ye game?"

He released me and spun past the sofa. I flopped down to watch him whirl. "I am caring for the lion cubs at Bruin's den today. Mayhap after—"

"I have to go with ye," he said. "I am yer guardian after all. I—Oh!" Samuel caught sight of the rest of his things on the table and raced to pick up his wand. He stroked the carved wood like a lover caressing his long-lost beloved.

"*Colligevirgorosas.*" He swept his arm in an arc around my suite. Instantly, the ceiling rained glitter and rose petals. Soft, velvet ovals of ivory, lavender, red, yellow and pink, fluttered and floated amongst a sparkling shimmer.

As Samuel spoke his magic again and conducted the rhythmic dance of roses, I leapt from the sofa and plucked them out of the air. It was like living within a snow globe of joy. It was pure and light.

I danced and twirled, free of worry and able to breathe easy for the first time in ages. The next time I twirled past Samuel, I raised to my tiptoes and kissed his cheek. "Such fun. Gratitude, Samuel—"

"*Lia!*" Galan's bellow echoed off the walls.

I spun toward the door. The petals and glitter vanished as quickly as they had appeared.

"Have you lost your senses?"

"I, uh . . . no." I hurried to meet my brother as he strode toward us. "Fash not, Galan. We were merely celebrating the return of Samuel's eyesight. He awoke just moments ago and can see well enough to do his magic."

Galan's glare slapped me with the force of a blow. "What do you mean he woke moments ago? Here? He spent the evening here in your suite?"

"He did, but—"

I grabbed for the suede of Galan's vest as he blew past. A bull in a rage, he lunged, struck Samuel's jaw and locked his fingers around his throat. My suite erupted in a blur of fists and fury, the pent-up animosity of nearly a year detonating.

Samuel thrashed, grabbing Galan's hair with one hand while pounding his face with the other. The two of them tumbled backward in a flurry of oaths. The coffee table stood no chance of survival as they landed full-bodied on its surface. With a mighty crack, it gave way to their weight and they lay in a heap of splintered wood.

"Stop this!" I yelled. "Please, stop."

Samuel's face had flushed as red as elderberry wine. He grabbed a chunk of the walnut table and struck Galan a sharp blow to the head. Blood sprayed across the rug and stained the silver of his hair.

"Galan, let go of his throat! Samuel cannot breathe."

The two of them continued to fight and kick and grapple.

The second crack to Galan's skull dazed him enough Samuel rolled to the side and gasped for air. Galan swiped blood from his eyes and tried to regain his hold. Samuel's fists flew in a wave, striking again and again. A fluid stream of his strange accent filled the air.

"Whoa! Whoa!" Bruin raced through the open door, grabbed Galan with one hand and yanked him from the brawl. His other hand he held out to keep Samuel at a safe distance. Not that there was any danger. The male was still on hands and knees, gasping for breath.

"Well, this is fun," Bruin said, glancing between them. "And I love a grand-ole donnybrook as much as the next bastard, but I think we'll call it a draw for today. Did either of you meatheads consider what this living room romp will do to my sister? Shit boys, Jade's supposed to be avoiding stress. How do you think she's going to react when Galan saunters up to her looking like he's been Freddie-fucking-Kruegered?"

Samuel crawled to the sofa, coughing in spurts, dragging wheezing breaths into his lungs.

"Anyone want to tell me what this is about?" Bruin looked from Samuel to my brother and back again. "No rush. I can play this game all morning."

Galan used the back of his hand to swipe at the unceasing blood trickling down his face. The scarlet stain bloomed from his scalp, transforming the lengths of his matted silver hair to the same deep red as his bridal braid. As macabre as it looked, it accented the purple mass swelling over his left eye.

Galan's gaze met mine. "Samuel took liberties with Lia."

Bruin turned to Samuel. "You can't be that fucking stupid, can you?"

I gasped. "He absolutely was not. Not stupid and not taking liberties. Castian set him unconscious on my sofa for the night after

Abaddon attacked us. He only woke minutes ago and discovered his vision was partially restored."

Samuel stood on unsteady legs and started another bout of coughing. His face flushed brilliant pink as he rubbed the finger marks on his throat.

Bruin smiled. "All right, Merlin. Congrats my man."

"Samuel took no liberties," I repeated, my fists clenched. "I kissed him on the *cheek* in congratulations. Galan insanely overreacted."

"Overreacted? You invite a male—a male who you know I despise —to sleep in your chamber for the evening and instead of asking him to leave the moment he awakens you show him affection?"

"Castian placed him here. It was not a planned event."

Samuel laughed. "So much for your heartfelt speech about owing me a debt of honor for rescuing your sister. That didn't last long, did it, Elf?"

"Only as long as it took for you to besmirch my sister."

I gripped the layers of my skirt. For the first time in my life, I fought the urge to strike my brother. "How dare you say such a thing? I did naught to deserve disapproval. Abaddon came for me while you were off tending to your other family. Samuel defended me and was struck down because of it."

"Defended you, did he? Are you so daft you cannot tell when a male is manipulating you?" He raised his finger and pointed over my shoulder. "That *Ud 'Raan* wants nothing more than for me to die a hideous death so he can bed my wife. If you think his overture of defending you is genuine, the Scourge addled you more than I feared."

The air in my lungs solidified. "Addled? For the simple sake that I kissed a male on the cheek? I have kissed Aust and Tham and a dozen males without you acting like a barbarian. And what of your sexual indiscretions, brother-mine? For decades, you pleasured the women of our village, trysts in the grotto, late nights in the forest. Did you think me so addled then that I did not notice simply because you entertained outside our home?"

Galan's shoulders drew tight and his gaze narrowed on me. "That was different. I was of the appropriate age . . ."

"As am I. My sixth-decade birthing day has come and gone. My time of courting is upon me and if I wish to kiss ten gentlemales on the cheek I am within my rights to do so."

"That wizard is no gentlemale. If you give him heed, he shall have you on your back and be pressed between your thighs in—"

The slap across his face was hard and fast. My palm and heart both stung from the impact. I pointed to the door, my fingers trembling and my knees about to buckle. "Get out of my suite. If this is how you wish to speak to me, I want you out of my sight before I say the hurtful things on my tongue."

"You cannot—"

"*Get out!*"

"This is *my* marital home, Lia. I am the male of the manse. You cannot order me—"

"Fine, I shall leave." I grabbed my jacket and scarf from the chair and raised a trembling finger into the air between us. "Know this, brother-mine, I worried and prayed for Jade and the young. I missed you, shouldering more heartbreak and loneliness than I thought I could bear. And when evil threatened me and I needed your support most, you failed me. I know not this male standing before me, but he broke something precious between us today."

Galan paled, looking stricken. "Lia stop. Apologies. I—"

I shook my head pivoting for the door. "Your apologies mean naught to me. Go be with your mate, Galan. Go be with your family."

"Stop! Where are you going?"

"Anywhere away from you."

CHAPTER EIGHT

*W*hen had my brother become a stranger? Running down the hall, tears obstructed my vision. I barely realized when I reached the open landing at the end of the hall and descending to the foyer three stories below. What, in the eyes of the gods, had I done to inspire such disapproval?

"Nothing," I said, retrieving Samuel's embroidered kerchief from my pocket. "I did nothing."

Raw heat burned inside me, suppressed anger that threatened to explode from within. The rhythmic strike of my boots to carpeted steps marked the closing of a door, a shift that left my heart physically aching. Where would I go? My home had always been Galan. Where he was, I belonged.

Now—*Oh, gods, now I truly am lost.*

My feet slipped on the tile as I turned the corner and slammed into someone. The impact knocked me backward, hands flailing. Strong arms came around my middle, grappling to save me from falling to the marble floor.

"Shit, Lia, I'm sorry," Nash pulled me upright in an awkward tangle of hands. He gazed at his firm hold on my breast and dropped his grip. His embarrassment filled my nostrils in a rush and he coughed to clear his throat. "Yeah, uh, sorry about that too—"

His eyes lifted, then widened. "Gods, Lia, what's wrong?"

I shook my head, my throat as tight as a clenched fist. Tears continued to stream in hot abandon. My breath hitched to the point of me gasping in spastic hiccoughs.

"Shit." Nash pulled me to one of the leather entry chairs in the grand foyer and knelt before me. Rubbing his hands up and down the sleeves of my dress, he looked stricken. "What can I do?"

"Lia?" Samuel's voice called from the staircase. "Ah, there ye are."

I forced myself to stand. "Yes. Here I am."

I dabbed at my eyes and drew a ragged breath. He had gathered his things, donned his coat and carried my satchel, packed and full.

"What have you there?"

Bruin spoke as he filed down the stairs behind Samuel and joined the mix. "First off, Galan says he doesn't want you to leave but understands he went off his rocker. If you need a breather from him, he won't stop you. I convinced him you should stay with us in the Dens 'til everyone cools off. That way you're with family and are still protected."

I let my breath out in a long rush. "That is a fine idea. Gratitude."

Samuel slung the strap of my satchel over his shoulder and reached for the crumpled cloth bunched in my fist. "It's going to be fine, duck," he said, wiping my cheeks dry. "At some point, everyone has a blowout with their family and strikes off on their own. Things will settle, and you and Galan will be right as rain before you know it."

He gave me back the cloth and settled my hair behind my shoulders. Normally it would be plaited with lengths of silk ribbon but with Galan bursting in on us first thing . . . .

My ears warmed to their tips. "I must look a mess."

"Hells no." Cowboy shook his head, coming out from the living room.

Samuel curved his palm over the back of my head, smoothing my hair. "The wolf's right. You could never be anything but stunning—"

"Whoa, back the truck up," Nash said, staring at Samuel. "Can you see her?"

The sad tension of in the foyer broke as Samuel and I told Cowboy, Bruin, and Nash about yesterday's attack, Castian's healing of him, and how he'd woken this morning being able to see the shapes of objects and auras radiating off things.

"It's not sight like before, but I'll never complain."

"It's True-sight," Nash said, looking awed and catching our curious glances. "My people believe True-sight is the ability to see things, not how they appear physically, but by the energy of what they are in essence. The colors mean different things and the radiance, whether it's a little fringe of color or beaming like a spotlight, also holds meaning. You need to figure it out. Fuckin-A, congrats, Merlin."

Cowboy nodded. "Cool. So, is there a *True-sight For Dummies* handbook?"

Nash shrugged. "It's subjective."

"S'all grand, boys. I'll take it and consider it a blessing. Now if ye'll excuse us, I think Lia could use some—"

As Samuel's words choked off, I followed his worried gaze in time to see Cowboy's eyes roll back. He crashed to the floor in a dead faint.

Nash knelt beside him, tapping a finger on the black stone of the bolo tie around his neck. "That one came on fast. Why the hell didn't the alarm go off on this thing?"

Samuel unsnapped the breast pocket of Cowboy's plaid button-down and looked stricken. "Where the fuck's his Auto-injector? Bruin, hold back his wolf."

Bruin closed his eyes and a surge of the Alpha's preternatural power tingled over my skin. Once a Were lost consciousness, he would shift to his base form. Then they were unlikely to be able to deliver Cowboy the help he needed. "I can't hold his shift off for long boys, so hurry up."

Nash joined the search patting and feeling over the planes of Cowboy's body. "Thank fuck," he said, pulling a fat, silver cylinder from the leather knife-sheath tied to his thigh. Without hesitation, he flipped off the cap and slammed it against Cowboy's muscled leg. "Come on, Wolf. Hang in there, buddy."

Samuel placed two long fingers on Cowboy's throat and closed his eyes.

Nash grabbed his phone and scrolled through his contacts. "Bree, we need you to Flash over to Jade's place. The Wolf's down in the foyer . . . good enough." He clicked the phone shut and within seconds the front door opened and Bree ran into the foyer with a small medical bag.

Samuel stepped back and let the Coyote girl in. Bree was petite but as deadly as any of the Weres. With cutting precision, she sent a claw down his sleeve and tied a long rubber band below the exposed bicep of his arm. Snatching something from her bag, she ripped open a packaged wipe and swiped the inside of his elbow. "How long has he been down?"

"Two minutes," Samuel said, pulling off the male's cowboy boots. "maybe three."

"Less chatter," Bruin said. "Holding back a shift here."

Bree stuck his arm with a syringe, the glass vial filling with a rising tide of burgundy. Jade did that in the clinic with Cowboy too. The wolf's blood held a mystery both healer and scientist were trying to unravel. Bree replaced the vial thrice before she removed the syringe and tucked Cowboy's blood into her bag. "Okay, Alpha, you're a go."

Bruin relaxed and the unconscious male shimmered with Were magic. His human body expanded to accommodate the coming animal. Bones popped and reformed. Fingers became paws. Nails became claws. His thick, tri-colored coat threaded through tight follicles in his skin.

Bruin laid a hand on the side of the magnificent beast. "Why the hell didn't the alarm on his medallion go off? And why did this hit so fast?"

"No idea." Bree snatched the bolo necktie Cowboy wore from the floor. The color of the stone lightened back from black to a lustrous turquoise. She laced her fingers through her short brown hair and sighed. "My best guess . . . it's the coming of moon madness."

"Moon madness?" Nash asked.

Bruin nodded. "Yeah. For a Were, a normal full moon is over-powering. Our animals come forward, aggressive and combative. It's a constant battle of control, but with the full moon falling within days of the Equinox in a few months—well, we're all feeling the effects."

Bree lifted Cowboy's eyelid with her thumb and exposed a piercing caramel retina. "It's too much for his body to deal with and still compensate for his condition. Give him some space, people. He's going to come out of this with his wolf panicked and snarling."

Bruin cursed. "And here he comes."

The wolf's eyes snapped open as Samuel tugged us back into the doorway of the lounge and pulled out his wand. Nash stepped away and did the same.

A crackle of energy lit the air. In a show of sheer power and grace, Cowboy's wolf lunged from flat on his side to land on all fours in a crouch. The magnificence of the movement rivaled anything I had seen thus far in the two realms.

"Easy, Wolf," Bruin said, holding his hand up to the Were-animal baring his teeth. "It's us, big guy."

Cowboy inclined his head and stalked over to Bree. She lowered her gaze to the floor and slowly curled into a squatting ball before the predator. The wolf bent and sniffed her hair. When he caught her scent the tension in his body eased and his eyes focused.

"Okay, guys," Bruin said in a quiet, even tone. "Bree and I have this. Nash, call Aust and ask him to come. His boy here is going to need a running partner."

Samuel backed us away, his wand at the ready. Instead of crossing the foyer to the main door, we walked out the mullioned glass doors of the lounge and across the back deck.

When the cool spring breeze crept across the back of my neck, I realized my jacket remained in the foyer. I had no intention of retrieving it.

"You okay?" Samuel asked. After slipping his wand into his pocket, he lifted his arm from his side.

I slipped my hand through the opening offered. "No, but I suppose I shall do."

We walked in a peaceable silence and it struck me our contact now remained out of habit and not necessity. Samuel's sight was restored. I tightened my grip and shrugged a little closer. He may no longer need a guide, but I needed the connection. I had never been at odds with Galan and the thought of being alone was more than I could bear.

The forest rustled with the scurry of squirrels, birds and woodland creatures emerging from the sleep of winter. Buds and sprouts replaced dried leaves. Grass sprung anew from brittle ground. The realm was in a state of rebirth. Creatures of the forest began again, foraging, forming alliances and building for the year ahead.

If only they could tell me their secret.

"What ails Cowboy?" I asked.

Samuel set his free hand on mine in the crook of his arm. "I'm no doctor, but it's something to do with his body not being able to regulate adrenalin. If it drops too low, his heart stops. Jade hasn't had much success treating it, I'm afraid. She's amazing at what she does, but it's a natural condition and her powers dinnae affect it. Bree's come on board with her sciences and hopefully, they can figure it out together."

"Does anyone in his pack suffer the same ailment?"

"No. That's part of the reason he lives here. His pack tried to kill him when they realized he had a health defect."

"His family tried to kill him?"

Samuel nodded. "Sent him out on what was supposed to be a hunt with the men. Turned out it was an ambush. They tore him to shreds and left him for dead."

A shiver shot down my spine and I shrugged closer to Samuel's warmth. "That is barbaric."

"Weres are animals. Animals prey on weakness. There's a poem by a man named Rudyard Kipling from the Modern Realm. It describes the law of survival like this:

Now this is the Law of the Jungle,

as old and as true as the sky,
And the Wolf that shall keep it may prosper,
but the Wolf that shall break it must die.
As the creeper that girdles the tree trunk,
the Law runneth forward and back;
For the strength of the Pack is the Wolf,
and the strength of the Wolf is the Pack.

A gust of wind lifted my hair and I shivered again.

"Cowboy was lucky Bruin claimed him," Samuel said, pausing to take off his long, worn duster. "It's the only reason he hasn't been killed."

He wrapped the coat around my shoulders and waited while I shrugged it on. The bottom hem hung below my knees, the arms well past the tips of my fingers. When he settled the weight on my shoulders, my knees almost buckled. "How do you wear this? It must weigh as much as I do."

"It's the weapons," he said, holding open the lapel and pointing out the pockets hidden within the lining. "You can never be too careful. Scourge can block magic. In which case, I want ye to know, I'm just as deadly with a blade."

I had no desire to think about battles or the need to remain prepared for unexpected attacks. I spun the blue-diamond ring once around my finger and squeezed the stone in my palm. Peering into the thin canopy of the spring forest above, I breathed deep and hoped the tightness in my chest would clear.

The forested path opened and we entered the meadow which bordered Glass Pond. Haven was home to many pocketed bodies of water, some magical, some not. One of the ponds deep in the forest was used as a portal just weeks ago for Lexi to enter the lost city of Attalos and find her Faery kin.

I rubbed my fingers over the velvet mourning band snapped tight around my throat. It was Lexi's mother, possessed by Rheagan, who ordered Tham killed. And though logical thinking dismissed Lexi as a contributor to Tham's death, part of me blamed her still.

I shuddered as a chill ran through me. "Tell me about where you come from, Samuel. Is it like Haven?"

He made a noncommittal sound in his throat and rubbed his eyes beneath his sunglasses.

"There's not much to tell. My Da is a Scotsman of the Realm of the Fair who lost his heart to an Irish lass of the Human Realm—despite the difficulties it caused. They raised his six sons and one daughter in a remote area in what is known as the Highlands. It's a beautiful country with culture, traditions and mischievous charm."

"Yet you hide your tie to your homeland?"

"What makes ye say that?"

"Your lilt rings far stronger when you anger. It is lovely, yet you choose to curb it. Why?"

His shoulders stiffened, pique tightening his brow.

"Apologies. I am ever too blunt. Galan always says—" My words choked off at the mention of my brother and my heart sank further.

Samuel shifted his arm to fall heavy across my shoulders. He pulled me close to his side and winked with a rascal's charm. "Aye, *A mhuirnin*. Ye can be a wee bit blunt, but I'll take it over shinin' me on, any day. And yer right. Ye see, I have a bit of a family rift myself."

"And what is yours about?"

"Let's say, Da expected me to follow in his footsteps but my love for magic forced me to my own path." He cast me a sideways glance. "Ironic really considering where I ended up. The Fates possess a twisted sense of humor. Crafty bitches."

I wanted so much to question him further, but the sorrow in his eyes spoke of a pain beyond my right to ask.

"Believe me when I tell ye, I know what it's like to feel cast out and adrift." He pointed to a group of birds with long black necks and ivory chins waddling beside the pond. "There's your gaggle of geese from the other day. See, they've glutted on the young grass and are ready to fly off and start their spring adventures."

The gaggle, as Samuel called it, pulled and snatched at the fledgling grasses around the edge of the pond. Aggressive little beasties. When one slighted another, they fanned out their wings, flapped in a fury and squawked their offenses.

Such odd creatures. Graceful in flight yet so awkward waddling along the pond's edge. How many survived their journey? How many fell prey to foul weather, exhaustion, or some unforeseen obstacle? Where was home for them when they were forced to migrate for survival?

Leaving Glass Pond behind, Samuel and I climbed the steady incline toward the peak that housed the Dens. The plateau was several hundred feet up, the climb a lovely exertion of energies. Bruin was sweet to offer me a place in his home, but again, it was his home. I doubted I would feel any more belonging there than at Jade's.

Would I ever find my place? Would I ever feel content to the depths of my bones?

I feared not.

CHAPTER NINE

I am a corpse, lain out on a slab, rolling through a maze of damp tunnels. The fuzzy hum circling my mind presses heavy. The flickering light of torches registers, their rhythmic interjection of golden strobes alternating with the darkness. My eyes are open, but I cannot see. Cannot move. The weight of impotence crushes my chest, forces air from my lungs until breath is a forgotten luxury.

My journey stops. I am aware of everything and yet nothing. Sensations burst through my fog until I am certain I will vomit from the bombardment: the scent of roasted pig, the sweet pungency of ale, the brilliance of light refracting off light fixtures above, the cacophony of male voices. . ..

Jeers and deep-throated laughter fill my ears as the stench of male lust fills my sinuses. The reek of it suffocates. I want to hold my breath, but gasp for air. I feel the vile touch of gazes upon me. They slither over my skin like cold-blooded serpents. I push against the weight, but my limbs are dead, my voice unheard. My eyes blur as I pray to my gods and my brother. No one comes. I am alone.

When my lungs collapse upon themselves I am relieved. With the coming blackness, I wait for death to take me. To release me from this nightmare.

I came awake to a shrill, horrifying scream. With my mouth stretched wide and my throat burning, bile rushed into my mouth. I bolted up to sit and clamped both hands over my mouth to silence the din. Movement in the far corner of the room had me scrambling in my sheets.

It took a split second to focus, but there was nothing. Had I dreamed it? Was some figment of my nightmare bubbling up to the surface of my subconscious?

Racked by a clammy sweat, I leaned to the side and grabbed the basin now standing vigil beside my bed. I propped it between my knees and when the muscles in my stomach tightened and pitched, I retched. Nothing came.

Four nights since Abaddon groped me in the forest. Four nights since I came to live with Bruin and his family of Weres. And after four nights of this nightmare madness, I stopped eating evening repast. Tears flowed silently down my cheeks. I sat in the darkness and waited, listening, hoping.

Down the corridor the cubs started to cry. First one, then the next, then the others. Stirred from their innocent dreams by my night terrors, I managed, yet again, to wake the entire den of Weres.

I threw the layers of bedding back and set the waste basket on the floor. After checking my balance, I clicked on the lamp, and swiped at my damp cheeks and forehead.

"Keep it up, Ryanne," I mumbled to myself, tying the belt of the robe. "You will be turned out before you know it."

"Dinnae worry about the quads," Samuel yawned, padding barefoot in his pajama pants across the threshold which joined our bed chambers. He picked up the robe Mika lent me and slipped it over my shoulders. "They'll settle soon enough."

I froze in place, my mind racing. Had Samuel heard me speak my soul name aloud? He scrubbed his fingers through his mish-mashed hair. Mayhap he was too groggy to register my words.

Please, gods, let that be the case.

Oblivious to my panic, Samuel rambled on still half asleep. I exhaled and listened to his running commentary. "—the new Prime Puma sent his niece, Ceri, to live in as a nanny as a peace offering. Cowboy said he's kissing ass after his predecessor refused Bruin's claim as king and helped Abaddon capture Mika. Anyway, I'm sure Ceri will settle them before ye know it."

"I am sure she is not ready for all four to be up at once."

"Good practice." Turning me by the shoulders, Samuel pointed me toward the bed and gave a gentle shove. When the knock came, he shuffled back the other way and reached for the handle of the door. He opened the portal enough to poke his head out. By the deep bass of the male grumblings, I assumed he assured Bruin all was well.

"Apologies, Bruin," I said. Samuel waved my concerns away, closed the door and shuffled back to where I stood. I brushed a piece of loose hair from my eyes. "It is my fault the young are awake. I should at least aid—"

He caught me around the waist and directed me back toward the bed. "What ye should do is mind yer guardian, crawl back into bed and try for some solid sleep."

Samuel stood in front of me, hands on his bare hip bones. My ability to speak vanished. The tiny nubs of his nipples peeked out from beneath dark chest hair. A short thicket of ebony covered his pectorals, thinned and trailed down to the waistband of his tartan flannel pants.

Highborne skin was bare, Samuel's was not.

My fingers itched to touch, to explore. Tight muscles. Tanned skin. Would the hair be fine or coarse? I was about to ask if I could touch it when I caught his frown.

With his hair standing up like a cockerel's comb, he raised a brow and pointed to my quilts. "Back to bed, please."

Giving in, I pulled the tie on the robe and tossed it back to the dresser. When he spun to give me his back, I laughed. "Why are Humans so bashful about nakedness? A body is a body. You have one. I have one. Elves give it no thought."

"I'm not bashful, Lia." The low, husky timbre of his voice quickened my pulse. "I appreciate naked as much as the next fella, but after what ye've been through and how yer family hates me, I'd never hurt Jade by giving them cause for upset. The last thing she needs is more Highborne drama."

Of course. It always came back to Jade. I folded myself into the fleeting warmth of my sheets. Reaching behind my head, I yanked the length of my braid free and laid it over my shoulder. "How can you say we are friends and, in the next breath, say *Highborne* as if my race were a disease you find yourself inflicted with? For a male appointed to guard my safety and my rights, you do nothing to guard my feelings."

Facing the wall opposite me, his head dropped and he gave off a rush of smoky emotion. When he turned, his opal eyes glittered with remorse. "I didn't mean you."

"Just my brother, the male who raised and cared for me since the day of my birthing."

Samuel bit his bottom lip. "Point taken. I'll do better."

"Fine. Now, if that is all, mayhap we could both get a little rest before the sun rises."

He stood his ground.

"Is there something more you wish to say?"

"Jade said insomnia can be dangerous for Highbornes. She said something about Aust and Scarlet Death? I promised I would ensure you were sleeping enough."

Ignoring the musky scent Samuel gave off when he spoke of Jade, I bit my tongue. The memory of Aust suffering from *scareg morttha* gave me chills. I gathered the blankets and pulled the bulk tighter around me. Though nightmares interrupted my dreams since I arrived, I was nowhere near the danger of that horrid affliction. Aust went without reverie for months before he began to exsanguinate back in August.

"Fash not. The next time I speak with Jade, I shall tell her you were intent on expressing her concerns. She will be so pleased with you."

Samuel frowned, pulling the mauve and black duvet high enough to cover my neck. Then he tucked down the sides of my body until I was snug as a first repast sausage. "Dinnae be catty, duck. I'm here because I want to be. I worry about yer well-being the same as hers."

None of the replies running through my mind were kind, so I remained silent.

He sighed. "Okay, so tonight let's try something different." Grabbing the throw from the blanket box at the footboard, he circled the bed. The mattress dipped as he climbed up on the other side. After angling the pillows until he was satisfied, he spread the blanket over himself, rolled on his side and stared at me. "Close your eyes."

I laughed. "You cannot seriously think you are spending the night in my bed. What if someone walks in? You saw how Galan reacted when you were clothed and slept on my sofa. He would lose his sanity if he found you in my bed."

He pulled his wand from the pocket of his flannel pants and spoke in his magic language. "The suite is now spelled for privacy. No one can barge in, so yer stuck with me."

Unbidden, my gaze traveled over the smooth lines of his shoulders, down the taut muscles of his abdominals to where his navel disappeared beneath the blanket.

He chucked my chin up to meet his gaze, the corners of his mouth twitching. "A body is a body, right? Highbornes think nothing of nakedness?"

My ears flushed hot. "Nothing at all."

Samuel smiled and yawned. "Besides, I'm on yer bed, not in it. And I'm staying. The nightmares started since ye moved here. I figure ye must either miss Galan or ye don't feel safe. Either way, a little company might help. We'll give this a try. If it doesna work, ye can wake everyone up in an hour with yer screamin, no harm done."

The last thing I wanted was to keep everyone awake again tonight, but if Galan caught Samuel in my bed there would be more than Highborne drama. There would be bloodshed.

"Besides," he continued, tugging at me until I relented and sank against my pillow, "we've a morning meeting with Reign and we'll both be useless if we dinnae get some sleep."

"A meeting?"

Rolling on his back, he closed his eyes. "Aye, lass. Reign's letting us use his private library to research some of the laws of what Abaddon's claim might mean."

My heart stuttered. "Did you hear from Castian? When do we appear before the Fates? Why did you not tell me?"

Samuel's chest rose and fell, his face relaxed. "Trust me, Lia. I'll tell ye everything I know when I know it. Ye do trust me, aye?"

"Yes."

"Right, so let's not get ahead of ourselves. Tonight, we sleep. Tomorrow we'll see where Abaddon's claim stands in the eyes of the Fates and realm law."

"How am I supposed to sleep now?"

He opened his eyes and sighed. "Exactly why I dinnae tell you. Now close those lovely blues and we'll think on it tomorrow. I swear there'll be time enough to worry when we're rested."

The genuine exhaustion on his face stopped me from arguing further. In the void of light and conversation, I lay rigidly still. It was strange though, that sense of comfort despite the awkward restlessness. Mayhap he was correct about his presence warding against my nightmares. There was something easing in the knowledge he was on the other side of the bed. I felt as safe with him as I had with no one other than my brother.

But Samuel was not my brother.

I inhaled, his scent triggering an entirely different reaction. Goddess, this was going to be a long night.

"All right," I said. "Tomorrow."

CHAPTER TEN

The haze of morning brought the most delicious sensations. The warmth of a touch moving from my arm to my waist. Lips on my throat. A gentle suckling at my skin. With closed eyes, I lifted my chin to grant access to my throat.

I liked this dream. My lips parted as a male groaned and waded through the sheets. With the barrier between two bodies eliminated, flesh met flesh. Something hard pressed into my hip. He groaned louder. A heavy leg shifted across both of mine, gathering me flush to his body.

His hips ebbed against me like a lazy tide advancing on the shore. The rhythmic surge of forward and back brought struck a tingle between my legs. The heat and the strength of him. The softness of his skin against the coarseness of his body hair. Something needy unfurled in my belly.

Strong arms wrapped around me as lips took my mouth.

My eyes flew open. Samuel. A luxurious hunger covered his face. The scent of arousal intoxicated. Neither tentative nor restrained he thrust again. Sure hands ran down my bare back and cupped the rounds of my backside.

Tentatively, I braced my hands on his chest. "Samuel?"

He drew back, his diamond white stare sharpening from sleep into full awareness. "Lia? Shit!" He wrenched himself away, flung off the bedding and leapt to his feet. I . . . uh."

My heart raced from the warmth of unbridled lust.

"I'm sorry, Lia. I never wanted ye. . ."

His words slapped me. Mayhap in his dream state, it had not been me he was pleasuring. With his back to me, he scrubbed his neck and exhaled.

"Was it Jade?" I wrapped the quilts around myself. "Was it her you dreamt of whilst lying next to me?"

He cast a seething glance over his shoulder before bolting for the ensuite connecting our rooms. "It was just a mistake. It just shouldna happened. I cannae say how sorry I am that it did."

It was nine when I trudged my way down the stone corridors of the Dens toward the dining hall. That this place was built deep inside a mountain amazed me. That it felt warm and homey, even more so. I rubbed my temples, my head having exploded into a migraine after Samuel stormed from my suite.

Why bring Jade into it? Samuel's thoughts and actions while sleeping were naught for me to judge. I should have allowed the awkward moment to pass. Instead, I humiliated him further by picking at old wounds. The warmth kindled in his eyes of late had extinguished in an instant.

Yet another thing ruined.

"Oh. She lives," Cowboy said.

As they always did, each of the males at the table rose as a female entered the room. This late in the morning though, the usual crowd of two dozen Weres had cleared out and only Cowboy, Bruin, Mika, and Bree remained. Samuel's absence hit me with crippling desolation.

Bruin strode to the empty seat opposite his mate and pulled out the chair for me. "We worried you weren't feeling well. You're usually up with the birds."

I rubbed my hand over my brow as they reclaimed their seats. Why choose this morning to make me the center of conversation? I selected a plate from the buffet and after collecting a napkin and cutlery, accepted the seat Bruin offered.

May the gods bless him, Bruin dimmed the lights as he strode back to his seat. The wooden chair creaked under his solid frame as he rested his arm across the back of Mika's chair. Absently, he played with her long chestnut ponytail. The two of them were lovely together. The ease they shared. Their affection.

Bruin held his hand up and a tall glass of offensive smelling liquid appeared. He flipped back his shaggy brown bangs, his turquoise gaze all too knowing. "A cure-all for a rough morning."

I squinted his way, my head drumming out an incessant rhythm. "Apologies?"

"This is your first headache since you got here, isn't it?" Mika asked.

I nodded and sniffed the rim of the glass Bruin gave me. My eyes burned and I thrust the glass away from my nose. "I think I would rather suffer."

"Nonsense," Bruin said. "Suck it back."

Not wanting to argue with the Alpha, I swallowed the first few gulps then let the rest slither down the back of my throat. My entire body shuddered and fought the urge to heave. Closing my eyes helped. I breathed in and out of my nose and after a few moments, the throbbing echo in my skull did, indeed, start to subside.

"Better?" Bree asked from the end of the table. Even in jeans and a t-shirt, the female of Aust's affections held an admirable strength. She survived the violence of the Scourge, but showed no sign of being left lesser because of it. Her warm amber eyes held sympathy, her coyote much too clever to mistake my state for a simple headache.

I speared fruit and pastries from the plates on the table and forced a smile. "Yes, gratitude."

She stood and gathered her lab coat from where it hung over the back of her chair. "Wolf, I need you in my lab this afternoon for blood work—no excuses. If you don't show, I'll track you down like the dog you are."

"Promises, promises," he said, reaching for a platter of bacon from the center of the table and tossing a slice at each of the lion cubs wrestling on the floor. The cubs, distracted by the meat bombardment, snatched up the bacon, swatting and growling at their siblings.

Bree rolled her eyes. "I'm serious, Wolf. Be there or face my wrath."

He barked out a laugh. "All the sass of a mate and none of the sugar." She smacked him on the back of the head and he laughed harder.

"Laters, everybody. Don't wait up."

"You working at the Hearthstone tonight?" Mika asked, slapping Cowboy's wrist as he made to throw another round of bacon to the four furry fiends now gathering around his chair.

Bruin stood to help Mika clear the breakfast plates. "By the blush, I say our little coyote has a hot date."

Bree's olive skin flushed brighter. "If you must know, Aust and I are going to run. He wants to let his tiger loose and it's been a while since my coyote really laid paws to earth."

"Sounds like fun," Cowboy said, finishing his coffee. "Want company?"

"No!" Bree leveled a glare at each of the males. "I moved out of the Hearthstone to gain some distance from overprotective men. You boys are going to give Aust and me plenty of space tonight. I mean it. If I catch one whiff of your scents on the breeze, I'll come back here and sink my canines deep into your haunches while you sleep."

Bruin rubbed his backside. "I don't know, coyote girl, my haunches are pretty tough."

Mika's hand cracked against Bruin's backside as he leaned over the table to clear plates. When his brow disappeared behind his shaggy bangs she shook her head. "Don't worry about them, Bree," Mika said. "Have a wonderful evening."

"Thanks, Ursa."

Mika reached for the remaining empty platters, but Cowboy jumped to his feet. "Sit Ursa, you cooked. The men will clean."

Mika settled back into her seat and smiled. "Who says chivalry is dead?"

I studied my plate of cut fruit as the males carried plates to the kitchen. "Has Samuel eaten?"

Mika sipped at her coffee mug and licked her lips. "Eaten no. He stormed out of here long ago. He told Cowboy to Flash you to Jade's house and escort you to Reign's office when you're ready. What was that about?"

I stuffed a spoonful of fruit into my mouth and shrugged.

She laughed. "I'm an investigative journalist, Lia. I can smell evasion miles away. If you don't want to talk about it, that's fine. Let me know if you change your mind."

Mika rose from her seat and untied the silk scarf laced through the belt loops of her jeans. Easing around the table she held it out to me. "If you want to avoid gossip and bloodshed, use this to cover up that love bite on your neck. The Talon gossip like old ladies at a quilting convention and even with your hair down, people will notice that hickey."

I touched the flesh of my neck where Samuel had been. In my haste to vacate my suite, I forgot to wear my mourning band. Not ready to face my suite again yet, I accepted her offering and pushed my plate away, appetite gone.

The scent of warm pastry drifted from inside Reign's private library. The smells rang of mango, lemon and apricot. Elora knew I was coming. Since leaving the village after Tham's ceremony, she had been spoiling me with baking. It was an indulgence in both sustenance and affection

One I missed living at the Dens.

My chest eased slightly as Cowboy pushed the heavy wooden door open and waited for me to enter. "One Highborne beauty delivered as requested," he said.

Samuel nodded but did not raise his gaze. Bent over the table in the center of the room, he continued running a finger over the faded sepia print in an ancient and likely priceless book. By the organization of the piles, I guessed he had examined a fraction of what he set aside to review.

His avoidance may have gone unnoticed to a human entering the space, but the scent of residual anger rang strong for a Were and an Elf. "That's all, Wolf. I'll let ye know when we're done. We might need to take a road trip, if yer game."

"Let me know what to pack. I hate bein' under-accessorized." Cowboy dipped the rim of his black hat and backed out of the door.

And then, the two of us were alone.

I understood his anger and from where it stemmed. I had embarrassed us both and it was only logical I be the one to calm the waters. I flexed my fingers and drew a breath. "Apologies, Samuel. This morning I—"

Samuel's palm jutted into the air, though his gaze remained locked on the books before him. "I told ye. It was a mistake. Let the moment die its final death."

I picked up a fabric-covered journal from a pile on the edge of the table. "And will your anger towards me be dying that death as well?"

He sighed. "It will. I promise. I hoped maybe the aroma of the sweets might cover that up."

I toured the room. Reign's private collection of realm books was astounding. His library, a two-storey room, rich in masculine tones of burgundy and midnight blue, housed floor-to-ceiling bookshelves brimming with scrolls, parchment and tombs. Beyond Elora's baking, a faint mint incense hung in the air, counteracting the musty scent of old parchment and stale magic.

"What are you looking at?"

Samuel gestured to the open books on the table before him. "I combed realm history, looking for precedent on a woman's rights over the act of mating. Highbornes aren't the only race with strict bonding laws. Weres, Sprights, and some shifters like Finfolk have similar beliefs about how claiming a body translates to claiming a mate."

"But there was no claiming of my body. No mating of any kind. Past cases will not come into argument. We should focus on how to prove that Abaddon lies."

He looked at me for the first time since I arrived and it was as if the entire realm faded from existence. His gaze held such a mix of regret and emotion. Was this about more than our incident this morning in bed? "What is it? Please, tell me."

He stepped around the corner of the table and bracketed my face with his hands. Wariness filled his gaze and he spoke too carefully for my liking. "Laws are laws, Lia girl. Ye cannae say for sure he lies, lass. Ye dinnae remember what happened in those weeks that Abaddon held ye captive. What if he can prove his claims?"

"He cannot." My heart thrummed heavy in my chest. "He cannot prove what never happened. He is sadistic and insane. We must expose him for the monster he is."

Samuel's lips pursed into a fine line and, after a few moments, he nodded. "Aye, we will. I'm just saying, we must look at every possibility."

"Because the asshole is evil hellscum," Jade said, striding in to join us. "We can't trust him to play by any rules when it comes to getting what he wants."

Samuel whirled toward the door and his body reacted unbidden. The air filled with the distinctive spice he gave off whenever Jade was near. I could not blame him. He had not seen her since the attack and with her sudden appearance—you love whom you love, after all.

With an easy smile, he gathered her in his arms and then stepped back to study her. "Gods, ye look grand, Luv. How are ye? I didn't know ye were home from Castian's Palace."

"Much better." In worn jeans, a thick ivory sweater, and her curls long and loose to her waist, she once again glowed with strength and health. "It's weird not having my powers, but since the Fates bound them, the danger to the twins seems to have passed."

"Then thank the Fates for that." I exhaled and hugged her myself. "That is wonderful news."

"Aye, it is." Samuel pulled a wing chair from the corner. "There now, sit."

She leaned over the mountain of volumes and scrolls lying on the table before us. "I'll sit. I promise, but being relieved of my teaching, Talon and healing duties has left me with way too much time on my hands. Let me help. Reign caught me up to speed and I'm all yours for as long as you need."

The vitality Jade gave off, eased a worry held deep in my chest. Until another thought struck me. "Will Galan be accompanying us?" Though I missed my brother, the thought of him being there while Samuel and I dealt with Abaddon's claim—What would I say to him?

"Not unless you want him to be." Jade's hopeful, emerald gaze dimmed as I shook my head. "Okay. That's okay. He'll give you all the time you need, but he is so sorry he said those things. He said if there is anything he can do—"

"There is." Samuel passed Jade a thick green book and backed her into the chair. "Abaddon's claim cites Highborne laws and, although Reign's collection rivals the Library of Alexandria, if Galan could go to the village and convince those elders to part with the texts dealing with mating laws and claiming, that would be grand."

A lump blocked my throat. "Is it not bad enough everyone here knows my humiliation? Why must those judgmental fools learn of Abaddon's filthy claim? My sire is one of the elders. Do you think I want him to hear of it?"

Samuel braced his hands on the table opposite me and sighed. "First off, not everyone here knows yer business. I bet no one beyond yer Elven family, Bruin, Cowboy and Reign know the details of Abaddon's claim. Stop worrying about that. Second, we need those books so we can shut the bastard down. No sense walking on eggshells. What's done is done."

I sighed. "Since when are you the logical one?"

Samuel smiled. "Yer rubbin' off on me, duck."

"So, do you want me to ask him?" Jade asked, her hopeful grin renewed. "I'll tell him to keep the reason private. He can make up something to satisfy those aristocratic windbags. He could be back in a couple hours."

My objection was ridiculous. Samuel needed those texts and until recently, I believed Galan hung the moon. More than my brother, he reared me from a sapling, protected me from our father and treated me with nothing but devotion my entire life. But his words from our fight still cut me to the quick.

I shook my head, picking up the yellow notepad Samuel used to make notes. "I cannot face him. If he were to give any credence to Abaddon's claim—if he even looked upon me with an ounce of doubt or judgment—it would rip my soul apart and I would never recover."

Samuel stepped closer and squeezed my shoulder. "All right, lass. We'll ask him to retrieve the books and leave them here for us to go through later. Ye don't need to face him if yer not ready. He'll be glad to help in any case, I'm sure."

Jade rose from her seat and moved to join us. "Whatever you need, hon. He'll understand and he wants to be involved."

Samuel's brow raised in an elegant arc. "He could say it's something to do with him being Sentinel of Souls. What do you say? It's yer call."

I rubbed my hands over my face. Though I would much rather hide in my room at the Dens or dunk my head in the river until the world and its troubles were carried downstream, I relented. "Very well, ask him. Please stress how important it is to me that the village not find out why we need them."

Jade nodded and strode toward the door. "Consider it done. And don't worry about a thing. Galan will not let you down again. I swear it."

CHAPTER ELEVEN

A few hours later, Jade received the call. Galan was on his way back to Haven with the Highborne law books. There had been no trouble and nothing about my situation came into the conversation. Spirits lifted at the thought I might once again be able to count on my brother, I left Samuel to receive the books and sought out Elora to thank her for the baking.

When I arrived in the receiving area outside Jade's kitchen, Elora sat engrossed in a book.

"What are you reading?" She jumped and let out a little yelp of surprise. "Apologies, I never meant to startle you."

Elora laughed. "No apology necessary, my attention was definitely elsewhere."

I looked at the black lace bra flung over the lampshade on the cover of the book and smiled. "30 days. What is it about?"

She swept a loose bit of hair out of her eyes and behind her flushed ears. "Lexi gave it to me and insisted I read it. It is about a girl whose husband passed to the After and the sexual adventures he left her to explore once she was ready to move forward. It is from the Human Realm but it seems the loss of love translates to any race and any realm."

"I know naught of the Human Realm but a love like yours and Cameron's shall forever stand as the perfect example. Even if it failed to last a lifetime, you were blessed to share what time you did."

She nodded and handed me the book. "Your age of eligibility is newly upon you. I remember the excitement of it. How badly I wanted to know about males, their bodies, my body and all the adventures in store. It must be even more confusing for you, living in a new place with so many males of different races to consider. Take it."

"But Lexi meant it for you."

"I have read it." She winked and refused to take it back. "Three times over. Allow your imagination to wander, child. Consider what sexual adventures you might like to have. And if you ever need to talk or ask questions, I shall be here."

I Flashed to the Dens with Kobi and Cowboy as my escorts and Elora's book tucked in my bag. Was I ready for sexual adventure? As a female Highborne, it was my privilege to call for males to tend to me. Pleasuring a female was an honor to males and would be a welcome invitation.

At least in our village.

I wondered how the customs in the Realm of the Fair differed. Did I have it in me to proposition a male? I eyed the two males close at hand. Kobi, lanky and dark. With his piercings and the black outline of his dark eyes, he was exotic and dangerous. Cowboy, broadly muscled and blond. His charm and humor warmed my heart. Both attractive in their own way. Both highly regarded by females if their banter was to be believed.

"Lia, sweetheart, see anything you like?" Cowboy's drawl stretched out the words as his smile widened. He was teasing me. He caught me blatantly staring at his body and was teasing me.

"Apologies. I, uh." I glanced around. "Oh, we are here."

The main entrance to the Dens was located in a jagged rise of Haven Mountain, a few hundred feet above the level of the castle and

Jade's home. The doors were not visible from a distance, inset and hidden in the shadowed contours of the rock formation. What was visible from the Academy grounds was the wide, flat ledge winding around from the east-facing entrance.

Encompassing almost the entire circumference of the peak, this ledge was the only access point into the royal home of the Alpha Were and his charges. Heavily guarded by Were-males, technology and magic, the plateau was the farthest point of access for Bruin's home by Flashing or climbing.

On the first day of my stay there, Samuel explained how he and Julian worked their collective magic on the extensive network of caves burrowing into the mountainside. The security had to be impenetrable before Bruin would consider allowing Mika to move in. Between Samuel's powerful enchantments and Julian's prowess with all things technological, the Dens was an impenetrable fortress.

"Honey, we're home." Cowboy's lazy drawl echoed off the rock face as we rematerialized outside the main doors.

According to Mika's Eduda, Grandfather Hawk, the main entrance faced east to welcome the rising sun for good fortune. And as the platform wrapped around the peak in varying widths, he and Mika created small vignettes of interest connected by gardens all the way around.

The plateau at the entrance was bare, for security purposes, but as you wound your way south, they had an herb garden, then a prayer and meditation landing facing the west and then an area with a gazebo and hanging gardens near the north vista. Samuel and I strolled the whole path two nights past and it took us over an hour to reach the end and return.

As my escorts and I rematerialized, Bruin stepped away from his conversation with two Were guards and met us as we approached the main doors. Bruin kissed the top of my head and held out a fist to bump knuckles with his friends. "Wolf, Demon, you boys want a drink?"

"Can't," Kobi said. "We're on rotation tonight. Just making a special delivery before we take off."

Cowboy pulled out a small, red package from the pocket of the plaid shirt he wore loose over his white muscle shirt. He removed two cigarettes and handed one to his Demon friend.

Bruin frowned. "I wish you guys would give that shit up. It's gonna rot your insides."

Kobi laughed, propped the cigarette in his mouth and held up his index finger. A flame burst from the tip of his finger and he lit his vice before letting Cowboy do the same. "Lost cause, Bear. Demons are rotten to the core."

"True, d'at," Cowboy tipped the rim of his hat and jogged to the door, exhaling a sweet-smelling cloud of smoke as he left. "Give me ten to shower up and grab my gear."

Kobi turned back to Bruin. "Hey Bear, you got a minute?"

"Sure, whassup?"

Kobi tilted his head to the side and walked the two of them to the rail at the far edge of the plateau. With heads close, they spoke in hushed tones. It was far enough for privacy from the lion guards but, where the Were sense of smell was superior to an Elf's, my hearing was far too acute not to overhear.

In an attempt not to be rude, I focused my attentions on the scenery below: the trees blooming with April life almost obscured the roof of Jade's manse and the Academy grounds beyond. I walked along the rail, watching the sun sink low in the sky, shivering as it took the warmth of the day with it.

Moments later Bruin's phone went off. "Yes, she's here, Samuel." Bruin winked at me. "They're here too . . . Okay, I will . . . Later." Sliding the device into the pocket of his ripped jeans he chuckled.

"What did Merlin want?" Kobi asked, exhaling a stream of smoke.

"He was supposed to get a call-back saying Lia arrived."

Kobi exhaled. "Like the Wolf and I were going to leave her in the forest somewhere and forget to bring her home? Gimme a fucking break."

I shivered as a gust of wind lifted my hair and swirled up my skirts. Though spring was upon us, the wind still blew cool. Instantly, a fitted hide jacket dyed the most perfect plum wrapped around me.

The gray fur lining rubbed against my chin as soft as Faolan's under-belly. "Gratitude, Bruin. It is beautiful, but you need not fuss. I am well enough."

The Bear-King strode over and eased my hair out from the furred collar, letting it fall to my back. "Castian appointed Samuel your guardian, but you're my family now. I gottcha, little sista."

The soft, rhythmic chuffing of wood being planed around the plateau caught my attention. "If the two of you will excuse me, I would like to spend some time in the butterfly garden watching Grandfather Hawk work."

The evening before, Grandfather explained the Native beliefs surrounding butterflies. If I were to capture a butterfly, make a wish and release the creature, it would carry my wish to the ears of the Great Spirit. What would I wish to be different? So many things.

Bruin gestured for one of the lions to follow.

I knew enough not to argue about the security. Other than inside the locked doors of Jade's home, the Dens or the Fae palace, I had been escorted by one hulking warrior or another every moment since Abaddon made his appearance. Like it or not, anonymity was a luxury the lost heir to the Queen's throne would never enjoy again. Rubbing the center of my chest, I headed around the side of the plateau.

Mika and a feline female were working amongst the second perennial garden along the path. When Bruin's mate saw us come around the bend, she straightened and tossed her chestnut braid behind her back. "Hey Lia, how'd your day at Jade's go?" She winced as she arched her back and stretched from side to side.

"It went well." I knelt on the stone wall bordering the plants and gathered her cuttings. "Samuel and Galan are working through the Highborne laws to determine what weight Abaddon's claim holds."

"Really?" she said, brushing off her khaki pants. "The two of them in the same room? So, who's there to break it up when they start killing each other?"

I rubbed my hands together to dislodge a dusting of dirt and stuffed them into the pockets of my new jacket. "Reign arrived before

I left, presumably to get an update on the research. More than likely he was inserting himself into the situation."

"Smart man."

I brushed my cheek to bring her attention to the dirt smudge on her own.

"So, what's next?" She asked, pulling off her gardening glove to clean her cheek.

"Samuel said we would hit the books early tomorrow until he had to go to the castle mid-morning. He is performing a mock duel for the fifth-year wizarding students. Did you know this class of Academy students is considered some of the strongest wizarding stock in three centuries? The things they can do are incredible."

"A mock duel sounds fun. Who's he going up against?'

"Another Talon wizard. An attractive Asian woman who has been filling in now and then in Samuel's absence since the explosion."

Mika's smile grew stiff. "An Asian Talon who wields magic? Did you catch her name?"

I shook my head. "I saw her practicing but did not wish to disturb her. Very talented. She moves with Elven grace and uses two bone-white sticks instead of a wand."

Mika cast a glance back toward the main plateau giving off a low growl, deep in her chest and the unmistakable sulphur scent of anger. "That would be Katsu. I hadn't heard she was teaching at Haven."

Taking the basket from my hands, she pushed it toward the blonde feline at her side. "Lia, this is Ceri, the newest addition to our little family. I don't think you met her at breakfast."

I greeted the female, wondering if I should apologize to Mika for whatever I did to anger her or mayhap I should apologize to Ceri for waking the cubs last night. "Merry meet, Puma. What a blessing you shall be to your Alpha and Ursa."

"It's my honor," she said.

Mika moved us further around the path to where her grandfather, G-pa Hawk—as Cowboy and the other Weres called him—was working on the second of three totems he designed to watch over their new home.

My step froze mid-movement when I saw who was watching him. The weeping girl from the forest tree lay on one of the reflection benches, her leg swinging.

Hawk extended his clasped hands along the log in a long smooth stroke. Curls of wood leaped from his drawknife and landed beside his fringed moccasins. When he caught sight of us, he straightened and flipped his wiry gray braid to his back just as his granddaughter did. "A man is blessed by the spirits to share the company of one beautiful lady. What have I done to deserve the attention of three?"

Mika giggled and kissed his forehead. "You're such a flirt, Eduda."

I chuckled, tightening my collar as an icy gust invaded our circle. "You mean four, Grandfather." I strode over to the girl and sat next to her when she sat up. "It is nice to see you again. Apologies, I do not recall your name? You are . .?"

The girl stared from behind shaggy brown bangs, her turquoise eyes fixed and focused. *You can really see me? Hear me?*

"Yes, of course. Are you well? We met before, remember. You helped me phone for aid."

Only the buzz of bees could be heard in the silence which descended. Looking to the raised brows and blank faces surrounding me, I wondered if someone said something and I failed to respond? My ears warmed to their peaks.

Grandfather Hawk's weathered face broke into a wrinkly, copper grin. "You see my spirit guest. I have long sensed her but cannot see or communicate with her myself."

"Spirit guest?" Mika said, her voice tight. "You didn't say anything to me about us hosting spirits here in the Dens."

Grandfather lifted a hunched shoulder and blew a puff of sawdust from the muzzle of the bear he was carving. The fresh earthy spice of red cedar bloomed in the air. "She is a gentle soul, merely keeping an old man company while he putters in the yard. I would like to know her name, though, as I cannot address her properly when she does visit me."

Mika stood behind her grandfather, her hand squeezing his shoulder. "Yes. I'd like to know who she is too."

The girl seemed as perplexed by the whole interaction as I. How was I able to see her when no one else could? "Who are you, my friend?" When she gave me her name I repeated it for the group. "Her name is Gemma Arthfael."

"I'm sorry, *who*?" The warm bronze of Mika's indigenous heritage drained from her cheeks. She leaned past the elderberry bush and the liquid in her belly splashed to the soil. Ceri rushed to her Ursa and pulled her hair back.

Just as her knees buckled, Bruin materialized and gathered her to his chest. Cowboy and Kobi Flashed in right behind him, daggers drawn, eyes sharp.

Bruin scooped his mate into his arms, leveling a harsh glare over the group. His usually turquoise eyes flecked gold, becoming more amber by the second. "What happened? Mika's emotions flipped off the charts."

All eyes turned to me.

Bruin lowered his gaze. "Lia girl? What did I miss?"

"I'm fine," Mika said, scissoring her legs. With her protestation, Bruin had no choice but to set her down. Even still, he kept his arm curled around her waist. "I uh, we had a bit of excitement. That's all. And it didn't sit well with my salmon sushi."

Again, Bruin's golden glare scanned the group.

Despite knowing Bruin was a male of worth, I was wary of his bear. The animal side of him was aggressive and dangerous. His huge, bulging arms, his thighs, thicker than my waist, were strong enough, fast enough to overpower a threat to him or his beloved Ursa. No. The last thing I would want is to anger his bear.

"All is well, my son," Grandfather Hawk said, setting down his adz to exchange it for a chisel. "There are many mysteries in the ways of the Earth Mother. It is not our place to question the why but endeavor to understand what comes."

Bruin blew a deep breath from his cheeks. "And what has come, Hawk?"

Mika placed her palms on Bruin's broad chest. "You know how I hear voices on the wind?" His shaggy, brown hair bobbed as he nodded, looking like he was soon to explode. "Well, Lia has a spirit gift herself."

"I'm listening."

"Lia seems able to communicate with spirits." Bruin's eyes narrowed on me, but Mika continued. "Do you remember the girl she spoke to in the forest before she found Jade?"

"Of course, we searched, but there was no trace of her."

"Because she is of the spirit world."

"She's a ghost?" Bruin's attention focused so solidly on his mate that I felt as though we were intruding on their privacy. "And what about her upset you so much? What the fuck's that look for, Mika?"

"This spirit says she's your sister—your twin, Gemma."

Bruin paced the great room, his heavy, thumping strides eating the floor in a frenetic circuit. Around the four couches set in a square, past the line of barstools tucked under the granite surface, past the doorway to the corridor . . .

"Bullshit," he said for the tenth time since he'd ushered us inside. He stormed behind the bar running the length of the far wall and banged a glass down. "My twin passed with the rest of them. She transitioned to the After with my parents and all our people."

He sloshed a liberal amount of amber liquid into the glass, swallowed it, then repeated the process. "No way could Gemma shadow me for fourteen years and I never feel her or know she's there. No. Fucking. Way."

He gave up on the refill approach and lifted the bottle straight to his mouth.

"Isn't it at least possible?" Mika asked.

Bruin looked first to her and then to me, his eyes filled with a feral fury. "Gemma was half of me. We were more than littermates. When those Scourge—" He growled. "When they did what they did to her, a huge part of me died too. I don't know who this ghost is, you see or think you see, but it's not my twin!"

My resolve withered beneath his golden glare.

I am so, you stubborn asshat. She went on in colorful detail, yelling at her brother.

I drew a deep breath and edited her message. "She says she passed three days later—after everyone crossed over."

Bruin's growl rumbled deep and long. "I remember."

I twisted and untwisted my finger around the tail of the scarf I wore. "She says she could not leave you alone and injured. She needed to stay, to ensure you were well."

Bruin's eyes pinched closed as his head dropped forward. "No. Gemma is with my parents Behind the Veil. That's been the only fact to give me comfort all these years. They're together. My family is together."

Wrong. Gemma said. *Most of them are together.*

No words would make this easier. I ignored the ghostly objections and said nothing.

Bruin continued to brood and drink, spiraling deeper into whatever nightmare he was reliving. Mika and I stood in silent vigil.

"Whoa, who died?" Samuel surveyed the large room and stepped in. His gaze narrowed on Bruin, shifted to Mika and me, and then Cowboy and Kobi by the door. "Ye all look like yer sailing the good ship Holy Shit. What did I miss?"

Bruin's growl filled the room, the vibration sending pictures rattling on the walls and the stained-glass shades chinking and chiming around the light fixtures.

"Right, Bruin's pissed and getting faced. Anyone else?" Samuel's expression darkened as he stared at me.

"I upset Bruin."

"Oh, baby." Bruin slammed the empty bottle on the granite counter and stormed around the bar, his claws extending from the tips of his fingers. "You haven't seen upset yet but it's coming."

Back off, Bruin. Gemma lunged from the sofa only to have her brother pass through her ghostly form. *Don't let him intimidate you, Lia. His bear is just broody.*

"Stand down, Bear." Samuel stepped before me.

The tension in the room crackled. Hostility singed my nostrils as harsh words volleyed and collided in the air.

Gods, what had I done?

"Enough!" Mika intercepted her husband and sent him back toward the bar.

My chest constricted, compressing until spots danced in front of my eyes. My trembling hands failed to untie Mika's scarf wrapped around my throat. I needed air.

Samuel turned and pulled me into his embrace. The moment his arms wrapped around me, the dam inside me broke and I began to cry.

"S'all right, shhh." His fingers sunk deep into the length of my curls. "Whatever it is, we'll make it right."

I closed my hand around Castian's medallion and the trembling in my body eased.

Samuel drew back, his face etched with anxiety. "Now, tell me what's happened?"

As Mika and I filled Samuel in on the discovery of my bizarre gift, Gemma sank back on the sofa and covered her face with the sleeve of her cable-knit sweater.

Samuel joined Bruin at the bar and, by the end of the story, he too clutched a bottle of spirits. "And yer sure it's the same lass ye saw the day Jade was attacked?"

I nodded.

"And has it happened before . . . seeing the dead? Other than that time?"

I shrugged. "At Tham's ceremony, we were given the ability to say our goodbyes, but . . ."

"But what?" Samuel set down the bottle.

"I saw Cameron, Aust's sire. I thought I imagined it, but at the river later Cameron spoke to me. Cowboy was there."

All heads shifted toward the doorway and the Oklahoma wolf raised both his hands. "She was talking across the river, but I thought she was sounding off. She had a pretty rough spell right before. Didn't blame her for letting off steam."

"But before that, nothing's happened like this before? In yer village? As a bairn?"

"No. Nothing."

"Because it's bullshit," Bruin huffed.

Gemma huffed back. *Take your head out of your hole, you stupid bear.*

Samuel looked to the other Talon Enforcers in the room. Could it have something to do with the soul capture spell? Her spirit was trapped in the Nether Realm for weeks. Maybe it did something to her, changed her somehow?"

Kobi blew a great gust of air from his cheeks. "I suppose it's possible."

What sort of aberration was I?

Cowboy leaned against the back of a leather sofa. "Would visiting Alyssa help? As keeper of the afterlife, and Galan's partner in the whole protector of souls industry, she might know something."

"Enough about the how," Bruin snapped. "I want the why. Why the hell is this female ghost saying she's my sister—and why is she here?"

Gemma growled and leaped to her feet once more. *I'm not just saying it, you stupid, stubborn bear. I am your sister.* Swinging the pillow she clutched in her hand, she batted him in the side of the head. His hair flounced when the cushion collided with his forehead and he stood there stunned.

"How'd you do that?" Bruin asked, touching his forehead.

"I did not. Gemma did. And she insists she is, indeed, your littermate."

Gemma stood beside her brother, hands fisted on her hips, her foot tapping the floor. *I've been communicating with you for years but you're too rock-headed to realize it.*

"Bullshit," Bruin said again, once I relayed the message. "I would've noticed if I was being haunted. Besides if she can hit me with a pillow, couldn't she lift a fucking pen?"

Oh, like it's that easy. It's fleeting. A passionate explosion of strength. It's not like I can write a letter. Gemma threw her arms to the air. *Ask him how many times he's been hit in the head by a cupboard door when he's acting like an insufferable jackass.*

"She says she has, indeed, made attempts to communicate with you, but it is a fleeting burst of strength. She said something about cupboard doors hitting you in the head when you are being . . . difficult."

Bruin's eyes widened. "That's her?"

Gemma sighed, rolling her turquoise eyes. *He's as thick as a tree trunk. Tell him that.*

My mouth dropped open and I shook my head. As much affection as I held for Bruin, he was the Were Alpha and King of the most volatile race in the Realm of the Fair . . . next to the Centaurs.

Gemma laughed. *Okay chicken, ask him about the chick flick marathons and eating Chunky Monkey.*

When I finished reiterating that message, Bruin looked nonplussed.

Mika burst out laughing. "Ohmygod that's hysterical. I love this girl."

Bruin navigated the room with the grace of a drunken Grizzly bear—verily because he was one. "Why didn't she go?" he asked, his voice a rumble deep in my chest. "Gemma should be with our parents and our sisters, not following me around for decades alone and unseen."

Samuel stepped behind me and squeezed my shoulder.

Gemma strode right in front of her unknowing brother. *I hid Father's signet ring during the raid and promised him Bruin would become the true and rightful king.*

Bruin sank to the sofa, elbows propped on knees, his face buried in his strong hands. When he exhaled and brushed his shaggy brown hair from his face he looked resigned. "Where," he asked. "Where did she hide the ring?"

With the excitement of the day over and Bruin and Cowboy off making plans with Reign, I slipped away to get ready for a quiet evening in my room. Gemma left to shadow her brother, wanting to be party to all the details of the recovery of their father's ring. Bree was out on her run with Aust. Mika and Grandfather Hawk were stargazing off the northern vista. And Ceri rounded up the cubs and corralled them into the nursery for bath, stories, and bed.

For once, all was quiet in the Dens.

"May I come in?"

I glanced in the vanity mirror, drawing my brush through the lengths of my curls. Samuel had changed out of his slacks and white collared shirt and instead wore jogging pants and a black t-shirt which clung to him in delicious definition. With his shoulder leaning against the doorjamb to our shared ensuite and his bare feet crossed at the ankles, he was just about the most intriguing male I had ever seen.

I cursed the warming of my insides and refused to think about it further. I had only read the first few chapters of Elora's book and already my mind and body were awakening to erotic new ideas. "You are always welcome."

"Even when I act like an angry arse?"

I fought a smile and continued brushing. "Yes, even then."

Pushing off the doorway he strode into my room and stood directly behind me. He gave my shoulders a gentle squeeze and sighed. "It wasn't yer fault. This morning I mean. I was angry, aye, but not with you."

I set the brush on the vanity surface and straightened it until it aligned perfectly with the spine of the comb. Sorting through the tangle of colored elastics in the little dish, I chose an ice-blue one to hold my night braid.

As Samuel waited for my response, he took the elastic and began dividing my hair.

My breath caught. The act of a male aiding me for bed was something Galan had done my whole life. Samuel repeating the same actions was vastly more intimate. "It felt as though your anger was directed at me."

"Gods, yer hair is like silver silk." He worked his fingers, twisting, dividing, and weaving. "I used to do this with my little sister. Braiding

112

her hair was the only time she'd sit still long enough for me to do anything with her. She'll not remember it, for she was a wee lass when I left, but I used to sneak into her room after chores and braid her hair for bed."

When he reached the ends, he twisted the elastic around to hold the braid together. "I hadn't thought about that in years, but that's my point, isn't it?"

"In truth, I have no idea."

He rested his hands on my shoulders and smiled. "Ye trigger something inside me, Lia. Something protective. As an older brother, I was never truly angry with my sister, just like I could never truly be angry with you."

I blinked and forced my gaze to meet his in the mirror.

"What happened this morning caught me off guard, ye see? I was dreaming and when I woke . . . it was a bit of a shock. I got bent outta shape and that was wrong. You dinnae want what happened any more than I, right?"

I did. I shook my head. "It was a mistake. Like you said."

"So, we're still friends? I'm yer guardian and you are my charge, aye?"

I nodded, my throat too tight to speak.

"Grand, so we'll forget all about it and carry on with me staying with ye to keep the nightmares at bay. No fault. No foul." He stepped back and glanced at my bed. "But to be on the safe side, maybe you could wear a nightie to bed. Just to keep things simple."

CHAPTER TWELVE

My brother is an idiot, Gemma said, stomping along beside me the following afternoon. *It took me fifteen years to tell him where the ring was hidden, the least I deserve is to help him retrieve it.*

I stepped around a massive mud puddle and headed for the clearing behind the Haven Marketplace. The neon sign at the Hearthstone flashed closed, Bree's father and brothers likely taking part in the cleanup. We walked the soggy path between the bakery and Iadon's tailor shop, the sounds of the clearing now audible.

"Bruin's objections were reasonable," I said. "The last time he and Mika were at your family Dens, Abaddon controlled the place. They were almost killed. It is safer for the warriors to handle the retrieval alone."

Great idea. Let the menfolk handle everything and we, the weaker sex, can stay here and work on our needlepoint. Do you really believe that shit? Gemma turned to Savage, my Talon escort of the day.

The nom de guerre system amused me. Savage, Rue, Terror, Agony. Most warriors picked names violently male and dramatic. Then there was Cowboy, Princess, Blaze . . . and, of course, Merlin.

Gemma curtsied low to the ink-covered Enforcer, waving her hand in a flourishing bow only I could see. When she rose, she huffed and rolled her eyes. *Helloooo, I'm dead. What could happen?*

I released the top toggles of my spring cloak and widened the opening at my neck to get some air. It was unseasonably warm for an April afternoon. Even more so since the storm two nights ago. "Bruin is protective beyond reason with those he loves. Mika suffers for it and you shall too. There are evils strong enough to harm even those walking the spirit world. He wishes to ensure your safety."

Nothing happened to me so far.

"How do suppose Abaddon and his Scourge minions never found the ring after all these years?"

Gemma waggled her brow, her ire replaced by a look of sly satisfaction. *Because I'm just that good. I hid it in our secret hideout. No adult could fit inside the tunnel opening, in fact, by the time Bruin and I were eleven, he couldn't fit either, so we gave it up. When Father told me to hide his ring somewhere, it seemed the perfect place. And I guess it was.*

"Lexi came from Attalos to go with them."

Gemma nodded as we neared the clearing. *She's tiny enough to get through the opening and down the tunnel. She'll have no problem retrieving it. Still, I should be there. Stupid, insufferable, overprotective ass of a . . . brother.*

I raised my gaze to Galan working in the open area ahead. "I know exactly how you feel."

Gemma followed my gaze to where almost twenty males worked on cutting and clearing two massive oaks which had been taken down by a freak wind and lightning storm two evenings prior. It was a tragic beauty. Many of the mountain's trees had snapped or had their roots unearthed under the pressure of the storm. Samuel and I had walked for an hour yesterday, taking in the magnitude of the damage.

Today began the cleanup, and many of the males from Jade's home, as well as the Academy and Haven proper, had rallied to join the task.

Gemma smiled. *Both our brothers might be idiots, but yours gets points for hotness. All your Highborne men do.*

Her words struck a chord. None of the Highborne males, save mayhap Galan, were mine. That would likely never change. What male of worth would choose to mate me when it meant a life of confinement and danger? "Highbornes are born of Castian's blood. It is simply godly genetics at work."

Gemma snorted. *What does a maiden from the Valley of Exiles know of genetics?*

"Bree speaks at evening repast. Her insights on the sciences are enlightening."

Uh-huh, she nodded, no longer listening to me. *And Aust's got it bad for her, eh?*

I smiled, our conversation returning to Highborne males. "He holds an obvious affection for her, yes, but waits to act upon it, as is only fitting."

Why is waiting fitting?

"He must establish himself. Males of my race must offer a potential mate security and standing in the community. Aust could never achieve that in our village, but here—a new world opened to him. With his determination to win Bree's heart, he is finding his purpose. He is, after all, on his *Ambar Lenn*—his journey of self-discovery."

A spongy bit of ground sucked at my boot and altered my balance. Savage caught my elbow and once my foot was freed, he stepped back to resume his position. I nodded my thanks. Though I resented being suffocated by male guards, at least he cared nothing of me speaking to a ghost.

Yeah, I can tell Bree's all about the coin in his pouch and his standing in the community.

Gemma pointed to where Bree stood amongst Mika, Jade and a crowd of other females gathered along the iron fence of the Haven Cemetery. The coyote's short hair flew free in the wind, exposing the sleek, sharp lines of her Were breed.

She was beautiful in her own right, captivated by the sight of Aust, Galan, and Iadon splitting the smaller branches from the fallen tree. With her hand hiding her mouth she leaned to Mika's ear and the two set off in a round of giggles.

Verily, beyond the magic and modernization of the realm, there was something primal about watching the muscular prowess of males hard at work. I stepped over to join them.

"The magnitude of the job is bigger than I imagined."

Jade gave me a quick shoulder hug. "Reign said these two trees are close to a thousand years old. Luckily, they fell toward the clearing and not the marketplace. It would have been disastrous if either one hit the Hearthstone."

Bree nodded. "Da sent Rys and Seamus to the Temple of the Gods with a huge offering yesterday morning. He's counting his blessings the Fates were kind to him for once."

Gemma bit her lip, her turquoise eyes dancing. *If the Fates were smart, they'd demand her foster brothers for the offering instead of food. Were-lions are seriously tasty.*

"Kind for once," Mika laughed. "They must have been having a good night."

"Or Zophia was there to rein them in," Jade said.

I nodded. "Zophia is lovely."

"Not what I expected from one of the Fates," Mika said.

"She's nothing like her sisters," Jade said. "Zana, Zora and Zinnea are cut from a different cloth—or tapestry if you will."

"Fingers crossed they don't mess with Bruin while he's retrieving the ring. He took an army with him but when the Fates are involved, you never know."

Right? Gemma said, shaking her head. *Okay, screw it. I'm going. Bruin won't even know I'm there and I deserve to be there. We women can't let the men have all the fun. Laters.*

Before I could object, Gemma was gone.

A feminine sigh escaped Jade's lips and I followed her gaze to where Galan raised an axe over his head.

He and Aust worked on a larger section of branches. In a long, graceful arch, his axe fell with a speed and accuracy I was accustomed to. He heaved down and chips of wood splintered off.

Jade sighed again. "I could watch him like this all day."

The females chuckled in resounding feminine agreement and I

understood their admiration. Since my coming of age, my body had grown highly attuned to the males around me. With the days warming, the majority of them wore only the thinnest of shirts. It was difficult not to get distracted by the corded musculature beneath.

I scanned the clearing—there.

As if on cue, a delicious wave of warmth flooded deep into my belly and expanded. I drew breath and smiled across the clearing to where Samuel, Kobi and Julian held large whining machines. As Samuel lowered the long, rotating blade to the tree trunk, his tool ate the meat of the tree like a sharp sword through flesh.

When he stepped back, he straightened and met my gaze. His expression softened as a grin spread across his handsome face. For the briefest moment, I ignored him comparing me to his sister and allowed myself the delusion that he felt something for me beyond friendship and duty.

Jade laughed beside me and another scenario came to mind. Mayhap his smile was for her and not me. Abruptly my warmth washed away and I felt nauseous.

"Lia?" Jade gripped my elbow. "What's wrong?"

A buzzing invaded my skull. Stumbling backward, I caught a rail of the cemetery fence as my knees buckled. The buzz in my skull rose to a hiss and I shivered as a frigid cold chilled my lungs.

I saw them then. A dozen spirits. Demented and twisted in anguished purpose, they rushed the iron fence from the inside of the burial grounds. I pushed back, but too late. Chaos erupted. Hands grabbed. Females screamed. Men shouted.

Icy hands clamped my arm as others grabbed my hair and yanked me up and over the fence. Iron pickets tore my skirts, and scored my legs.

Across the clearing, a warrior's cry rose over the din. Kobi hurled himself from the crowd, his body exploding into a tidal wave of black smoke.

Savage wrapped an arm around my shoulders. Sword swinging, he cut the air, the evil specters unaffected.

Blue bolts of magic zinged through the ghosts.

A great winged demon with flaming eyes landed beside me. Wood chips pelted as he hit the ground like a meteor. His mutated howl vibrated in my bones.

Kobi in his true form.

Savage fell and knocked me to the ground.

I struggled to roll out from under him as a sinister weight crushed my lungs. Evil slithered inside me, edging beneath my flesh like a dark serpent tunneling inside.

My throat closed.

Something . . . some invisible thing slid into my body like an icy hand into an empty glove. A dark euphoria filled me.

Kobi threw Savage clear of the battle and crouched above me. His leathery skin exhaled smoke, his lips black as night. Compound eyes flickered orange and scarlet as the fires of hell burned in his skull. Speaking in tongues, he dragged a jagged yellow claw down my bodice.

Galan dropped to my side and grabbed my hand.

Samuel knelt by my head and a blue field surrounded the four of us. The cemetery silenced—all but the evil entity inside me held at bay.

Kobi hissed a stream of guttural sounds. The dark spirits fought to get to us, beating against Samuel's shield. "Hold still," he growled, his voice not his own. "This will hurt."

Jagged yellow claws closed to fists against my chest. He pulled his fist back like he had hold of an invisible rope. My shoulders arched off the ground. The entity within me sent wiry tendrils into my organs, rooting itself.

Laughter rang in my skull, the dark soul amused.

Samuel chanted incantations. Louder. Harsher. Kobi gripped again with his other hand and heaved. My lungs burned. My spine felt like it would rip from my body.

"Stop. I beg you, *please!*"

The demon yanked. Veins stood defined on his arms. Time and

again, Kobi grasped and pulled and grasped again while Galan held my shoulders to the cold, wet ground. I went numb, beyond the agony. Distant from reality. Kobi pulled again, his smoking skin glistening with sweat.

"Let me die—"A violent roar erupted inside my skull and a funnel of evil spewed from my belly.

CHAPTER THIRTEEN

I came awake to the scent of blood, foul magic and male sweat. A claustrophobic darkness cocooned me. My night vision failed to come. I blinked and opened my eyes wider.

"I cannot see."

"Give it a minute," Kobi wheezed, next to my ear. He shifted his body a little to give me space, the two us lying side by side on a small bed. I welcomed the closeness, the warrior's body heat thawing the chill from my bones. "Probably residual dark magic. It should clear."

Should? His assurance held more doubt than certainty. What if my sight failed to return? Was this vulnerability how Samuel felt? "Where is Samuel?"

Kobi shifted again and I caught his troubled scent. Our close contact was uncomfortable for him. "Relax. We're at the clinic. Merlin spelled this room to keep safe while he got someone to heal us. Apparently, even flirting with the Grim Reaper I'm still your best bet against your threat of the day."

"And what of Savage?"

"Patched up and miserable. Nothing new."

I exhaled, thankful the warrior had survived. "What was it you pulled out of me, Kobi?"

"A nasty spirit wanting to possess you. I connected with the thing. Powerful."

"Was it Rheagan?"

"No fucking clue."

"What about the others? Was anyone else hurt?"

A racking cough took Kobi over and left him gasping for breath. "Sorry . . . too busy coughing up a lung to notice."

Judging by the liquid rattle in his throat and the fresh wave of blood tainting the air, his quip rang too close to the truth. In the darkness, I followed the contours of his frame snug against mine. He was drenched with sweat and blood, his body trembling with fever or mayhap the aftermath of saving my life.

"Kobi, what can I do? I am no healer, but after working with Jade, I might be of some aid if you tell me what your injuries are."

He coughed again. "Advil and bandages won't do it for an incubus, Lia. Samuel's gone to find what I need."

I blinked and saw the outline of his pained face coming into focus. Thank the gods. My vision cleared more moment by moment. There was something I could do. I heard the evasion in his voice, smelled it in his protestations. "Tell me. Verily, I wish to aid you."

Kobi stared at me through half-lidded eyes and cleared his throat. When he spoke, his voice was low and rough. "Incubi heal by leaching sexual energy, Lia. You know, crotch mingling, getting horizontal. You still want to aid me? You saw what I am. You want to snuggle up to that monster?"

"You heal during coitus?" My ears flushed to their tips.

He ground his teeth and closed his eyes. "Just one of the perks of being me. And no, I'm not asking you."

No. Of course not. Samuel's rejection echoed in my head, *you didn't want that any more than I did.* Had being close with me been so distasteful? And now Kobi refused me?

Kobi? The most indiscriminately promiscuous male of all the warriors, would rather risk death than approach me.

My blood boiled hot. "What about me is so undesirable to males?

Am I homely or too inexperienced to consider? Am I that pathetic a female you would refuse to touch me even to save your own life?"

Kobi's mouth gave a bitter twist. "You're pissed at me? For trying to do right by you?"

"Yes. I am. Verily, I have what you need . . . all the correct parts and pieces which arouse a male, yes?"

"Of course, . . . I mean, you are . . ."

"And does it have to be coitus? Will not some . . . sexual pleasure ease your injuries?"

"Ahhh, I'm not sure. I never hold back."

Until now. "So, it is me."

"I am a demon, Lia. Hellspawn. One of the damned. My Pantheon is different than yours. My gods feed on death, conflict and kill to absorb the rush. You saw me back in the clearing. Do you really want that inside you—"

Stupid male. I stopped his protestations with my lips on his. In this dark cocoon of privacy, I seized his rugged, stubbled jaw in my palms and kissed him. He tasted of blood and sorrow, loneliness and self-loathing. His outlook on life may differ, but a Highborne's attitude toward sexual pleasure differed from other members of the realm as well.

To save a male's life . . . where was the question? I would give what I could.

His lips started tentative, but as the surprise of my advance wore off and our connection heated, his body met my offering with greedy abandon and claimed what it needed.

Nervous I would fail him with my inexperience, I let him lead. He kissed with passion, the intensity of it stole my breath and fluttered in my insides. Once I grew certain he would not refuse my help, I ran my hands down the contours of his body and the flavor of his kiss changed. The sorrow replaced by hunger.

Strong hands ran the nape of my neck and across my lower back. It was me who closed the space between our bodies, sending a hand down the curve of his spine and to the round of his backside. He moaned and I felt the magic of his healing tingle through me.

My inexperience proved less of an obstacle than I imagined. Kobi kissed a blazing line down my neck, a decadent purring rumbling in his chest. "Gods you taste good, Lia girl."

Lia girl. My chest tightened hearing Samuel's voice instead of Kobi's. Though I wished it was Samuel pulling my braid loose and combing through my hair with strong fingers, it was not. Kobi needed this. Kobi needed me.

And what a wondrous thing, to be needed, to have purpose—no matter how small.

The magic tingling over my skin ceased and the pain of his injuries remained rife in the air. His healing stalled. He was aroused. I could smell his desire, but his caress and attentions remained politely restrained.

In the past year, there had been little within my control, but I would be damned if I let this male's sense of propriety inhibit his health. If there was some situation I might affect for the better in my life—I intended to affect it.

To that end, I ran my palm down the front of his leathers. His hips thrust forward and he groaned close to my ear. "Fuck yeah . . . oh, gods rougher. That's it."

The magic zinged over my flesh again and I continued my exploration with a surge of triumph. I pulled his shirt up so I had access to his skin. I had never touched a male, but the excitement of it burned in my blood. He moaned as I found the little hoop piercing his nipple and toyed with it.

With my bodice ripped down the front from the attack, Kobi's hand slid up my ribs and over my breast unimpeded. At the same time, his teeth nipped the sensitive tip of my ear and I shuddered against him. He hissed as the pulse in my neck jumped against his thumb. "Like that do you?"

I did. Undeniably. Uncontrollably. I tilted my neck so he had better access to my ear and sighed when he brushed back my hair and continued. Gods, if the preamble to relations with a lover felt this good, what would it be like to share body and soul with another?

He kissed me a long while, caressing with a honed touch. The combined scents of our arousal created an intoxicating aroma in such an enclosed space and since sexual energy was the balm Kobi needed, we were in good stead.

After a long while, Kobi made a male noise deep in his throat and pulled away. He kissed me once on the tip of my nose and sighed a long and languid sigh. "That, my sweet, young Highborne, was just what the doctor ordered."

It took a moment for the adrenaline rushing through my veins to slow enough so I could speak. "Are you healed? Why have you stopped?"

He drew a deep breath looking puzzled. "Better. Much better than I should be. And as much as my darker demon impulses demand I pin you down and continue, our private time has come to its end. Merlin is back and has brought me a friend. It would be bad form to greet his efforts indisposed."

He shifted to separate our bodies once more. "Catch your breath before he sees the flush in your cheeks and realizes we weren't unconscious and dying in here. I may be reckless, but I avoid having high-level wizards wanting to kill me."

I pulled the sides of my bodice back together. "Why would he care? He regards me as nothing more than his charge. That is why I am grateful to you, Kobi."

He chuckled and it was a low, sultry sound. "You're thanking me?"

I brushed his cheek and ran my fingers down the line of nickel piercings in his ear. The male projected an image of cocky self-possession, uncaring of the reputation of villainy that followed him. In truth, he was emotionally isolated. Adrift. I knew that ache all too well.

I bit my lip and searched his face. His eyes were once again smoky, charcoal-grey.

"You saved my soul today and likely my life. You exposed your true self, valuing my well-being above your privacy. So, yes, I am grateful."

When he opened his mouth to speak, I pressed my fingers over his lips so I could finish. "This interlude has been the only time in near a year when someone treated me as a competent, mature female. You let me make my choice. Your touch held no pity and you let me express myself. I hold no talent or experience with males but, still, you wanted me. It felt wonderful. Liberating. Empowering. You, my brave friend, are a male of great worth."

"Anytime you need empowerment . . ." Kobi grinned and ran his fingers through his blood-matted, night-black hair. "As for that male of worth stuff, your wires are crossed there. I've got an image to protect. Emotionally unavailable bad-boys score more women and scare more men."

I smiled. "Your secret is safe."

By the time Samuel released his spell and stepped into our recovery room, Kobi had given me his t-shirt and I had wiped what blood could be removed from the both of us with the tatters of my blouse. I sat, still a little shaken, on the edge of the bed and Kobi stood facing the window.

Thankfully, Samuel looked none the worse for the attack, stressed and flustered, but beautifully whole. His jaw tightened as he glanced from Kobi to me, and back to Kobi. "I expected ye to be in worse shape, demon. Ye seemed to be knockin' on death's door a half hour ago."

Kobi shrugged and the metal ring pierced through his nipple caught moonlight. "Can't keep a demon down for long. We're like cockroaches. Resilient."

Samuel made a disparaging noise and scowled. "Yeah, well, since ye've made a miraculous revival, ye should be well enough to cut yer healing session short. Yer lady friend is in the next recovery room, and Jade and Rowan are waiting to check Lia over. When the two of you are well, Reign's expecting us in the war room. He's holding the debriefing of Bruin's ring recovery now and Lia's attack is up next."

Kobi nodded and strode out the door.

Samuel frowned at me, his face dark with anger as he headed out to the main part of the clinic.

CHAPTER FOURTEEN

The Talon war room was located on the fourth floor of the castle and the clinic was on the first. After both Kobi and I were given a clean bill of health, the three of us had a long, awkward climb up the spiral steps until we arrived at our destination.

"Good, you're here." Reign stepped back from a conversation with Julian and Savage. Cowboy and Bruin were there too—as well as Galan. "Let's get started."

Samuel closed the door behind us. "The sooner we get started, the sooner it's over."

Reign strode to the head of a long, oval table and took a seat. "For the sake of expediency let me recap. Bruin's recovery of the King's ring in his abandoned childhood home was successful and uneventful. And while he had three squads of enforcers with their thumbs up their asses in Alaska, Savage was being Ginsued in the clearing, unable to defend against angry ghosts taking possession of Lia."

Samuel pursed his lips and exhaled. "Aye, that pretty much covers it. If not for Savage holding her back and Kobi and I being in the clearing, she would have been taken and possessed before anyone knew what was going on."

"And how did you know what was going on?"

Samuel shook his head. "I didn't. I saw the demon shift and figured if he was showing his true self in public, something monumentally bad was going down. I followed along until I figured out what was happening."

"And, Kobi? How'd you know? You were across the clearing, right?"

Kobi shifted forward in his seat and tapped his fingers on the surface of the table. "Distance wouldn't matter. I felt the energy surge. A call for dark souls."

"Felt it?"

He nodded and cleared his throat, flashing a heated gaze. "Evil energy is an aphrodisiac to an incubus, like waking up with someone sucking on your cock. It's hard to ignore when it's happening and easy to pinpoint where the pleasure is coming from."

Reign set his elbows on the table and tented his fingers. "And this call for dark souls rang through the air? From who? From where?"

"Could Abaddon be behind it?" Galan asked. I expected him to cast me a glance, he did not.

Kobi shook his head. "No. The call came from the entity trying to possess Lia. The others were summoned to secure her for the taking."

Reign rubbed his palm across his eyes and cursed. "All right, what about the attempt at possession?"

All eyes turned to me and I tried to recall everything from the moment Gemma and I arrived at the cemetery fence, to the icy presence slithering into my consciousness, to waking up in the recovery room with Kobi. Samuel stiffened at that point of my recount and I ended my story. "Kobi and I wondered if it was Rheagan."

Julian pulled out his phone and held up his finger as Reign began to speak. When Lexi's voice picked up on the other end, I was even more confused.

"Hey Wiseass, whassup?" she said.

Julian pushed a button and laid his phone flat on the table. "Princess, listen, You're on speaker. I'm in the war room in a meeting of minds. Are you here or back in Attalos?"

"I'm downstairs with Jade and Rowan at the clinic. We're talking about grabbing dinner at the Hearthstone, why?"

"'Cause I need you to come up and tell us what it felt like when Rheagan tried to possess you. Specifically, what her presence felt like."

We heard her working her way through the student-filled corridors of the castle. "Eew, creepy, is that what went on?"

Reign leaned forward. "Your brother's wearing that look he gets when he's about to wow us with his intuitive brilliance."

"Ahh, I know that look. I'm on my way."

Samuel rolled his eyes, but only I noticed. Then it occurred to me. The room was filling with his least favorite people and one more was on the way. Lexi and Galan were openly hostile with him, and Kobi and I had offended him back at the clinic. I wondered where the problem stemmed. Protectiveness? Did he disapprove of my actions, or did he disapprove of the demon I had chosen to pleasure?

Lexi arrived and Reign stood to greet her.

The contrast between the massive six-foot-six mountain of a male with long brindle hair and his petite, adoptive daughter with short, ebony spikes remained as jarring as the first time I saw them side by side last summer. Lexi reached up and hugged her father, her black velvety wings flexing as they embraced. She cast a warm, amethyst glance around the room but avoided Samuel completely.

I found myself offended on his behalf.

As always, Lexi was less the petite Faerie female and more the warrior of her family. Even in designer jeans with a glittery gold halter top, she wore a large knife sheathed against her thigh and another in a shoulder harness.

"Thanks for coming, Lex. Now, back to the question at hand." Julian pointed to the chair across the table from him, but his sister waved it away. "When the bat-shit queen attempted to possess you in Attalos, you told us what happened, but what did it feel like?"

Lexi unsheathed the knife from her thigh and began a slow stroll around the table as she twirled it around her fingers. "At first it was like a shadow edging into my dream. My heart raced and a buzzing built in my ears. A slither of icy awareness snaked through my skull, down the nape of my neck and into my chest. As it spread, my vision dimmed. I couldn't breathe, suffocating on frigid cold as it leached through my lungs into my arms and legs. I felt her to the depths of my soul—an evil strength, luring, coercing, growing more seductive every moment."

As the images danced in my memory I choked. Cowboy strode to the cabinet at the wall and returned with a glass of dark red wine. The fruity bite eased the twisting knot in my throat. I sipped some more.

"What about laughing?" I asked. "A confident, maniacal laugh which makes your insides churn."

"Not the first few times when she came in my dreams, but when she grew more confident, yeah. Nasty laughter bubbled up from nowhere and echoed inside me until it vibrated in my bones."

I nodded to the group. "What Lexi describes is what happened to me. Exactly. Do you believe Rheagan tried to overtake me?"

Reign frowned. "With her powers stripped and cast into the sea, she shouldn't have been able to do any of this."

Kobi stroked his goatee and scowled. "She's not powerless, Boss. If I hadn't been right there to rip her from Lia, she would've overtaken her within minutes. She's got a shitload of evil mojo if she can raise the dead, control them during an attack and attempt a possession at the same time. If she'd taken root inside Lia, I'm not sure we'd be able to weed her out."

My head grew light.

Lexi took a seat next to Reign and leaned on the table in a pose identical to his. Though not related by blood, Julian, Bruin, Jade, and Lexi all carried traits and mannerisms of their adoptive father.

"So," Reign said, taking his phone from his leather vest and texting someone, "how do you suppose she was able to take root in Lia in the first place?"

Julian scrubbed his palm over his short afro. "What if Abaddon's soul capture spell was intended to make it possible for another soul to take possession of Lia's body. Like vacating the house for the new tenant. And now Rheagan's trying to move in."

With the total absence of mirth, I laughed, my heart pounding in my ears. "Abaddon wants to give Rheagan my body? He's taking me before the Fates, claiming me as his mate, so we can rule together once Rheagan possesses me?"

Galan cursed a long, colorful stream of Elven profanity. "Castian cannot let this happen. If that is where this is headed he must put an end to it."

Reign cast my brother a dispassionate gaze. "The God of gods is sworn to support the rights of all his charges, Galan. You still don't quite get it, do you? I know you look up to the guy, but his stance gets damned frustrating. Regardless of right and wrong, Abaddon's claims will be heard and the laws will dictate the outcome, not Castian."

Reign's seat creaked as the warrior leaned back. "All right, boys and girls, assuming our theory on the possession is correct, what can we do about it?"

Kobi wrapped his knuckles against the surface of the table. "Merlin wants me to stick close, but at best, it's a short-term solution. Our best option is capturing a Hell Hound and bonding it with Lia."

Reign's neck cranked around so fast it must have hurt. "A Hell Hound?"

Kobi shrugged. "They're territorial when they claim a master. They consume evil souls like candy. And they generally scare the piss out of everyone with half a brain."

"Any other ideas?" Reign said, glancing around the table. "Maybe something not involving demonic canines and sending people to scale the fiery pit of hell to separate it from its mother?"

"Castian could ward her," Galan said, raising a hand before Reign could argue. "To be true to his position of non-interference, he could ward her against possession from members of his or any other Pantheon. That would include his sister, Rheagan, anyone from Behind the Veil and any deities from other Pantheons. It would not, however, protect her from earthbound souls."

Samuel nodded. "That's a solid idea, Galan. It won't keep spirits from attacking her, but it would dash Abaddon and Rheagan's plan to rule through her."

Seeing Samuel and Galan agree on something highlighted just how dire my situation was. Ignoring how they failed to ask me my opinion, or speak to me directly, I added my thoughts. "I fear for the safety of those guarding me. Savage fought and yet had no effect on the evil spirits."

What about me serving as one of your guards, little one?

I jumped and spun around to the doorway. Tham sat perched on the bureau behind the entrance swinging his suede boots in a lazy pendulum. He winked, appearing as strong and capable in death as he had in life. He hopped down to his feet and strode closer. *Following Lexi around is growing old—though if you repeat that, I shall deny it—but if Sav had no effect because what attacked you was spirit-based, mayhap having a spirit guard is an answer.*

I pushed my chair back and looked to see what Galan thought of the idea. Galan nodded and repeated Tham's plans to the rest of the room.

"The logic is sound," Samuel said. "Tham is strong in a melee and ye trust him, aye?"

"But I what if something more happens to him because of me? How do I live with that?"

Tham squatted down beside my chair, his smile dimming. *Surely, the Fates freed us from the village for me to do more than get cut down before proving my worth. My future may not be what I envisioned, but I shall make the most of who and what I am.*

When Reign and Kobi broke into the conversation, Galan and I discussed the idea more with the others. Lexi despised the idea of Tham standing between me and evil spirits, and Samuel's scowl deepened even further. The rest of the room thought the idea had merit.

And so, it was decided, for a trial basis, Tham was named another of my personal guard.

CHAPTER FIFTEEN

Over the next few days, Samuel remained distantly polite and annoyingly efficient in his duty as my guardian. He stayed in my room each evening as we had established, but no longer slept on my bed. He brought in a pallet and had taken to sleeping on the floor.

Regardless of my confusion as to why he was still so angry at me, I tried to give him space to work through it.

Verily, that's what friends did. Or so I assumed.

It was decided, too, that I was to remain indoors as much as possible. So, when Samuel left each day, I busied myself at the Dens reading and being of aid where I could.

The recovery of Bruin's signet ring raised a buzz of excitement within Bruin's home. Though it had yet to be announced to the Were population at large, the impact of Bruin taking his proper place ruling the Weres rippled through the halls. Bruin was inviting the thirty-eight Primes of the race to a summit to be held on the solstice moon in just over two months' time. If all went as planned, he would perform the customary challenges of skill and strength, and formally assert himself as the true and rightful King of Weres.

Smiling at the pile of completed invitations mounding the dining table, I stretched my achy fingers and poured myself a cup of hot cocoa. Bruin had reluctantly accepted my offer to pen the invitations. It was least I could do after all he and Mika had done for me.

With my mug of comfort in hand, I headed for the main corridor to return to my room. A metallic *thunk-thunk-thunk* of footsteps on a ladder drew me to the inner vestibule. Mika was elevated high above the inlaid floor, her sleek chestnut ponytail swinging as she climbed. Judging by the way her worn t-shirt hung, even tied over one hip, it was Bruin's.

"Mika, may I be of aid to you?" I skirted the round foyer table and looked toward the ocular domed ceiling.

"No. I'm good . . . great. Damn. Great. Why wouldn't I be?" The growl in her tone and the scent of her pique spoke differently. I grew more accustomed to the human tendency to use sarcasm every day.

On a small shelf near the top of the ladder perched several tins with wooden handles sticking out of them. "Whatever are you doing?"

Mika barked a laugh. "Ding-ding-ding, that's the million-dollar question. What am I doing?"

Elevated fifteen feet in the air, Mika brushed the curved wall before her with a soft rag. The stone arch of the entryway had been chiseled and sanded smooth and now was being stenciled with a missive of welcome. After tracing the inside edges of her lettering, Mika filled in the outline with long flourishing strokes. The message wrapped the circumference of the circular foyer and said:

We believe in the right to bear arms and the right to arm BEARS.

"I used to be a well-respected journalist."

I sipped my drink, remembering the flurry of discussions when Bruin first brought her home. Some liked her straight away like Aust, Galan, and Julian, while others took some convincing. One of the key arguments against her was the visibility of her career and how that might affect the realm laws of secrecy.

"I tracked down criminals, shadowed poachers and wrote award winning exposés. I held the respect of most, if not all my peers."

She dipped the brush back into her pigment and scraped the excess off on the edge. "I testified in federal cases." She finished filling in some letters, climbed down the ladder, shifted it a few feet then stomped back up to the next section.

"The last thing I did before coming here was expose a black-market ring decimating Were populations across both realms. In fact, it was me who figured out Abaddon and the Scourge were selling Were pelts to raise money for their war."

Mika cursed as a wayward drip trickled beyond her guidelines and grabbed her rag. The cloth smeared the spot into a darkened smudge and she cursed louder. After tipping a foul-scented bottle against the rag, she began a frantic attack on the unwanted blotch until it disappeared. Sighing, she reloaded the brush. "So, you ask, what am I doing?"

The light coming in the transom dimmed as the sky clouded over.

I flipped the switch and the brilliance of the entryway chandelier illuminated the space. "May I make an unsolicited observation?"

"Thanks," Mika said, gesturing to the light as she returned to the ground once again. After shifting the ladder into its next position, she raised her bare foot to the first rung. "Sure, go for it."

"It is none of my affair, so mayhap I should hold my tongue, but having a male love you so completely that he is devoted to your safety and well-being seems a blessing, not a burden. The two of you hold differing opinions on your role as Ursa but you love each other. Many relationships are resolved with less."

Mika growled and resumed her climb. "I've shown him I have skills in business and can take care of myself. I want to take part in the summit. Hugh told me Bruin's mother was actively part of his Father's rule. But *noooo*, he wants his mate safely out of the line of fire."

"And is there a threat of danger?"

Mika bit her lip and focused on the curlicue she was working on. "Several of the Primes are pissed Bruin is taking a more active role. I think he's worried that when he presents himself with the ring, they might challenge his claim. He wants the Weres united against Abaddon. Disgruntled species means the race isn't as strong as it could be."

"What is their objection?"

"Male ego mostly. They've been free to run their own camps for almost fifteen years. Some of the dominant species don't want to be told what to do by Bruin or anyone for that matter. And I don't think him mating a human Mundie wins him any points."

"Does he anticipate these hostilities are a danger to you?"

Mika stopped painting and looked down upon me. "Bruin thinks everything is a danger to me. It's frustrating as hell. I'm lucky if I can go hang out with Jade in her fortress. Gods forbid I visit my girl-friends in the Mortal Realm and not have an armed squadron surrounding me."

"I am familiar with that particular frustration myself."

Mika looked and me and frowned. "Lia, forgive me for saying this but stop letting the men in your life decide what's good for you. Speak your mind. Get angry. Get involved. You've led a sheltered life, I get that, but you can't let people live your life for you. Take control. What do *you* want?"

I honestly had no idea. I sipped at my hot cocoa and thought about that.

Hey ladies, whasssup?

I squealed and jumped.

Gemma giggled, pointing at the cocoa splash down the front of my blouse. *Geez, Lia, Jumpy much?*

Mika assessed the situation and tossed me down a clean rag. "Hey, Gemma, how's things in the Nether Realm?"

Boring, Gemma said, pushing out her lips. *Everyone's so busy, there's no one to talk to. It's like I'm invisible.*

I rolled my eyes and gave up on the stain. "You can talk to both Mika and me. What's on your mind?"

She twisted a piece of her frazzled brown hair. *I was thinking about boys.*

"Boys?"

Yeah, Bruin's mated and if I were alive, I think I'd have a boyfriend or maybe be mated. Kobi and Cowboy are always talking about their sexual encounters and—

"You should not eavesdrop on the sexual lives of those two. They are promiscuous and likely thought themselves alone if discussing their encounters."

Mika snorted. "The demon and the wolf I presume?"

I nodded, saddened to see Gemma so lonely and isolated as she had been for all these years. "Did you want to pass over to the After and join the others now that your promise to your father is fulfilled? Bruin has the ring. Galan and I could take you to join your family and friends."

Mika looked down at me, her color draining. "Gemma, please don't make any decisions about leaving yet. Bruin just found you and he'll be heartbroken if you—"

Mika's expression faltered a moment before it totally blanked out. Her eyes rolled back and in the next second, she keeled and toppled from the top of the ladder.

"BRUIN!" I screamed, running forward.

In a split second, males Flashed into the foyer. The doors flew open as two Were sentries burst into the entrance as well. It happened so fast. One moment she was falling and in the next heartbeat—Bruin scooped Mika out of the air and rematerialized with her cradled in his arms.

On a run, Aust and Tham flew around the corner. Aust blew through Gemma's spectral form and headed straight to his best friend. Tham collided with Gemma and they both tumbled into the stone wall.

Apologies, Tham said, straightening them both and looking confused. *Nothing like being mowed over during a moment of crisis, is there pretty one?*

I'm fine, Gemma said, her turquoise eyes locked on my Highborne brother. *Mow me over any day of the week. Seriously. I volunteer as tribute.*

"What happened?" Bruin asked, bringing my attention back. He searched Mika's unconscious face as the other Weres scanned the entrance.

"I don't know. She was on the ladder and swooned."

"Put me down," Mika said, her eyes flittering open. "Really, every-one, I'm good. Just a little dizzy. No biggie."

"No biggie?" Bruin ignored the scissoring of her legs to gain independence. "If Lia hadn't Banshee-screamed and if we hadn't been within earshot, you would've hit the floor and broken your neck." The words hung heavy in the crowded foyer. "I swear you'll kill me, Mika. One day, my heart will just give out."

Mika leaned her head against Bruin's broad chest and closed her eyes. Her rich coloring had yet to return, but beyond that, something was different. "My stomach was off, so I skipped lunch. Lesson learned."

Bruin's eyes narrowed. Laying Mika into Aust's arms, he fished out his phone. The text he sent was quick and the replying beep came almost immediately. "Okay, I'm taking you to the kitchen to feed you. Jade is on her way."

"Jade? Don't bother her. She's supposed to be resting." Mika squirmed again and Aust reluctantly set her on her feet.

"If you're fine, it won't hurt to have her check you out."

"Jade can't use her ability," I said. "It's bound to protect the twins."

Bruin pulled Mika tight to his hip and with a strong, muscled arm wrapped around her waist, he nuzzled her hair. "Just a routine once-over, nothing magical. I'll feel better if my sister tells me not to worry."

Mika scowled. "But you don't believe it when *I* tell you not to worry?"

Bruin shook his head, his eyes flecked gold. "No."

Before the two of them devolved into a heated scene, I interrupted. "Mika's right. There is nothing to be alarmed about. I am surprised you Weres failed to notice it sooner."

"Notice what?" he snapped.

"Mika's scent has altered. It is subtle but discernable."

Bruin, Aust, Cowboy and Tham all drew in deep breaths and Mika raised a brow looking like we had all lost our sanity.

"Well whatta you know," Cowboy drawled. "We got ourselves another announcement for the summit. Our Ursa is pregnant. Let there be cubs!"

CHAPTER SIXTEEN

As the excitement of Mika's pregnancy ramped up and Bruin was even more insistent on Jade's visit, I slipped away to bed. Too much joy for one day. Mika was loved beyond all sense, adored by her male and carrying her mate's young, so too was Jade. Though I loved them both, their happily-ever-afters struck a chord too close to the ache in my heart.

Having endured Samuel's disappointment and anger for days, I had no interest in either seeing or smelling his affection for my brother's wife when she arrived.

"*Ughhhh.*" I pulled the tie from my braid and shook my hair out. Was it so wrong to want love? I waited six decades for my age of eligibility and since its coming, the only males to show interest in me were a dying demon I forced myself upon and a psychotic monster who wanted my body to house his even more monstrous queen.

Abaddon's claim filled me with such an overwhelming sense of shame and dread I could not breathe. The Fates could call us before them at any time and once again the course of my life would be decided by someone else.

Mika was right. I needed to get angry. I needed to get involved in my own life. But how?

Mayhap Samuel had an idea. He had been studying realm and Highborne laws for days. Deciding I'd sleep better with answers, I headed through my suite toward his.

Turning the door handle of our shared bathing room and the sputter of falling water registered. An unobstructed view of Samuel's profile in the mirror stopped me mid-step, my intake of breath lost in the sounds of his shower.

Well-toned, his musculature shifted and shone as water cascaded over his body and he laved soap into his palms.

After replacing the frothy bar to its ledge, he skimmed his hands over the dusting of dark hair covering his chest and down the trail which led to his navel

And down farther still . . .

My breath caught. Samuel naked was a magnificent decadence. Standing out from his abdomen, his sex rose thick and proud. When his hands skimmed over his length, his head dropped back and his eyes closed. A moan rumbled out of his chest as his erection kicked in his hand. As he focused on his ministrations, his hips rolled forward and a spicy cinnamon scent filled the air. He licked his lips and swallowed hard.

What was he thinking about?

A low groan escaped my chest as he swept beneath his staff and palmed his sac.

"Lia?" Samuel's eyes flew wide and his feet squeaked on the tile floor of the shower.

I started to retreat but what was the sense? He caught me staring. His anger had become such a constant between us I knew this would only add to my offenses. "Apologies, I . . . uh, forgive the intrusion."

I dropped my gaze to the floor as he shut off the water and watched the last of the soapy froth gather and swirl by his feet. My ears burned. I wished I could back away and return his privacy to him. My limbs ignored my request.

"Is there something you wanted?" He grabbed a towel and wrapped the square of fabric tight around his hips. The thick quality of the textile did nothing to hide the jutting out of his erection. It simply pushed the fabric away from his body and highlighted his graceful lines. Sweet Shalana he was a beautiful male. Broad in the shoulders, slim in the hips with thick muscular thighs—

"Lia, eyes up here, please. What did you want?"

I raised my gaze. "I wondered about your research and came to ask." I swallowed as tears burned my eyes. "I failed to notice you were bathing until I stepped into the room. Please, finish your shower . . . forgive me."

"Nothing to forgive. Is everything all right?"

"Yes. I . . . uh, am embarrassed."

He shifted his feet, reaching for a second towel. He made as if to dry himself off, but stopped once his body was shielded from my view.

My tears brimmed and warmed my cheeks. "Verily, I angered you yet again. That was not my intention."

I strode back into my chamber. The room we had shared every night for the past weeks, large enough for the both of us minutes ago, suddenly felt far too confining.

"Lia, dinnae cry. Ye did nothing wrong." He moved before me and took my hand. "I may have been a little embarrassed myself but not angry."

I swiped at the moisture on my cheeks. "Mayhap not about this but you are most definitely angry with me. You have been for days."

He rubbed his hand over the scruff on his jaw and cursed.

"Fash not." I said. "You are free to feel however you feel. I simply wish things would return to the way they were."

He cupped my jaw and raised his fingers to smooth the lines of my brow. "We're good. Everything is fine."

I swallowed as a drop of water trickled a path from his collarbone down his chest to the tiny pink nipple of his breast. It rolled down his body, a marvelous sight as it kissed all his sharp angles and smooth lines.

"You lie to spare my feelings." My ears flamed hotter. Gods, his naked body destroyed my focus. Mika's words rang in my head and caught in my throat.

Take control. What do you want?

"I want to invite you to my bed." Both of us froze. It took me a moment to realize I voiced my thoughts. My first instinct was to cover up. To apologize and say something to ease the awkwardness but the intensity in his gaze gave me hope.

"Studying Highborne laws as you have, you are surely aware that I am within my rights to invite you to enjoy sexual pleasures and a degree of intimacy with—"

There was a hard edge to his face as he touched a fingertip to the burn in my cheek. "No. I, uh . . . just no. I'm sorry."

His words stung. I could not breathe. It was as if my heart was being squeezed by my lungs. I turned toward my bed chamber. "No. I apologize. You made yourself clear. I . . . let my imagination hope for more. We are friends."

Head high, I strode back to my room. Moments away from falling apart, I needed to gain some distance.

"Friends," he repeated, following me. "Aye, that's what we said but it hasna felt like that the past few days."

"Then tell me what I did."

"Ye healed Kobi." His jaw clenched, his fist gripping his towel. "I held back, ye see, thought I was doing what's best for ye, considering. To know he . . . that the two of you . . ."

He placed a wet hand over his heart. "I want to kill the bastard for laying hands on ye. I want to scream for ye letting him. I have no right to either reaction."

"But he is your friend."

He shook his damp hair. "Kobi may be a fellow Talon and a warrior I respect, but the demon is no one's friend. That goateed pincushion is as dangerous as they come and feeds off pain and suffering. Remember that."

"He saved my life."

He turned and braced his palms against the surface of the dresser. After exhaling a long, uneven breath he nodded. "Aye. When I did nothing but watch ye writhe in the dirt, he saved yer life. He excised that evil bitch. That's why he's here and the only reason he's still breathing. It's selfish and verra unkind, but the fact ye returned the favor and saved him boils my blood."

"How could I not? He bled for me."

"Aye, he did. I've thought of nothing else since, and nothing—no weapons, no acts, no words have cut me so deep in a long while. So, I ask ye . . . do ye feel something more for the demon? Now that ye've lain with him?"

There was a horrible silence, during which Samuel stared determinedly at the sand-colored stone wall behind me.

"You think I joined with him?" I raised my hand.

"Are ye tellin' me otherwise?"

"I certainly am. Kobi and I shared nothing but a few playful pleasures to right his health. We were not intimate."

His opal gaze met mine as if gauging my sincerity.

"Nothing passed between us beyond stolen kisses to aid in his recovery."

"So ye didn't . . . I mean, I know how Incubi heal . . . and I know Kobi. The man is . . . Christ, and I have no say in the matter if ye had—"

I lifted my chin and clenched my fists. "No. You do not. By your own declaration, you hold no interest in being intimate with me, yet you judge with the same assumption Galan did when he thought the worst of me. What is it about my moral character which has the males in my life expecting me to mount any male who stumbles into my path?"

"I never meant—"

I grabbed the fabric of my skirt and held it out to my sides. "Is my dress not tasteful, with all my provocative private parts covered?"

"Yer a vision, as always—"

"My intellect then. You think me simple or compromised mentally. Unable to control my base female urges."

"Of course not—"

I threw my hands in the air, my body humming with fury and hurt in equal measure. "I must have done something to warrant not only Galan's censure but yours as well."

"I'm an arse. I'm sorry—"

"And for you to judge me is worse. You know how Galan hurt me. You wiped my tears and I confided my heart to you. He at least was governed by his prejudice of you and his rage. And yet still you repeated his mistake."

Samuel rubbed his bare chest and winced. "Lia, duck—"

I thrust my hand in the air. "I am not your *duck*, I am not your, *luv*, I an not your . . . *anything*. If I were yours in any fashion, you would come to me as an equal and voice your concerns. You would show me the respect I deserve. Instead, you treat me the same way Galan did . . . as a naïve child."

As he started toward me, I braced my hands on his chest. "You are not the male I thought you to be, Samuel Murray. I want you to leave."

"Lia no, don't—"

"Get out." I choked on the words and shoved him toward the bathing room door. "Sleep in your own room. I refuse to place my heart in the hands of males who hold me in such low esteem. I shall manage on my own from now on."

CHAPTER SEVENTEEN

I am a corpse again, lain out on the rough slab, rolling through the maze of damp tunnels. The hum in my mind expands beyond thought and understanding. Torches flicker. My eyes are open but I cannot see. Cannot move.

The weight of impotence crushes my chest, restricts air from entering my lungs.

My journey stops and sensations bombard from all around the large hall: the rich smell of roasted meat, the pungency of ale, the brilliance of light refracting off a dazzling chandelier above, the cacophony of male voices. . . .

Deep-throated laughter fills my ears as the stench of male lust fills my sinuses. I feel the touch of eyes upon me, slithering over my skin like cold-blooded serpents. I push against the weight, but my limbs are dead, my voice unheard. I pray to my gods. I pray to my brother.

No one comes. No one.

My eyes flip open and the nightmare ends. Staring at the chiseled stone ceiling above the bed in my suite, my breath saws in and out of my lungs. I listen. Did I wake before screaming? Did I manage to exit my night terrors before I woke Bruin and the rest of the Dens with my cries?

Yes. Thank the gods, I had managed on my own. No need for Samuel to race in looking all protective and worried and annoyingly handsome. No. He need not return under the guise of it being for my own good. I had no want of a caregiver bound by duty. I wanted a male who wished to stand by my side. If he was not that male, best we ended our arrangement before either of us became too involved.

I rubbed my fingers over my lips. The moment of becoming too involved had long passed—at least for me. I closed my eyes and relived the passion of Samuel's kiss when he came to me in his waking moments. He had not kissed me like a guardian. His lips had consumed me, his hips pressing forward, wanton. He had kissed me as a male would kiss a female. Passionate and hungry. And then he had woken and declared the entire moment a mistake.

I slapped at the coverlet and exhaled.

Why now would my Elven logic fail me? It was senseless to pine for a male who, by his own admission, held no interest in me. The humiliation of rejection washed over me anew.

I wondered if my fruitless fantasies could be some strange side-effect of the queer tingle of my skin. Since the night I moved into the Dens weeks ago, the sensation had increased incrementally each night. At first, it had been nothing but a tickle, like a tiny bug crawling across my flesh. It had grown until my skin hummed like my hormones had awakened, resonating at a vibration all their own.

No one spoke of the mysterious kinetic energy in the air and I wondered if the others sensed it. My theory: Were Magic. At night, when in their base forms for sleep, the magical essence of Bruin's bear, Cowboy's wolf, Bree's coyote, the cubs, and the dozen security and support Weres living within the mountain filled the space with a sense of restrained wildness.

And as the full moon of the summer solstice grew ever nearer, the frenetic energy built.

Anticipating.

Aust said, with the coming of the solstice, the animals of the Weres prowled much closer to the surface. I wondered what build-up of power and aggression would mean to the Weres living in Haven. I wondered if their restlessness could influence my own sensations.

After ages of twisting in the sheets and growing more frustrated with my life, I liberated my legs and threw back the blankets. The t-shirt Samuel had given me to wear as a night shirt lay flung over the upholstered bench at the foot of the bed. After pulling it over my head, I tugged my braid free and headed to the kitchen for some hot cocoa.

When I opened the door, I startled and jumped back.

"Hey, Highborne," Kobi said, his fist raised as if he were about to knock.

"Sweet Shalana, Kobi," I said, my hand over my chest. "What are you doing outside my door at this hour?"

He swaggered forward, shirtless, his nipple baring a nickel ring similar to the ones pierced his brow and lip. Reaching up, he gave my braid a gentle tug where if fell over my breast. "I heard you stirring around by yourself. Wondered if you wanted some company? Demons haunting you again, little girl?"

I swallowed. The *little girl* reference had worn thin long ago, but by the scent of him, Kobi was intoxicated and upset, so I let it pass. "You are the one up drinking alone in the darkness of night. Mayhap, something haunts the demon."

"Touché." He raised the tumbler in his other hand, his eyes flashing with fire for the briefest moment. "If you had a drink with me, I would no longer be alone."

I stepped back. He followed, closing the distance between us once more. "I, uh . . . though to go to the kitchen for some hot cocoa. You are welcome to join me."

"Cocoa? Lightweight. This is a hell of a lot more effective than cocoa." When I shook my head, he shrugged and emptied the glass himself.

"Kobi, not to be impolite, but what can I do for you?"

He bit his bottom lip, his mouth twitching in a crooked smirk. "Glad you asked. You see, after our little make-out session in the clinic, I realized something was different. I don't go for the whole Victoriana librarian thing—ever—but there's something about you."

He slid a hand across the small of my back and pulled me against his muscled chest. "You soothe something inside my demon nature, Highborne. Something which has burned away at my insides my whole cursed life."

My ears flushed. "I am pleased I eased your discomfort but our moment together was for your healing. We cannot—"

The piercings in his dark brow pinched as he frowned. "Don't cock-block me yet. Think about it, Lia. You're of age, inexperienced and unattached. I spend a lot of time at Haven. We could keep things casual, spend some time having fun."

I opened my mouth to answer and his lips were on mine.

His tongue penetrated, the taste of alcohol strong. His hands ventured down my back and under my nightshirt to stroke my bare buttocks.

I braced my hands on his chest and pushed back as far as his strength allowed. "Stop, please. Apologies, but no."

He kissed my cheek, my jaw, my neck. "You sure? You're hungry, little Lia. I can taste it. There are advantages to being friends with benefits."

I pushed again and he released me with a curse.

Kobi was a highly sexual male—an incubus demon. The primal part of me he had awoken in the clinic wanted more, wanted all Kobi offered, hungered for that kind of connection, longed to be wanted with an all-consuming passion.

Yet not by him.

"Mayhap you should excuse yourself before something happens we both regret."

Kobi chuckled and arched a pierced ebony brow. "Demons don't do regret. Waste of fucking time. Live for the moment, Highborne."

I drew a deep unsteady breath and stepped towards the bed, thought better of it, and strode back towards the bathroom door. Remembering who lay sleeping on the other side of that shared bathroom, I changed course once again and wound up standing back with

Kobi. "Highbornes are not casual lovers. Consummated means committed—for life—forever more. I doubt that is your desire."

He wagged his finger. "Don't toss "forever" bullshit at me. Tham talked about pleasuring the females in your village a hundred times. We could be creative and keep it casual and you know it."

"And do my feelings enter into this arrangement?"

His sultry smile triggered warmth deep in my belly. "Trust me, Lia, you'll be feeling things. So, will I. Even after one kiss, the relief is exquisite."

"So, I am to be the balm on your pained existence? How romantic. It is a far cry from the all-consuming love I dreamed of in my youth."

Kobi's jaw clenched tight. "Romance is an illusion for naïve school girls. Don't buy into that shit. It'll do nothing but wear you down."

I envisioned the passion shared between Galan and Jade and Iadon and Nyssa. Yes. I absolutely did believe in love. "I am sorry you suffer, Kobi. I wish to ease you but you are not the male my heart desires. Go now, please."

"I'll go, but not far. We will be together, Highborne. I get what I want in the end. Always do." The slam of the door echoed through the sleepy silent halls. I winced and studied the bathroom door.

If Samuel heard the noise, he would race in to check on me. What would I say about Kobi's visit? He was already angry about my first private encounter with him. I smoothed my hair and waited. I would make him understand. I would apologize for losing my temper and make amends.

I waited. Nothing.

My heart sank. Mayhap he was merely lost to slumber. Verily, if I meant to stand on my own, I needed to stop depending on well-meaning males. I nodded to myself, resigned to my original course of visiting the kitchen to fix myself a cup of hot cocoa.

"Lia?" Zophia said right beside me.

I staggered to the side, collided into an ornate gold plant stand, and scrambled to right it before dirt spilled over the polished marble floor. After setting the vessel back, I scanned the vaulted ceilings of the room, the vignettes of ornamental vases and bronze statuary and the thick, floor-to-ceiling brocade tapestries hanging from black irons rod running the length of one long wall.

"You Flashed me to the Fae Palace? How? I thought the Dens were protected against magic."

Zophia smiled, her midnight blue eyes filled with amusement. "Protected against realm magic, maybe, but my abilities are a little more powerful."

I had never considered Zophia a particularly powerful female: elegant, educated, regal—yes. But verily, as one of the Fates and a member of the Fae Pantheon, she would be very powerful.

Zophia stepped forward, her long dark hair piled high on her head with little escaping tendrils falling next to her glowing pearl face. Her ice-blue gown kissed the sheen of the sleek floor as she practically glided to stand before me. "Lia, I know it's late, but I need to speak with you privately and have been watching for a moment to find you alone."

I smoothed my fingertips along the hem of Samuel's t-shirt where it met my thigh. "Speak about what? Has something happened? Are your sisters tormenting you?"

Looking dreadfully serious she waved her hand through the air and a cool breeze sprang up out of still air. The tapestries hanging against the long walls leaped to life, sliding along the rod as they shifted position. Flapping and rearranging themselves, they bustled like magic carpets until one woven tapestry settled deliberately to the front.

Zophia stroked the weave of fabric and nodded, her dark gaze falling everywhere except on me. "Lia? Do you recall my station as one of the Fates?"

I did—Keeper of the Lives in Progress—Sweet Shalana. "Oh, no. Galan's young? Are they well? Have you seen something? Galan and Jade will be heartbroken if—"

She waved her hand between us. "No. The babies are doing as well as can be expected. This is not about Galan's young. I came to speak about you . . . about Abaddon's claim and about my testimony when you face my sisters."

The bitter taste of bile rose and caught in my throat. "Your testimony? You must to speak to his claim?"

"Yes. I'm the Keeper of Lives. I was asked to study your tapestry and disclose the truth of what happened during the time Abaddon held you in his compound."

My heart leaped. Zophia could access what happened and refute his accusations and prove Abaddon spoke nothing but lies."You can testify I am a newling and he is a liar. Despite his claim, he cannot force me to be his mate—"

Zophia had yet to smile.

"What am I missing, cousin? This is good news, is it not?"

She turned to the tapestry and the lights dimmed. "Lia? Did you mean what you said to Samuel? You want everyone to stop tiptoeing around you?"

I bobbed my head. "Please, yes, if you have something important to say, I wish to hear it."

With a grim nod, she waved her hand over the fabric of the closest tapestry.

Another breeze came up and the loveliest scent filled my senses. Where Castian's powers smelled of bergamot and mint, Zophia's smelled of spring rain. She turned to gaze at me. "Galan said you don't remember your confinement. It's against our basic tenet to interfere but you should see this before you're in a room full of people. I thought it might be better this way. To prepare yourself."

Zophia took my hand and drew my fingers back and forth across row after row of the weave, unwanted memories unlocked in my head: being laid out on a rolling cart, positioned at the front of the Scourge dining hall, Abaddon's weight over me, the stench of his triumph and lust singing my nostrils, reeling against the stillness of my body as he penetrated to my innermost depths. And not once. Evening after evening, for the entertainment of his army.

Violated. The depravity of it . . .

I raced to the closest niche and vomited into a vase. The images persisted. My insides gripped and twisted as every hormone-filled scent, guttural sound, and callous touch washed over me. Whatever levee of denial my subconscious had erected, crashed down around me.

I wanted to run, to get away from Zophia's gaze and the woven authentication of my shame. My trembling legs would never hold my weight if I attempted to move. I sank to my knees on the polished floor, the soiled Fae antiquity in my lap. "Apologies, I, uh—"

Zophia rushed before me and ran a hand down my arm. "Don't worry about that old thing. How can I help? Tell me."

I wiped the tears from my cheek and drew an unsteady breath. "Would you mind . . . could you please send me back to my suite?"

"Are you sure you want to be alone?"

I nodded. No words spoken could change the truth.

Zophia rested her arm across my shoulders and hugged me before she stood. "I'm sorry, Lia. I wish . . . well, I wish a lot of things had been different for you."

"How long?"

Her head tilted to the side, a long, dark tendril falling against her breast. "Until you're called before the Fates?"

I nodded, my breath coming in rough hiccoughs.

"A few days . . . a week if I can push them off."

I closed my eyes and waited until the silk of my coverlet replaced the cold of polished stone beneath my shins. How had this happened? I knew. A part of me had always known. It was the reality I had fought inside myself for months, the darkness I had denied—the truth.

I had been mated by a monster.

CHAPTER EIGHTEEN

*M*ated by Abaddon.

I crumpled into the folds of my bedding, the tightness in my chest excruciating. Agony burned. Physical. Mental. Spiritual. It surrounded me. Consumed me. Injected lava into the marrow of my bones.

Abaddon had taken me against my will and bound us forever. The only male who could ever claim my body was the sadistic sorcerer destroying the Realm of the Fair and killing the innocent.

I would never know the touch of a true lover. I would never be caressed or cherished as I had dreamed my entire life. Samuel's words came back to me. *"Stick to yer story and I'll never say a word, but remember, Lia, I was there."*

The pit of my belly went cold. The last hope I had kindled for Samuel to grow to love me extinguished.

He had worked covertly to gain access to the Scourge compound. He had played his part and bided his time until he was able to rescue me. He was there. He had seen.

Knowing his heroic nature, his kindness was likely tantamount to him feeling responsible in some part. Black spots flickered in my vision. Gods, was it any wonder he held no interest in me. And if he was there in an official Talon capacity, they all knew. He would have made his report and they would have discussed it in one of their Talon meetings.

I staggered to my feet, my head a cyclonic jumble of thoughts and images. I needed air.

Stumbling behind a wall of tears, I padded down halls, stairs and emerged out on the rain splattered plateau. The night was windy, a tumultuous spring rain whipping eddies at me from all directions. I blinked up at the three-quarter moon and down on the slick steps leading from the Dens to the Haven grounds below. My bare toes curled over the edge. Descending, I followed the silver trail of moon-light as quickly as my feet would carry me.

Vaguely I registered voices shouting behind me. Male voices. Bruin's sentinels guarding the entrance no doubt. I ignored the calls and continued my descent. They would not follow. They must needs guard their Alpha's home. I could not face them regardless. I had nothing more to give to anyone tonight . . . or mayhap ever.

I wiped my eyes and cheeks as my feet met each step in rapid succession. The turning tide of my evening left me hollow. Abaddon mated me. And in a few days' time, the Fates would declare it. I had lost my brother . . . my friends . . . my innocence . . . my choice and my future.

My inner construct shattered. The jagged edges of the break tore at my insides never to be whole again.

Rain-sodden ground squished under my feet as I reached the base of the Den's rise and stumbled on. My energy flagged and still, no amount of distance helped. No matter where I ran, I remained trapped. Mayhap Abaddon's intention to vacate my soul and allow Rheagan to claim my body was a blessing. My shame would end. My soul would soar free.

Gods how I wanted to be free.

I rounded the bank of Glass Pond. The moon's reflection fractured and fragmented on the mirrored surface. I drew closer and stopped on the water's edge, my mind drifting back to the last time I stood in this spot. Samuel had explained the formation of Canadian geese in the sky. *"The lead bird bears the wind resistance as long as it can, while the others ride in its stream. When it tires and can take no more, it'll fall back and another will take its place."*

I fought to breathe through the constriction in my lungs. As the only heir to the throne, if I were gone, there would be no other to take my place. Abaddon and Rheagan would be foiled, the people of the realm would have one less thing to threaten them. And I would be free.

"I can bear no more, Samuel. I am sorry."I glanced down at the Academy t-shirt and sobbed. How I wished Samuel had claimed me. I peeled the t-shirt over my head and drew it to my face. His scent was trapped in the fibers and I breathed him in for the last time before I set it on the bank.

Icy water rose around my calves. Shivers racked me as it crept over my knees and up my thighs. Three more steps and the surface enveloped me.

Angry water, black in every direction, closed in. The silence dazzled. The rushing of the wind, the hiss of the rain, the echoes of my anguish all silenced. That solitude . . . that isolation . . . was the reason I found comfort under water.

Aching cold numbed my flesh, prickling hot.

I blinked in the darkness as a vision of Tham appeared before me. Peculiar, as my life ebbed away, he was the male delusion my mind conjured.

He looked frantically around the darkness, his ghostly apparition as perfect as the real male. I passed a hand through the image of my beloved friend and brother in all but blood. *Amin mela lle*, Tham.

My lungs burned for oxygen. My muscles cramped from the cold. I remained at ease. Months of headaches, denial and anxiety had worn me down. Black spots bloomed across my vision growing larger by the moment.

Tham disappeared and I missed him immediately. I missed Galan too. The ache of disappointing my brother sliced me to the core. What would the loss mean to others? Galan and Samuel would blame themselves. Jade would be overwrought. Might she lose her young? Even unborn, I loved those twins with all my heart.

I would never cause them harm. Any of them.

I forced my legs to bend and tried to push. My strength waned. My arms hung heavy. My head spun. I tried to kick, to breach the surface, but it was no use. My decision to live had come too late.

A thousand sharp, icy spears prickled my flesh as warmth surrounded me. Lethargy and confusion hung heavy in my head. No longer was I surrounded by darkness while freezing water filled my mouth, nose and lungs. I stood shivering in a small golden alcove off a royal bed chamber.

My gaze skipped over the ornately carved bed, the velvet drapery, the fabric-covered walls and settled on an ethereal female wearing a sheer champagne gown. She lay on a raised platform before me, her hair a rich burgundy I had seen on only one other person.

I sputtered for air and looked down at myself. Naked except for my mourning band, I clutched Castian's pendant, Pond water dripped in a steady stream from my braid, my fingers and everywhere else.

Standing at the side of his unconscious wife, Castian looked murderously annoyed.

"Am I dead, Sire?" I coughed again and pushed my voice past the burning in my throat.

Castian drew his fingers along the woman's face and curled a wayward lock around his finger. "You tell me, *Ryanne?*"

I winced. Usually, when Castian spoke my soul name, it filled me with an intimate sense of peace. Instead, his dry clipped tone gripped me, his pretense of civility veil thin.

I steadied my slippery footing on the marble floor. Was I passing to the After to join the dead of my village? Had my momentary loss of hope cost me everything? My mind whirled with a multitude of questions, but

"Has Jade spoken to you of her mother?" He rounded the foot of the platform. The powerful fury seething beneath the surface of Castian's gaze took me aback. "I asked you a question. Find your voice and speak."

My gaze flashed up to meet his. "Uh, yes, some. Her name is Abbey. She remains dormant after a Scourge attack though her body is healed. Jade holds hope her spirit will find its way back and you three will be reunited."

His square jaw flexed. "Do you know what she suffered to leave her in this state?"

I hated to speak of the pain that haunted his emerald glare. "She was violated, tortured to gain access to Jade but she protected her daughter until Reign came upon them."

Castian nodded. "Do you believe it was her fault . . . what those men did to her?"

Who was I to hold an opinion on such matters? He was the God of gods. I was . . . no one. I barely knew the male and could not speak to what happened two decades ago. Still, he stared at me awaiting an answer. "No Sire, of course not."

He crossed his arms and looked down at me. "Do you think I reject her and find her unworthy because some vile men forced themselves inside her?"

"No, my lord, it is obvious you cherish her to the depths of your soul."

He raked his fingers through his long, brown hair and turned to his mate. "I believe the torment of her state is my penance. I saw the horror unfold and refused to stop it. And as much as everyone despises the Fates, every event affects another along a long chain. For Jade to survive and claim the life meant for her, I couldn't interfere. And so, I left Abbey to those animals."

"It was an impossibly horrible choice to make. You must not blame yourself for her condition."

Castian frowned. "Fate and free will are poised in a tenuous balance. Image two twining vines growing and thirsting towards the same source of light. Both are needed to create the whole. Abbey's body is healed, yet, on some level, she chooses to abandon our life. Is it punishment because I failed to save her from those monsters?"

My stomach knotted.

He brushed his knuckle against her cheek. "I watched as evil took something precious from us. Do I love her less for it? Does it change her in any way in my eyes?"

My mouth dropped open, closed, opened again. "I cannot speak to your feelings, Sire, but I think not. Your feelings exceed the circumstances, no matter what you were made to bear witness to."

A grim smile curled his mouth as if my answer spoke more than my words. "Yet here she lays, a shell of the woman I once loved. A beautiful husk for me to mourn. She gave up. On me. On Jade. And now, I ask you, why?"

I shook my head. "I cannot say, Sire."

His emerald gaze narrowed. "You hold no insight as to why a woman in her position would surrender to oblivion rather than fight to claim life?"

I clasped my shivering hands before me and dropped my gaze. "Forgive me. I cannot begin to tell you . . . to express how I wish I had chosen a different course. When I learned the truth of Abaddon's claim—when the images overtook me—to be mated to such a male . . ."

Energy snapped in the air. He clasped a hand around my wrist and tugged me to his beloved's side. Clasping the back of my neck, he held my gaze fixed on Jade's comatose mother. "Is this what you want? To be dead in all ways save the most final. To have Galan and Samuel mourn you and relive the ways they failed you for decades to come. Do you blame them? Wish they had done more, said more—"

"No."

Castian held me fast and leaned close to my ear. "What will you do about it?"

Tears burned my cheeks. "What can I do?"

"Change. Change your course. Change your mindset." He released me and I spun around to look at him. The fury ringing in his voice was absent in his expression.

He looked composed. Calculating.

Taking my hand, he led me away from the raised platform and sat me on the edge of one of the two upholstered chairs in the alcove. "Harness your pain and fury. Let it fuel the fire within you to grow stronger. The life you envisioned as a child is gone. Forget it. Take charge of your destiny and forge your path as Queen of the Realm of the Fair."

I blinked back the tears blurring my vision. "You cannot truly believe I am the woman the realm needs."

He opened my clenched fist and twirled the blue diamond from my palm to its proper place on my finger. "Will you do this, *Ryanne*? Do not let atrocities define you. Seize control of your life and lead the realm."

Castian produced a silk handkerchief and gave me a moment to wipe my eyes.

"You will not be alone. Reign will help you. So too will Galan, Samuel, Bruin and countless others. Accept your destiny. Seize it. Make the Realm of the Fair a safer place in which to live. Think of the lives you can save."

Gooseflesh raised on my skin. "I *was* thinking about the citizens of the realm in my despair. With me dead, Abaddon's plan to vacate my soul for Rheagan would be moot."

"Rheagan is my problem, not yours," Castian said.

"Until she possesses me. How do I focus on a future when I wait in terror for her powers to grow strong enough to take control of my body?"

Castian pressed a hand to my forehead and an electrical charge tingled from my scalp through my body and sent goosebumps prickling along my skin. He placed his other hand over my heart, and the instant the circuit connected, a white-hot fire spread across my shoulders. I gritted my teeth, the scent of bergamot growing until it was rife in the air.

A moment later the burn was gone. I glanced down to my shoulder at the crescent moon tattoo inked on my skin.

"Safe from possession, now your task is to fight. Become Queen of the Realm and steer the course of your life. Stand for those who suffer at the hands of the plague of the realm."

I stared at him, numb. "Where shall I begin?"

He moved back to his wife and brushed his finger along the line of her jaw. "Tell Samuel of your intentions, my sweet niece. Tell him what you want and he will make the arrangements."

CHAPTER NINETEEN

I was drowning again—my world filled with frigid darkness. My feet compressed into the thick muck at the bottom of Glass Pond and I pushed with all I had. My limbs, heavy and useless from my time underwater, refused to get me off the bottom. Despite a renewed conviction to live, my body remained numbed by its prolonged exposure to the cold.

No, no, no. *NO!*

Raising my spotty gaze to the darkness above, I fought to hold my breath—to save the oxygen locked within me. While I held an ounce of breath left in me I would do as Castian asked. I would fight to become the Queen the people of the realm. I would fight to ensure Abaddon and his disgusting army of monsters never won another battle. I would fight to reclaim the two males I loved most.

The thought of Samuel agonizing over my death for decades like Castian twisted my gut. A male of worth, sworn to protect me, he would take on the responsibly of my stupidity. He would blame himself, isolate himself from friends and family, sink deeper into his despair than before.

Samuel. I shuddered as his handsome image appeared before me.

He was there. My mind had heard my heart's call and conjured the proper illusion this time.

Samuel—my *garda síochána*.

The apparition of Samuel scowled. His dark features creased and pinched, his luminescent eyes glowing and swirling with emotion. If he were real and could speak, he would lash at me, his lilting accent thick.

I would have welcomed his chastisement.

Strong hands grappled under my arms. He yanked hard and we broke the surface as one. Samuel's grip shifted as he pulled us toward the pond's grassy edge. Was he real? I collapsed, coughing and sputtering, onto the rain-sodden ground. I grabbed the folded t-shirt and curled around it.

On one knee, he rolled me on my side and struck the center of my back in a sharp rhythm. "Jaysus, Lia, what the feck were ye thinkin'?"

Water thrust from my lungs. It gushed forth in alarming volume. It spewed from my mouth and nose.

"Breathe," Samuel snapped.

Wave after wave wracked me. It burned my sinuses and tore at my throat. The expulsion failed to give me enough time to inhale.

"Dammit, Lia, breathe." Samuel's voice, wild and angry, rang sweetly in my ears. His fury did not frighten me, it stemmed from fear. If I survived this, he could rant until the coming of the equinox moon and I would not utter one word of complaint.

Galan and Samuel both postured around her as a cockeyed expression of affection. Stupid males. I felt sick with despair, the distance between me and the two of them unbearable. Another tide of water convulsed from my belly. I retched again.

Samuel groaned, hovering over me as rain dripped from his shoulders. "Christ woman, look at me. Are ye all right? What can I do?"

I tried to focus past the spots in my vision. Samuel's face was close, his eyes too wet. I raised a shaky hand to his face and he pressed his cheek into my palm. My teeth chattered. My lips quivered. "M-m-make c-c-cocoa and I shall love you f-f-f-forever."

Something flashed across Samuel expression and he scooped me back into his arms. "Aye, I can live with that. I'll tan yer beautiful bare arse once yer warmed up then, shall I? Dinnae think fer one minute this is finished between us."

I let my cheek fall to Samuel's chest. The heat of his words and the scent of his panic seeped warm under my skin. Nothing was finished between us. "Agreed."

~

Samuel's accent snapped thicker than I had ever heard, his body more rigid than I had ever felt. After Flashing us back to the upper plateau of the Dens, he stormed past the guards and then Bruin, Cowboy, and Kobi without a word.

"Dinnae move," he said, dumping me unceremoniously on my bed. He tugged his wet t-shirt from my grasp and wrapped the coverlet around me tight. Before straightening, he glared, finger pointed. "Not an inch, lass. I'm warnin' ye. I cannae take it. Not. One. Feckin'. Inch."

I did not even nod.

He stormed through the bathroom door, his flannel night pants hanging low on his hips from the weight of pond water. Water thundered into the bathtub in a rush. A moment later, he returned, wearing a dry pair of boxer briefs and a towel in hand. He scrubbed the towel over his head in a flurry as he paced back to the hall door and slammed it shut.

"Ye took twenty years off my life tonight, Lia. I swear it. What the hell was that about? Jaysus fecking Christ." He wrenched the towel from his hair and slung it to the floor.

"I uh, lost hope for a moment."

"A moment? *A moment?* Ye nearly lost it fer good." His hands flew into the air as he strode back into the bathroom. The water shut off and he was back. His gaze bounced around the room landing on everything and yet nothing at all.

"Samuel, let me explain—"

The door to my suite flew open and Galan raced inside. He stormed to my bedside in a pique that could only be equaled by

Samuel's. "Tell me Tham is mistaken, little one. Tell me you would never intentionally end your life."

Sweet goddess, I loved these males.

I worked my hands out of the blanket mountain tucked around me and shoved my hair from where it stuck to my face. Tham stood behind my brother looking equally pale, if not more so, for the fact that he was a spirit.

So, he *had* been with me down there. "Apologies, brother mine, but I cannot speak that which is not truth. I had a lapse."

Galan hissed, wringing his fingers through his hair. "A lapse? What in the two realms would possess you to harm yourself?"

Samuel nodded. "Aye, I asked her the same feckin' thing."

Galan swung to see Samuel standing beside the bed in his boxers and tensed.

"Galan. Stop!" I squeaked, my throat raw and sore. "If you wish to stay, you will neither say nor act against Samuel in any way. He saved me just now. If you value my feelings at all, lay aside your anger and hear me out."

The muscle along Galan's jaw clenched but he settled.

"Now, if you could close the door, it has been a difficult evening and I think it best to explain from the beginning."

Tham took my request for privacy to heart and left Galan, Samuel, and I to speak.

Where to begin? My fight with Samuel would only exacerbate Galan's mood. My encounter with Kobi was liable to send Samuel over the edge. I drew a deep breath. "Zophia visited earlier this evening, to prepare me."

"Prepare ye for what?" Samuel asked.

"During Abaddon's hearing with the Fates, she must read the tapestry of my life and testify to the factual account of my incarceration last summer."

Samuel's mouth narrowed into a hard line. "And what did yer cousin say about it?"

I met his anguished stare. "I believe we three know what she told me, or showed me, rather."

"Showed ye?" Samuel turned, his shoulders and fists clenched tight. "Feckin' Fates! Why would she want ye to see such a thing? Ye said she was different than her sisters."

"She is," Galan said, his voice flat. "Zophia would never bring it up if avoidable. If she must testify to the validity of Abaddon's claim, she has no choice."

Samuel rounded on him. "Then she shoulda' done it when we were there, not leave her alone in her grief 'til takin' a midnight swim seemed a good idea."

I squeezed the coverlet tighter around me. "Samuel, my actions are my own. After I saw . . . once I knew the truth, I asked for privacy. Zophia respected me enough to leave me. She is not to blame."

Samuel was a Celt kettle about to boil. I patted the bed and was thankful he acquiesced. He took my hand and his eyes rolled closed. "Ye coulda' died, Luv. Do ye understand what it does to my insides to know how close ye came to drowning? If I hadn't found ye . . ." He bit his lip and shook his head again.

I stroked his cheek. "How did you find me?"

Galan pulled a chair to the bedside. "Yes, Samuel, how did you find her? Tham heard the guards call out and saw Lia enter the pond. He came to wake me. How did you know where she was?"

Samuel exhaled heavily and caught my dripping braid with a corner of the bedspread. After squeezing its length within the fabric, he removed the elastic at the end and began to comb it out with his fingers. "Ye told me ye like to sit under water of yer river when the world closed in on ye. Then, when ye went back to the village for Tham's ceremony, ye scared Cowboy half to death with a similar impulse."

"He told you?" I asked. "Am I a general topic of conversation?"

"No. When I became yer guardian I read every report the Talon has filed on ye." He grabbed my chin and forced me to look at him. "Dinnae fash. It's important to keep a record of what happens during a Talon shift. No one's spying on ye, if that's what yer thinkin'."

I pulled my jaw free of his hand. "Did you file a similar report on what happened to me in the caverns last summer?"

His frown deepened.

My breath froze in my lungs. "You told me once you were there and you knew the truth. Did you report to your Talon friends what Abaddon did to me? Is that why everyone looks at me with such pity —if they can look at me at all?"

Samuel scrubbed a palm over his face. "I'm sorry, I—"

"You need not apologize." Galan glared at me. "Reign brought me that report. What Samuel said . . . well, he left you with as much dignity and privacy as possible, considering his position and his duty."

So, I was right. Everyone knew. Galan. Samuel. Reign and the Talon. That included Jade and Lexi. Zophia and Castian as well. My stomach twisted as Castian's words for Abbey rang in my head. *"Evil claimed her body and something precious was taken from each of us."*

Taken. Not given.

I may have been mated but the images in my memory were distant glimpses. I had been drugged. What Zophia showed me was horrible but not me. The embarrassment was mine. Anger. Shame. But that helpless maiden bound to the table bore no resemblance to the person I was or wanted to be.

How much would I allow Abaddon's evil define me?

Should I retreat from family and friends because they knew something I would rather die than think about? I made that mistake and almost lost my life. That would never happen again. Abaddon and his evil meant nothing next to my life.

Knowing the entire truth, no matter how painful, liberated me from the cocoon I had been living within. A spring of anguish escaped the deepest part of my soul, streaming to the surface like bubbles in a glass of soda. It carried with it the darkness and despair which had weighed me down for the better part of the past year.

Breathing in, I filled my lungs and flopped back on the bed, half dragging Samuel with me. We fell in a tangle of bedding and clunked heads. I giggled and broke out in genuine laughter. Samuel's baffled expression broke my heart, the anxiety of the night etched into every chiseled line of his face.

Galan cleared his throat and I realized I was lying, half on top of

Samuel, naked on my bed with him a mere three feet away. I kissed Samuel's cheek and sat up to face my brother. "Fash not, I have had an epiphany."

Galan arched a graceful brow. "Pray tell, what would this realization be?"

"Castian told me, fate and free will is a tenuous balance. Both are needed to create a whole. Whether what Abaddon did to me was his free will, the Fates toying with our lives, destiny or something in between, the result remains the same. My life changed the day Scourge raiders entered our village. I cannot go back. I can never again be a naïve maiden living unaware of the realm around me."

Galan shook his head. "No, little one, you cannot."

I scooted to the edge of the bed and set my feet on the floor. "And just as your destiny with Jade began the moment you tackled her to the forest floor and knew your place was at her side, my destiny lies in me being the heir to the throne. I cannot be the female I need to be, here with you at Haven. I gave my word to Castian. I accept my place and shall try to be the Queen the realm needs. To do that, I must needs go."

Galan ran his fingers through his hair. "Haven is your home. Where will you—"

I pressed two fingers over his lips, my resolve more concrete with every word I spoke. "No. Haven is *your* home. And though I have always followed you, trust that I am grown and capable of forging my own path. Support me. Love me. Disagree with me if you must, but do not try to stop me."

He moved my fingers from his lips and kissed them. "Is it because of our falling out over Samuel? I shall do better, I swear. Look. We are in the same room and neither of us—"

I shook my head and cast a glance back to Samuel. "Could you give us a moment?"

Samuel rolled to his feet and nodded. On his way past the dresser, he opened a drawer and tossed me one of his long-sleeved shirts. "Put that on before ye catch yer death. I'll go make the hot cocoa I promised ye."

In the chair beside the bed, Galan sat, fists clenched against his suede pants. His straight silver hair hung loose with the burgundy braid of his binding brushing the side of his chiseled face. How long had it been since he fought with Samuel in my suite at Jade's? Weeks? A month? More?

Aside from racing to my aid in the clearing and again tonight, he had been absent from my life. Now, with me leaving, we must needs mend our rift.

His glance flickered from the shirt on my lap, to the dresser and locked back on me. "Why does Samuel keep clothes in your chamber?"

"Because he has slept in here since almost the first night I left Jade's manse." I pointed to the pallet of blankets and pillow on the floor by the wall. I kept the details of our time sharing a bed to myself. "My night-terrors do not overtake my sleep when he is near, so we share a chamber."

I waited for the furious accusations—they did not come.

Gods, he looked weary. So—lost. Lines of stress creased his brow, ageing him far more than his century and ten. Jade's attack, the uncertain fate of his unborn young and the difficulties with me—life was wearing him down.

I pulled Samuel's shirt over my head and rolled up the sleeves.

With an expression of somber purpose, Galan opened his mouth. "I missed you, *sweeting*. Gods, I ached to make things right between us. I respect your decision to keep me away, but," he closed his eyes, "do not leave. Let us figure out your destiny together. We have spent too much time apart already."

There was an awkwardness between Galan and I that never existed before. I took his hand and leaned close. "I gave Castian my word."

Galan cleared his throat. "I practiced what I would say to you a thousand times over, to apologize for my behavior. Now, I am at a loss." He stared at me, his brilliant blue eyes, so much richer than the rest of the Highborne race.

I squeezed his hand. "When you lashed out and questioned my

honor, I was all but ruined. I need you to realize that. You tore my heart and soul from my chest and left me an empty, broken shell."

A strangled noise escaped the back of his throat as he leaned forward and pressed his forehead to mine.

"You were my horizon, Galan. My guiding point. Without you, I have been adrift for almost a year—lost though rescued, isolated though not alone. You moved us to Haven, giving me no say in the matter, and restricted my movements. Then, you assigned males to guard me."

He straightened. "For your protection."

"You were always my protector, Galan. *You* were my 'Haven'. Though I understand Jade moved into the largest part of your heart, it hurt to be replaced."

"No, *Ryanne*. Not replaced. Never. I love you as much this moment as ever."

"Until that morning in my suite, I never questioned that but the things you said—"

"I take them back. All of—"

"You cannot," I said, the last of my energy seeping from me. "Mayhap we needed the distance to realize our paths cannot continue as they have. The balance of fate versus free will made itself known."

Galan exhaled a labored breath. "What are you saying?"

"I am saying I am no longer your little one, nor do I care to be. My coming of age has passed. It is time you treated me as an adult, and it is time I behave as one."

"I know nothing other than to take care of you."

"Please." I nearly hissed the word. "Removed from the village, friends, and afraid of everything in this chaotic new world, I have fended for myself since my capture. Do you know what it is to be overwhelmed every minute of every day trying to live up to what others expect of you? Do you know how exhausting it is?"

"I do." Galan rose and started to pace. "I am mated to the daughter of our god, and gods willing, shall be a father. I am also Sentinel of Souls responsible for all lost and displaced lives. Apologies if you feel I failed you, but you could have told me how you felt."

"You should have *known*." I swiped at the unwelcome tears warming my cheeks. "You have always known my heart. I never acted inappropriately with Samuel and you should have known that. I was kind to a male who suffered and sacrificed his own happiness so we could have ours. In return, you were a—a—an arse."

His brow arched and his mouth twitched up. "I never heard you utter a curse."

"Well, I shan't make it a habit, but the occasion warrants it." I rubbed my temples, the dull ache behind my eyes taking root. It was hard to know what was bringing on the headache this time. There was so much to choose from.

Galan closed the distance between us and sighed. "*Ryanne*, you are a lovely female with strong virtue. I regretted my words even as they spewed from my mouth. Abaddon came for you, claimed his right to you, and while I was caught in a fit of fury and panic, I found you embracing Samuel in your suite. I behaved deplorably. You have my deepest apologies."

I slid my arms around his waist and embraced him. "I accept your apology but know this, since you drove me away, Samuel and I have grown close."

He fingered the shirt I wore. "Do you love him?"

"Does it matter? I am mated to Abaddon and Samuel stood witness. Whatever I may or may not have hoped for is unimportant."

He kissed my forehead. "Your feelings are important to me. And though Samuel sets me off half-crazed, he feels for you too. You realize that, yes?"

I rolled my eyes, a familiar ache tightening in my chest. "My sense of smell is as keen as yours. However, neither attraction nor affection constitutes romantic interest. He made it clear there is no future for us. He holds no intentions to pursue me."

Galan gathered both my hands in his. "Though I dislike the male, Samuel has been kind to you, a friend when you needed one."

I sighed. "Do you understand why I must needs go?"

He wrapped his arms around me and squeezed until I thought my spine would crack. "Not entirely but I respect your decision. When will you leave?"

"In a few days. There are things I must sort out myself before I go."

He kissed my forehead and nodded. "When you settle, I shall visit and ensure you are being well cared for. And I shall stand for you at your tribunal."

I smiled against his neck. He smelled of outdoors, suede and, to my heart's relief, Galan. "I expect nothing less."

CHAPTER TWENTY

*L*eft to my bath, I closed the door. Steam condensed on the mirror and humid air hung thick in the small space. Immersing myself did little to warm me. For months, life had swept me along in its cruel current. Despite finding the shore, I still felt the power of the undertow dragging at me.

What was I to do now?

I rinsed the last of the pond water from my hair, brushed my teeth for the third time, and wrapped myself in an oversized towel. Dimly lit beneath the glow of bedside lanterns and with the Dens quiet in the dead of night, the silence of my bed chamber echoed back at me.

"And how are ye feeling now?" Samuel sat propped in one of the club chairs in the corner, his silhouette barely discernable from the shadows. As my vision adjusted, I could see remained ready to explode. "Ye all right?"

I accepted the mug of hot cocoa he offered and sat in the chair opposite him. Curling my feet beneath me, I readied for his fury to unfurl. "I am as well as you might expect."

Samuel shifted forward, leaning his elbows on his knees. At some point, since he'd left me with Galan, he'd showered and put on another pair of flannel pajama pants. I wondered if he had been able to warm up any better than I.

I eased the mug from my lips and blew across the surface, the chocolate ambrosia yet too hot. "I am mated to a monster. In days or mayhap a week, I shall stand in front of the Fates and they will declare me Abaddon's female. I shall never know the love of a gentlemale or raise a family. I must needs come to terms with that."

"So, ye've given up, have ye?"

"To face what I must is logic, not despair."

"Right. Of course. Your life is forfeit because a madman drugged ye and pinned ye down, is that it?" Samuel scrubbed the back of his neck looking rabid. "Why am I bustin' my balls combing through Highborne laws if yer gonna throw up yer hands before we stand before the Fates? We've got some bite to our objections, ye know? We could win this."

"Facts cannot be argued."

"Luv, I'm a Celt—*anything* can be argued." Crouching on the floor before me, he placed his hands on my bare knees and squeezed. "Abaddon will never get near ye again. I swear it. I'll fight the Fates 'til I'm blue in the face and come back for more with my wand if need be. I'll protect ye with my life."

The sweet spice of truth vibrated in his words and I loved him for it. That thought pierced my chest. I *loved* him. Though it changed nothing. "You are a true friend and a valiant guardian, Samuel. No matter the outcome of my fight with Abaddon, I made a promise to Castian and cannot stand as Queen of the Realm of the Fair if hiding behind my warrior protector."

"Friend," he said, a violent edge to his voice. "There's that feckin' word again."

"Yes, there it is." And friends was all we could ever be. "At least now I understand why I am such a pariah to males. When no one would dance with me at Tham's life celebration, I was saddened. That not one male inquired about courting me since my coming of age was hurtful. But when you kissed me and regretted it so deeply, despite our obvious attraction, it cut me to my depths. Knowing the truth is a relief."

Samuel's opal gaze flashed. "You think I dinnae want ye?"

"You told me as much. Now I understand why. You saw what was done to me. As a male of worth, you tend to me as you would any innocent in your charge. It was me who mistook your attentions for more."

He slid the mug from my hand and set it on the round table beside my chair. With my wrist still in his grasp, he shoved my hand against the front of his pants. His erection kicked as my hand pressed against its length.

Samuel's gaze locked on mine. "I'll argue with ye on that. Yer perfect to me, inside and out. Abaddon's cruelty does nae affect my feelings in the slightest. And they *are* feelings, Luv—not duty, not guilt and not friendship."

I reclaimed my hand and sat deeper in my chair. "The truth remains, I am bound to Abaddon." The intensity in his eyes forced me to break from his gaze. "I am ruined."

Samuel leaned over me, gripping both arms of my chair. "Yer not ruined. Yer as vital and whole as any woman I ever laid eyes on. Dinnae say such a foul thing again or I'll tan yer sweet bum rosy."

I laughed. "Your charm is odd but appreciated."

He tapped the end of my nose with his finger. "Listen to me, Lia, and use that Highborne gift of yours to smell the truth of my words. I've wanted ye every night I spent in here. In bed, I fight not pull ye beneath me. Ye fill my dreams. Ye consume my waking mind. I want ye every way a man can take a woman. On yer back pressing you into the sheets. On yer knees with me driving home from behind. I want my mouth on yer core lapping at ye until ye shatter into a million pieces. I want ye beyond all reason."

I swallowed, the images he described dancing in my mind. He coaxed languid warmth inside me with just his words. Was that normal? "Yet you refused me without explanation when I asked you to be my consort."

"Because it was nae right."

"Was it right to make me feel unwanted and invisible?"

"How could ye think yerself invisible? Yer all I've seen since we started up together. And that was even before I got my sight back."

He rose on his knees and leaned close to my chair. With his body between my thighs, our faces were just inches apart. "With the panic attacks and the headaches, I realized ye weren't hidin the truth like I thought at first. The drugs had either left ye with no memory or ye'd blocked it out. It was a hateful act and it was nae right to allow anything physical to happen between us when ye dinnae know the truth."

"And what of my opinion? Knowing you cared for me would have been a lifeline. I was adrift. Alone." Heat burned to the tips of my ears and I gripped the arms of the chair. "I shall decide what I want and you, my brother and the rest of the Realm of the Fair need to remember that, Mr. Murray!"

His ebony brows lifted as the corners of his mouth twitched. "Well, dinnae stop there, Miss Caleblasse. Tell me what it is ye *do* want." His opal eyes sparkled and made my heart beat faster. Gods he was a lovely, virile male. Even when he infuriated me.

"Do you truly wish to hear it?"

He laughed darkly. "I wait with bated breath."

"And will you listen? Listen and hear me?"

"Ye've got my undivided attention."

It struck me that he was teasing, flirting. How easy it would be to join him on the floor and ease my suffering. I wanted to erase the images of Abaddon in my mind, to replace them with pleasure filled experiences and wanted memories.

To be Queen, a true and strong leader, I needed to stand on my own before I joined with another. "Going forward," I said with more resolve than I felt, "I shall make my own choices. No males shall ease my way or keep things from me. I want full say in my trial, in my future and in my personal affairs."

I leaned forward and gave him a quick kiss.

If Samuel was surprised I kissed him, he showed no sign. His

Adam's apple bobbed as he swallowed but his attention remained locked. "And what do ye want regarding yer personal affairs, Luv?"

Everything you mentioned. "In truth," *I cannot believe I am saying this,* "I ask that you return to your chamber and leave me to find my way. Give me a few days to figure out my own mind. In the meantime, make arrangements for me to claim the throne. Castian said you know what to do?"

He nodded. "Aye, I do. Three days, Luv, and then we revisit this and see where we stand."

I nodded. "Three days."

Scattered moments of sleep filled the hours until dawn. For the first time in almost ten months, nightmares had nothing to do with my restlessness. Excitement kept my mind awhirl while my determination solidified. I was stronger than people gave me credit for. I was stronger than *I* gave me credit for. The understanding of that, coming so late, left me racing to catch up with my life.

I had three days to build the foundation of who I was and what I wanted. Abaddon might have mated an innocent girl to use in his plans but he would learn the truth of his error soon enough. I may be his mate but I would never be his pawn.

I strode down the halls of the Dens to first repast. The moment I reached the dining room, the clink of cutlery to plate and male bravado silenced. The table was full. A dozen Weres plus the cubs, Mika, Grandfather, Aust, Tham and Gemma. Samuel was absent. No doubt giving me the space I asked for.

The males stood when I joined them.

"Sit, please." Awkward gazes danced across the golden stone walls as they retook their seats. It became apparent that each of them had heard about my pond escapade. "Yes, well, let us air things out, shall we? Last evening, I learned I am indeed mated to a monster and had a lapse. I now have three days to pull my life into focus. Pity is of no use to me but I would appreciate your understanding and your aid."

"Anything, anytime," Bruin said. He stalked over and pulled me into his embrace. The strength of his hug squeezed the breath from my lungs. "Everyone in this room has been kicked in the nuts by the Scourge. We get it. Whatever you need, sista, you just ask."

"Gratitude," I reached up and kissed Bruin's cheek and then addressed the table. "After we eat, I would like to speak with you, Grandfather Hawk, if you have the time?"

Mika's grandfather bowed his head, his silver braid falling forward. "My time is yours, young one. For however long you need me."

With that, I made my plate and smiled as the table burst back to life.

~

My morning with Grandfather Hawk proved to be far more grounding than I hoped. The wisdom of the male and his serene outlook on life helped me sort out many conflicting emotions.

We walked the ledge, sat in the meditation garden, gave thanks for the rebirth of spring and the coming strength of summer. We talked about my life, old and new, the males who loved and protected me, the gods of his world and the lessons they brought him, and who I needed to become to survive a future with Abaddon.

I was his mate but I would never succumb to living in one of his compounds of evil. As Gemma said, soon I would be the freakin' Queen of the Realm.

I would decide where and how I lived.

When Grandfather tired, I walked him to the entrance and then wound back along the path to the gazebo on the far side of the mountain. Sitting alone in the afternoon's serenity, I soaked in the warmth of the sun's rays and thought about Galan and my sire, about my Highborne and Haven families, about my emotional and sexual awakenings and about who I was and who I wanted to be.

"Hey there," Bree said, her smile tentative as she rounded the bend carrying a small tray. "Mind if I interrupt?"

"No. Please." I gestured to the bench beside me and accepted the tray. It held a plate of salmon with grilled vegetables and two bottles. With the scent of grilled fish fresh in the air, my stomach growled. "Is it evening repast already?"

"Long over, actually. I thought you might be hungry."

I picked up the cutlery, pleased at my day's accomplishments. "Gratitude. I failed to realize the day had slipped away."

"Contemplating life can do that." Her gaze flashed gold as she spoke, a sign that her Coyote-self rose close to the surface. "Know that what Bruin said is true. Every one of us at Haven have lived through the violence of the Scourge. Rape. Murder. Torture. I'm not comparing our injuries to yours, because everyone has the right to mourn what was done to them, but know that the darkest hours will pass."

We sat in companionable silence for a long while. I ate my meal and she drank from one of the two bottles. She watched the sky redden to a brilliant champagne but I wondered what she actually saw.

When I finished eating, I sipped my alcohol and decided there had been enough contemplation of sorrows. "Bree, I know what I want to do next but need you and Mika to come to my chamber to aid me."

Bree brightened and upended her bottle. "Sure. What's up? What do you want us to do?"

"My life shall take a serious turn in a few days, but before that happens, I wish to make some cards."

CHAPTER TWENTY-ONE

As it turned out, my chamber was not big enough to hold our evening. Once I explained my curiosities and showed Bree and Mika the book Elora had given me, they squealed and called in the other women in my life.

"Ladies night has officially begun," Mika said, raising the blender from behind the bar in the living room. She set it atop the counter and Bree handed over several bottles from the lit wall of alcohol. "Let margarita madness ensue."

Jade opened the heavy wooden doors and rushed in waving video cases in the air. "The research material is here."

Nyssa and Elora followed carrying trays of food.

Gemma sat perched on the back of one of the sofas, smiling from ear to ear. *What's the research material?*

I relayed her question and Jade held the covers toward the seating area. Magic Mike and Magic Mike XXL.

A round of whistles and laughter sounded as ladies accepted their drinks and milled around the room. Bruin and Cowboy poked their heads in to investigate and were shunned and sent away.

Bree held her glass up. "Here's to Lia. May the doors opened to her tonight never close. And may her cards bring her everything she deserves."

Mika raised her virgin margarita and smiled. "Long live the sex cards." Another round of laughter erupted. "But before we get ahead of ourselves, Lia, why don't you tell us what you want from tonight."

I drank and waited for the icy lime chill to cool my insides. "Tonight," I said, addressing my friends, "is about discovery and redis-covery. From my hair and clothes to my thoughts and taking control of my path. Tonight, we plan how I emerge a more confident and happier me."

"Did somebody say extreme makeover?" Lexi skipped through the doors and behind her, Rowan and Cowboy carried bins, bags and what looked like large kits. "And lookie-lookie, I came prepared."

When everything was set down, the men were once again shooed out of the room and the doors closed tight.

"All right," Lexi said. "Let's unleash your vixen."

The evening progressed with both hilarity and abandon. Bree cut and styled my hair. Lexi showed me a braid that the women of the Modern Realm used. And Jade demonstrated how to apply makeup and yet appear I wore none. Then they glued tiny purple gemstones in a flower and vine pattern across my breast and down my side.

Jade's movies captured both my fascination and imagination. Gemma whooped the loudest though no one heard her but me. Even the mated females found Channing Tatum and his band of dancing brothers titillating.

"Lia, repeat after me." Bree's words slurred with drink. "Dude, nice ass."

I laughed and waved my pen. "I could never say that."

"Why?" Mika asked. "Samuel has a great ass."

Hells yeah, Gemma said. *The way his slacks cling to those curves makes me want to lick him like an ice cream.*

I threw a cushion, but it passed straight threw her.

"The line works every time, I swear," Bree said. "Maybe you're not an ass girl."

The others laughed, and Elora passed me another drink. "What do you notice about a male's physique, child? What warms your core and makes your mouth water? Broad shoulders? Banded arms? Piercing eyes?"

My ears flushed hot, right to the tips.

"Don't be shy," Jade said, holding up navy lace lingerie. "No one will repeat a word spoken in the confidence of the margarita confessional."

"Here, here!" Lexi said.

What fueled my inner fire? Samuel possessed each of the attributes Elora mentioned, yet what truly held my sexual fascination was not listed.

I wet my lips. "Samuel wears lounge pants in the evenings. What whets my appetite is the way they hang on his bare hips. They show off the fine hair of his navel and how his hip muscles angle down beneath the waistband of his pants."

"Yesss," Bree hissed. "The mighty V. Gotta loves a man with tone."

"Okaaay," Mika said. "Where are we with the cards? Do we have anything about following the treasure trail down the might V?"

I shifted to the beginning and cleared my throat. "Pleasure your-self. Shop for sex toys. Touch a naked male. Wear underwear that feels sexy. Grind on a dancefloor. Give a full-body massage. Fondle a partner in a summer rain. Give a blowjob. Get naked within risk of getting caught. Tie him up and have your way. Skinny dip. Sex-play in the moonlight. Whisper something dirty in his ear. Ride 'em cowboy."

"But not necessarily our Cowboy," Mika added.

Bree whistled. "Though don't rule it out. You can choose anyone to consort, right? Well, that man is ripped like nobody's business. Have you seen him naked?"

There was a digression while the room discussed Cowboy's attrib-utes. As a Were, we had all seen him naked. Everyone agreed I should consider him as consort material.

Nyssa pointed to a page in the book. "Sex with food."

My pen remained poised above the next card. "What?"

Nyssa nodded. "Write it down. Sex with food."

My mouth hung open as the others just laughed. "I shall consider food part of the ambiance of a sexual moment but not as part of sex. I draw the line."

Nyssa laughed. "The line is yours to draw. As you wish."

I wrote that down and waited for the next idea.

"Go dominatrix on his ass," Lexi added.

"Have him perform a striptease."

In the end, I had twenty-three sex cards, ten self-empowerment cards and absolutely no idea how many drinks I consumed.

The next morning, I leaned my head against the cool tile wall of our shared bathing room. "Gods Samuel, no matter how I hold my head it never hurts any less. This is worse than when I was being possessed."

I struggled with the cap of the toothpaste and squeezed a dollop onto my brush. "And my mouth feels as if Mika's bearcat, Orville, has climbed in and curled itself around my tongue. Is that normal?"

He cocked a brow. "Aye, that's the morning after for ye."

I finished brushing my teeth and scooped some of the running water with my hand. It was cold and after I rinsed, I drank down a couple swallows.

Samuel filled the glass at the edge of the sink and offered me two white tablets. "Take these and drink every drop."

When I had done as he asked, he passed me a cool hand towel and I pressed it over my face. It smelled like the almond soap Mika stocked in the laundry and for some reason I found that remarkably soothing. When I looked up, his gaze danced with amusement.

"Stop laughing at me." I flopped the towel over the side of the sink. "I feel like an imbecile."

His laugh was deep and sexy. "Why, because ye got shit-faced with the women?" He shook his ebony hair, guiding me to my small primping station outside the bathroom. Angling my shoulders, he sat me into the dainty make-up chair and moved to stand behind me. I tugged the hem of my night shirt down to cover my legs. "Everyone has the right to let off steam. It's perfectly understandable that ye let loose. Ye did it in the safety of this fortress surrounded by yer kin and yer friends. There's nae a thing wrong with that."

I reached to the vanity counter and retrieved my hairbrush.

Samuel leaned over my shoulder, hand out. The scent of his cologne, faded from the passing day, filled my sinuses. I handed the brush to him, closed my eyes and then popped them open again and waited for the world to stop spinning.

"As ye say all the time to me, dinnae fash. At least ye dinnae throw up on me again this morning."

I covered my face with my hands. "Oh Gods, did I vomit on you last night?"

He laughed against my back. "Seriously. Yer fine. A little water to re-hydrate, a few more hours of rest and other than a touch of quease, you'll be a new woman by noon."

"If only," I whispered and headed back to bed.

Samuel's council was, as usual, accurate. At 11:20 am, I woke, showered and dressed. If not completely well, I felt quite near to it. I nibbled a bit at the cinnamon bagel he left for me and by the time the knock came at my door, I was ready to receive.

"Julian, come in." I held the door open wider and he joined me in my suite. Though dapper in his dress, Julian's wardrobe was not as formal or crisp as Samuel's. Still, a well-dressed male always held a certain attractiveness. "I appreciate you coming. Did Jade explain to you what I want? About helping me with my cards?"

His teeth, straight and white, shone as he smiled. "She did and I got you covered."

"Wonderful, where should we start?"

~

It was well past seven when Julian and I finished for the evening. I stretched up and hugged him, my confidence boosted immeasurably. Tall and athletic, he had a similar build to Samuel though the two smelled nothing alike.

"You are a wonder, Julian. You have taught me more than I thought possible in one session. Gratitude."

He shrugged and stepped to the side as Samuel strode in to join us. "Those cards are fun. Anytime I can help, I'm game."

He winked and gave me a wave as he stepped out into the hall. "Catch you later, Merlin."

I closed the door, my heart lighter than it had been in months. "What a day. Julian is a marvel. A true marvel."

"I'm sure he is," Samuel said, facing the far wall, his hands on his hips. The line of his shoulders was rigid, the drape of his white, pressed shirt rumpled after a long day. "So, ye had yer fun, did ye? Sowed some wild oats?"

I had no idea what that meant but his scent and voice told me it was bad. "What happened? Why are you so angry?"

He turned and the pain in his glare took me aback. "When ye said ye needed a few days, I dinnae think it was to take up with other men. I heard about yer cards, ye see. Bruin was chuckling about them with Mika, tryin' to get her to tell him what was on them."

Part of me thought to let him suffer a little for not simply asking me what had gone on. Only a very small part of me.

"But *Julian?*" he said. "Why in the three realms would ye turn me away and go to him? Ye barely know the man. Is this because I turned ye down the other day? I explained that to ye. I thought ye understoo—"

I stepped before Samuel and handed him the two white cards Julian and I had chosen for our afternoon. "Please read them aloud and stop panicking."

"Embrace communication and information technologies," he said. "Learn how the Talon works to protect the Realm."

I nodded.

"That's why Julian was here?" He shuffled the order of the cards and read them both again. "But Bruin said the cards were about sexual conquest and such."

I went to the hutch by the wall and opened an ornate keepsake box. From inside, I took out the remaining cards. "The ones in green ink are personal goals. The ones in red ink are sexual goals."

I handed him the small pile. He did not look at them, his attention still focused on me. Unable to discern if he was still angry or not, I started at the beginning, Elora's book and how I thought if I could take small steps to claim things I wanted, both sexually and in my everyday life, they would be steps toward being the person I wanted to be.

I managed to get through the explanation, pausing only long enough to breathe. I made no attempt to hide my embarrassment. "When I say it aloud, it sounds like objectifying males to my own end but it was fun to talk life and love with the others. I never had a mother and I . . . needed female perspective."

Samuel stared at the top card.

I pulled my new silver phone out of my pocket. "Julian aided me with two of the green goals. Self-empowerment. I need to embrace this realm if I am to understand what the citizens need. Does that make sense? Please say something. I cannot tell if you are still angry."

Samuel swallowed. "Aye, I'm angry but at myself."

"Nonsense. What did you do?"

"Exactly. With all the changes and everything ye've been through it's obvious ye'd need to build yer confidence and want to learn things. I should have helped ye. I'm sorry, lass."

I waved away his apology and pointed to the cardboard in his hands. "I still have much to learn about myself and there is only one male I want involved for the red cards."

His smirk melted away my anxiety. "Anyone I know?"

I wrapped my arms around his waist and laid my cheek against his chest. His heart beat a steady rhythm in my ear. Was I a strong enough female to take what I wanted?

In truth, what I wanted went against the very nature of my raising and Highborne beliefs. Yet, Highborne beliefs were the crux of my life's turmoil. I more than the laws of my race. I was an individual with the right to choose.

I inhaled passed the lump in my throat and spoke my heart. "The cards were simply for fun. What I truly want is to erase the vile images playing in my mind. I want you to aid me in replacing them with something passionate and welcome. I want to be devoured as a female should be by her first encounter. And . . . what you said . . . I wish for you to take me every way a male can take a female."

Samuel inhaled and when he spoke, his voice was rough and deep. "I'm afraid to ask, but are ye sure? What about being Bound and all that? Highbornes are only allowed—"

I leaned back to see him. "I reject what was done to me. In a few days, I may well be living a different life. If so, I want something of my own choosing to remember." I traced the pulse racing down his neck and my own pulse quickened to match the pace. "Only we two need know. I want you to be more than my consort. Would you deny me a second time?"

After a long moment, Samuel groaned. "I want that too and so much more but—"

I placed my fingers over his lips and blinked back the sting in my eyes. There was so little time. Soon I would be swept away by fate's cruel reality.

"Please, Samuel. I need you."

He tucked my hand in the crux of his elbow as he had dozens of times. His stride, strong and sure, led us to the bed we had shared so many nights and yet never truly shared. Backing me against the mattress, he eased me back onto the bronze coverlet and claimed my mouth.

His kiss continued deep and slow.

Before Kobi, I had never truly been kissed. Boys. Family. Friends. I was thankful Kobi and I shared some affection because I knew better what to expect. The mechanics were the same, yet kissing Samuel ignited things inside me. Powerful things. The wanton scent of him was addictive, his manly spice no longer guarded.

"Sharing yerself with a person ye feel for is incredible, a physical and spiritual bonding of two bodies and two souls. I want that for you . . . to erase what came before."

"And you feel that for me—could share yourself despite what came before, what you witnessed—you still want me?"

Looking down on me, he smiled. "Ye'll tell me if ye need to stop or slow things down, aye? No fault. No foul. If something doesna sit right, say the word and we'll deal with it." He waited until I nodded before he reclaimed my mouth.

Stretching out beside me, his lips moved in hypnotic rhythm. He kissed his way across my jaw and tugged the hem of my skirt up my thigh. "I want rid of this thing, *mo chridhe*. I dinnae want anything between us."

"Then let us be skin to skin."

There was nothing gentle in the way he tore my clothes from me only raw desire. When I lay bare upon the blankets, he inhaled and grinned.

"You stare as if my body is new to you."

He bit his bottom lip. "Before now, I was in no position to take in the sights, ye see?"

I brushed a fingertip across his tight pink nipple.

"I cast a few lingering glances yer way from time to time but now I can enjoy it. Ye take my breath away. Ye know that, right?"

"And I thought my feminine wiles had been lost on you."

A soft blush warmed his cheeks. "Why do you think it took me so long to get out of bed each morning? I could hardly saunter around with a cock-stand as thick as an oak."

Samuel's slacks hid what he pointed to and that set me to task. "You need to be naked. I hunger to see your body."

He winked and laid back. "If yer new resolve is all about taking control and men not paving yer way, I say work for it. If ye want my clothes off, have at it. Isn't one of yer wee cards to touch a naked male? I think ye'd get extra points for strippin' him down yerself."

I licked my lips and shifted up on my knees. Samuel was a fit and tightly muscled male and unlike him, I had not resisted the urge to gaze in passing. I knew well what awaited me.

I pulled off his shoes and socks and tossed them to the area rug. Gathering the leather of his belt, I loosened it and freed it from its buckle. After the button and zipper were taken care of, I slid his slacks down his legs.

My fingers caressed the fine dusting of dark hair which followed the contours of his muscular chest and down further. "Mika calls this the treasure trail."

He chuckled, watching me trace the line until I reached the juncture between his thighs. His erection stood thick, the tip glistening with moisture. The sight of him sent a shimmering bolt of energy through my body and stole my breath.

Samuel became eerily still.

"Is this all right?" I asked, pulling back my touch. "Have I overstepped?"

He shook his head, his diamond eyes glittering. "More than all right. Go ahead. I'm good."

My hands glided from his knees, splayed over the tops of his thighs until they met at the juncture of his pelvis. His skin was soft and warm, not smooth like a Highborne. "Your body hair tickles my fingers. It is incredibly stimulating."

"Good. Stimulating is good."

Working my courage up, I drew a deep breath and closed my fingers around Samuel's arousal. His hips surged forward as the length of him bucked in my grip. His head dropped back. Despite my inexperience he seemed rapt. My body tingled, heated with an urgency which claimed my insides.

"What do I do to increase your pleasure, Samuel?"

He moaned. His hips rolled, as his hand closed over mine. "Here, like this." His hand guided mine from base to tip, slowly, oh so slowly. He made the most wonderful noises when my thumb lingered at the small opening at the crown.

"Ye'll have to stop that, darlin'."

"Why? I enjoy touching you."

Samuel's stomach flexed under my ministrations, the dim light of the lanterns catching the ridges of his physique. His hand came down on mine and he choked out a rough laugh. "I'm glad about that, but yer going to make me come and it's far too early yet to get there."

"Do you mean release?" My confidence bolstered. My touch aroused him. I controlled his pleasure. "Are you nearing your release?"

"It's more than near. I'm biting it back with every ounce of strength I've got."

"Why ever for?"

He cupped my jaw and ran his thumb over my bottom lip. "Because, this moment is about you, my sweet lass. Let me show you how wonderful it can feel to be a worshiped female. You can play more after. I promise."

One thing I learned weeks ago, Samuel always kept his promises. "All right, but we will come back to this soon."

"Soon," Samuel said.

I laid down beside him and tugged on him to cover my body. Ignoring my invitation, he remained on his side. Facing me, he pulled my leg to drape over his hip and shifted closer. Closing the gap between our two bodies, the heat of his flesh pooled against my belly.

"Again, if ye need to stop or slow down, ye swear ye'll tell me, aye?"

I cupped his jaw, the stubble of his day's growth a seductive prickle against my palm. Close like this, the rich scent of him drove me to wanton madness. "I welcome your touch. I welcome everything you and I share."

His lips against mine were gentle, exploring, sweeping me away into dreamy contentment.

I sank my fingers into his hair. Soft. So incredibly soft. He growled into my mouth as I raked my nails against the back of his skull. He nipped at my bottom lip, teasing, coersing. The wet heat of his tongue swept against the seam of my lips.

I allowed him entrance into my mouth.

The swordplay of our tongues hit me right between my thighs. I fisted my hand in his hair. Kissing Samuel was a pleasure in itself. He was playful and affectionate. His hunger enveloped me, yet he refused to be rushed.

Tight in his embrace, his hands roamed a seductive circuit down the valley of my lower back and over the curves of my backside. With each returning caress, his fingers came achingly close to brushing my core.

The pulsing of my wanton made me feel bold and aggressive. Desperate. "You are driving me to madness. Please, Samuel, I ache for you."

He smiled, his lips returning to mine. "And where do ye ache, my beautiful, lass?" He drew his finger down the side of my neck and across my collarbone. "Here?"

I bit his lip, my agitation growing. "Lower."

His ebony brow arched, and he eased back a bit to watch me. "Lower, the lady says." His hand swept down my shoulder to my breast. The warmth of his palm cupped the mound as his thumb brushed and fondled the tip. "Here? Do yer breasts ache for me? Shall I focus here for a bit?"

He was enjoying himself far too much. Did he not know how I yearned for him? "That would be glorious, but I need you lower still."

His manly growl added another flood of warm moisture to my core. My back arched and I stiffened. Samuel's smile faltered. "Are ye all right?"

I pushed my breast harder into his palm and moaned at the zing of sensation it sent through my body. "I am having a problem in my most private parts. My body weeps for you, yet you take no notice."

"Oh, I noticed." His palm slid down my belly and cupped my mons. "It's exactly where I want ye to be. Wet and aching for me—Oh Christ," he gasped, and his hips rocked against me. "I forgot ye'd be bare."

"And is that good?"

He bent forward to capture my lips again as he curled a finger through the silk of my sex. "Yer burning alive . . . and yes, everything about ye is good to me."

His fingers circled and stroked. Lightning tingled beneath my skin, building, consuming. My hips arched upward. He slid a finger inside me, and I moaned into his mouth and squirmed. How could a simple touch make me feel this much?

"What is happening to me, Samuel?"

"It's your release. Remember the pleasure yer touch gave me? This is how it feels."

I meant to respond but had no idea how to speak. My mind was a blur of erotic colors, sensations and scents. I was naïve to think I knew what sex with Samuel would be like. He had experience and I knew nothing. He had been with females who knew their bodies and minds.

What if he needed more from a female than I could be?

"Lia? Stay with me. Are ye all right?" His hand stilled, his fingers retreating. "Do ye need to stop?"

I wanted to cry at the injustice of losing the sensation, of doubting this perfect moment. "Stop asking me that. Do you ask that of all your lovers? Am I so broken you cannot simply be lost in the moment?"

The sting of his hand on my bare backside stole my thought. His spank was not hard, yet shocked me to silence.

"I told ye, not to speak about yerself so. Yer not broken. Not unworthy. How in the two realms did we get from me pleasuring ye back to that?"

Strangely, the sting of hand on flesh brought a new pulse to my wanton. "We are there because I want you inside me. Not preparing me. Not gauging me. You said you desire me, yet you make no move to join with me. If I were a female seducing you from the Hearthstone or one of your warrior lovers, would you be so cautious? I think not."

Samuel pulled me over his chest, and in a blur, his feet came between my ankles and spread my legs. The crown of his erection pulsed and prodded at my damp core. Gripping my hips, he undulated his body upward, easing inside me inch by succulent inch.

"Christ yer an infuriating female. I told ye, yer perfect. Courageous. And passionate. I cannae help but want to protect ye. It's my instinct. It's what I was born to do."

My head kicked back as he filled me to my limits. His hips rose, burying inside me to the root. He pushed my shoulders until I sat straddled over his hips. He lifted me a few inches and brought me down firmly as he thrust upward.

I cried out.

"Never mistake my concern for thinking ye weak or lacking. Yer the feckin' air I breathe. And if ye need me to bed ye rough a hundred times to prove it, be ready to stay in bed tomorrow, cause ye'll be too sore to get out of it."

I was lost.

"Lia, stop thinking so damned much and let yerself sink into me." Slipping his hand beneath my hair, he pulled my lips to his. Kissing me in earnest, his tongue penetrated my mouth in the same aggressive rhythm as his hips rose and bucked beneath me. His hands returned to my thighs, his gripping fingers guiding me up and down as sensations built inside me.

I soon learned the way of things, the rhythms, where he liked to be caressed and when he preferred the scrape of my nails to the soft pads of my fingers. Sex was heady. Surprising. It brought me to a place both powerful and vulnerable.

Sweat covered us, mixed together between our bodies as I rode him. Samuel's thumb stroked the sensitive nerves at the base of our joining. I dug my nails into Samuel's shoulders as I ground down. My chest tightened as the muscles in my legs began to quiver.

"Yes, that's it. Let the sensations explode within you. Set them free. Ride me. Take from me."

The demand rolled off Samuel's tongue like warm honey. I trembled as everything around me blanked out. I cried out, writhing over him. It was bliss. And oblivion. It was throbbing triumph. And a loss that it would end. My body clenched and pulsed around him as I uttered Elvish nonsense.

Samuel hips bucked harder, his grip on my thighs verging on painful. I did not care. The small fissure of discomfort was worth the way his body came alive beneath me. His breath escaped in a rough hitch as he stiffened. His muscles clenched taut, his chest rising and falling under the strain of his own release. I had always thought Samuel a handsome male, but in the throes of orgasm he was utterly breathtaking.

How could anyone survive a sensation like this? How was it even possible?

CHAPTER TWENTY-TWO

Samuel was out. Completely. Blissfully. Out. His soft breathing created a gentle rise and fall of his arm where it lay on his chest. I gave thanks that Elves needed half the sleep of humans, for the extra hours of quiet gave me time to sit in the reading chair across the room and memorize him as he slept. His lean strength, his ridges and curves, and the way his expression relaxed in slumber.

Despite Zophia hoping to hold the Fates off for a week or more, they might well call me to appear at any time. I studied him—the mate my heart had chosen. And though he had threatened to bed me rough a hundred times until I learned my worth, he had tended to me most thoroughly and then insisted I get some rest.

Samuel rolled onto his side. The sheet dragged across his hip, working hard to cover his essentials. His arm reached up and flopped to the pillow above his head, elongating his position. Another shift and the sheet would be irrelevant.

Simply breathtaking.

A feminine gasp had me turning.

Ooh, don't you just want to lick him? Her tongue dragged across her upper lip as she skipped to my side. *This is new,* she whispered, though being a spirit, there was no need for the precaution. *Have you ever had a boy-girl-sleepover before?*

I giggled, trying not to wake him. "No, this is a first."

Gemma tiptoed to the bedside and peered over Samuel's prone body. The bed frame was a bit too high for her to get a good view, so she floated off the ground a foot. *Is it totally inappropriate to say your boyfriend makes me want to—*

"Yes," I said, shooting her a look. "Please keep your thoughts to yourself."

Just sayin', that body could give a girl a serious case of the swoons. Gemma shrugged and took the seat opposite me. *Speaking of male hotness, is your blond Highborne friend single? Think I might have a chance there?*

I rolled my eyes. "Well, he was unmated when he was killed and I doubt his death has presented him with a vast dating pool. I assume his status remains the same."

And he's a good guy?

"One of the best males you could ever meet. He is fun, loving and a true gem."

Gemma's mouth curled in an uneven grin. *Fun, a gem, and super sexy. Sounds like a destiny trifecta to me.*

The shuffle of sheets silenced our conversation. Strong hands searched beneath the sheets. When Samuel found nothing, his eyes opened and found me in the small sitting area. "Good morning. Did ye sleep all right?"

"Very well and you?"

He curled his finger in the air and tossed the sheet back. His erection thick and ready. "Slept like the dead but woke with a wee issue I need yer help with."

"Wee ye say?" I said, imitating his speech. I rose from the chair and hoped Gemma would take the hint and leave. "I beg to differ with ye 'on that one, Celt."

Gemma clamped her hand over her mouth and burst into hysterics. *Wow. Big day in the life of you, eh girlfriend? Okay, I'm outtie, but I want details later. Lots of details.*

Thankfully, Gemma jogged through the wall as I strode back to the bed. "I slept soundly and am deliciously sore. Oh, that we could stay in this bed for days."

He chuckled and kissed my collarbone. "If that's what ye want, I'm game."

I shook my head. "No, we have plans. No time to be lazing about having sex."

"And that's a pity—"

The knock on the door was loud and offensive.

"Lia? You awake?" Bruin asked from the hall. "Breakfast has come and gone. Did you still want to work on self-defense with me and Cowboy?"

I giggled as Samuel flicked my nipple with the tip of his tongue. "Apologies, Bruin. It slipped my mind. Do you mind if we meet up later?"

"No, that's fine. Is everything all right?"

"Oh yes, glorious, Bruin. Fash not."

"Glorious?" There was a long silence before he cursed a low oath. "Lia, honey, is Samuel with you?"

Samuel raised his head, looking piqued. "Aye, I am. We'll be out in a bit, Bear. S'all good."

Bruin's bear growled long and low. "Dammit, Samuel, do you think she needs this? For fuck's sake, I'm supposed to be watching out for her. Galan's going to shit kittens if he finds out you're fooling around with his sister."

"Our business, Bruin. Not yours. Not his."

"Yeah, I'll remind him of that when he shoves his fist through your chest and rips your heart out."

I winced as Bruin's heavy stomp receded down the hall. Propping myself up on my elbow, I flung my hair out of my face. "Should we ready for our day or would you like to complete another card?"

Samuel laughed. "If we keep selecting cards, we'll never make it out of this bed. We've preparations to make and a journey ahead of us if yer going to be queen." Scooping me into his arms, he headed for the bathroom. "Besides, showering together works on both fronts. We'll get cleaned up and have fun doing it."

~

Less than two hours later, showered, fed and dressed for travel, Samuel Flashed us to a rolling green landscape much like the one by the stream weeks ago. In the distance, an elaborate, labyrinth hedge wove its way across what appeared to be the entire countryside. Acres of perpendicular paths cut in a mesmerizing maze as far as I could see.

Tham materialized by my side and we studied a grand fortress dwarfed the center of the labyrinth. It glowed against the darkness of the coming night, an imposing set of standing stones rising up as sentinels all the way around it.

"Where are we?" I asked, though I feared I knew.

"Lothendril," Samuel said, "The Silver Citadel."

The Silver Citadel. Aptly named. For as the last of the day's light sunk behind the horizon it reflected on the stone architecture. Lit by the heavens, the building and monoliths radiated a silver sheen as if the walls were carved from the finest crystal.

I fought to draw breath. Highbornes once stood as the great guardians of the Queen's palace. Corrupted by the seduction of magic and their complacency, they failed to realize when Rhegan's motives shifted and she became the danger to the realm. The Silver Citadel stood as monument to my race's legendary fall from glory.

A swirl of black mist brought Kobi to our group. Wearing his Talon leathers, he nodded to Samuel, swaggered over and winked at me. "Demon on board. Let the party begin."

Samuel drew me closer with a firm hand at the small of my back. "Yer here to warn us if ye sense a possession, demon. That's the only reason. Do yer job."

I brushed a hand over my crescent tattoo and realized I had yet to tell anyone Castian warded my body against possession. Samuel had kissed it a few times last night but neither of us were interested in chatting at the time.

Kobi's pierced brow arched as he broke into a taunting smile. "You hate that I'm here, don't you Merlin? Afraid I might sample your goods again? Did our little Lia tell you about my visit to her room the other night?"

My ears heated. I looked up at Samuel, who now glared quite murderously at Kobi. "I said nothing because nothing happened worth mentioning in a night filled with far more important issues."

Kobi raised his palm to his chest. "You wound me Highborne. That kiss wasn't nothing. I have a healthy frame of reference, and you and—"

"Stop," I hissed. "Why do you insist on causing turmoil?"

Samuel's fingers gripped into my hip. "Because he's a filthy demon. And if I learn he had any part in the upset that led to yer pond adventure, he'll be a feckin' dead demon."

Kobi laughed. "What, you think I . . ."

A far-off rumbling caught my attention. Three males on horseback approached at a gallop.

Jade's childhood attack ran through my mind. Ambushed by Scourge raiders in exactly this fashion, men on horseback raped and almost killed her mother. They also slaughtered the man she believed to be her father.

Night thickened around us, offering few places to hide.

The thundering of hooves created a weighty rhythm in my chest. Tham drew his dagger and stepped before me. A sweet gesture no matter how ineffective.

Samuel drew his wand and pointed it at Kobi. "Are ye finished being a prick?"

Kobi winked at me. "Sure. Let's go with that."

The riders were nearly upon us. I gripped Samuel's arm and pulled toward a nearby bush. The blessed male did not budge. I tried again, but he held fast and flashed me a hot look. "Stop yer fussing and stand behind me. This is why we're here."

His tone stung. So Kobi had brought us back to that, had he? I ruffled my hair forward to cover the points of my ears and hide my hurt. To me, panicking seemed the only option. The riders stopped just short of our group. The horses stamped and plodded the packed earth.

Peering out from behind the shoulder of Samuel's slicker, my pulse hammered through my veins.

The three males were alike. Dark features, dark eyes and by their menacing scents—dark hearts. The largest of the three leaned over his horse's neck, the leather of his saddle creaking with his shift in position.

No fetid stench of Scourge Raiders filled the air. Mayhap they were simply local folk passing by.

"Weel, what have we here? Look lads, a filthy Highborne rabbit caught in our snare."

Or mayhap not.

Samuel pocketed his wand. "Clap yer gob, the lass has done nothing to deserve yer venom."

The two other males dismounted, each wearing pleated tartan skirts that came to their knees.

The male still seated on his horse smiled. "She's Highborne scum. That's reason enough. Then there's the bit about you gents bringin' an exiled Elf on our land, so trespassing seems to be another offense."

One of the men on the ground nodded. "And ye riled our stock by Flashing in. Magic's outlawed here."

"True enough. Ye cannae be upsetting the animals," the third one said, their taunts bouncing from one to the next. "So, we ask ye. What tithe shall ye offer in compensation for our troubles?"

I eased a step back, my heel stopping when it met Kobi's boot. The demon smiled down at me, his eyes glowing red, and then cast a glance to the three. "You overestimate yourselves, boys. You need to apologize to the lady. If not, I don't see things ending well for you."

The three burst into a fit of deep laughter.

One of the males rushed forward. Samuel met the advance and matched the male with every shift and scramble. Move for move. Strike for strike. Samuel blocked, punched and countered, as if he anticipated every blow.

The attacker's dark eyes widened. "Ah Jaysus, is it you?"

"Aye," Samuel said. "And I have a mind to shove a tithe up yer sorry arse with my boot for insulting the lass."

The largest of the three dismounted and approached. "And why would ye care, Sammy boy? She's a bloody Highborne. Are yer loyalties so far gone ye lost sight of the cause completely?"

Samuel scowled and gestured to the males. "Lia, meet Deaglan, Nolan and Chad, three of my younger brothers. Lads, meet Lia Caleblasse, the lost heir of the Queen and the woman ye've all sworn yer life to protect."

CHAPTER TWENTY-THREE

I woke atop a bed the size of my entire bedchamber back home. I blinked, the plush velvet canopy above washed in mid-morning light. How long had I slept? Where was I? It came back to me in blurry memory, bit by bit.

After meeting Samuel's brothers, they leant us one of their horses to ride with them to the Citadel. By way of starlight, we wove through endless turns and corridors of the living maze. Even mounted on horseback we saw nothing but the night sky above. The monotonous plodding of hooves and clinking of bridles lulled me like a babe in a cradle. And soon enough, my eyes grew far too heavy to fight.

The arborous walls offered no markers to guide our path, yet the Murray brothers knew the way.

Samuel included.

What did he know about my calling as Queen? How was he so familiar with this strange, isolated place? And why was his family here at the Silver Citadel? It made me wonder if the past failures of my race might be part of the reason Samuel held Highbornes in such disdain.

"Samuel?" I searched the room. "Tham? Kobi?"

A parchment on the opposite pillow rustled when I sat up. Addressed to me, it was written in Samuel's hand.

Lia, sleep well, for yer as safe as ye've ever been.

Deaglan and Nolan are outside the door standing watch. I think I sent Tham on an errand last night—hard to tell when speaking to thin air if he heard and ventured off.

I know ye have questions. We'll find yer answers.

For now, I have some details to tend to.

Meet me in the small hall at your leisure.

Until then,

S.

I re-read the name Deaglan and wondered at the spelling. Samuel pronounced it Deklan. Seeing it written out made me smile. *At my leisure.* I laughed. Little leisure had graced my life in a long while. I was not about to start soaking in tubs when there was so much to be done.

I swept the fancy throw aside, thankful that in my filthy, post-horse-riding state Samuel had settled me on the bed and not in it.

The chamber held a regal charm decorated in gold and black, with rich purple accents, smooth stone walls, and wide wood beams high overhead. Light streamed in from the three long, leaded-glass windows, casting a kaleidoscope of colors across the opulent space.

Rolling across the mountain of golden, silk blankets, I exhumed my legs from my crumpled skirt and headed to the ensuite. At the vanity, I washed my hands and glanced in the mirror. My gods, the journey had taken its toll and *phew*, I smelled most pungently of horse.

I flipped on the water in the shower and set the temperature. A quick wash then. I stretched as I undressed, wincing at the strained muscles between my legs. Riding a horse did nothing to aid my already stretched muscles after a night of sex with Samuel.

A warm awareness woke throughout my body.

I shook myself. There was no future with Samuel. Despite the hours we had stolen making love, I remained bonded to Abaddon.

Leaning closer to the mirror, I eyed a sheer, blue gown and matching ribbons hanging on the dress-stand behind the door. And another note.

Can't have you looking like I dragged you through a keyhole. What kind of guardian would I be then, aye?

I thought the blue would look nice with your hair.

S.

My shower was quick, and the dress fit like a second skin. The midnight blue bodice was embroidered with silver cross-hatching and sparkly gems where the lines intersected. The skirt and sleeves, were sheer and flowed and fluttered, the fabric resembling the finest gossamer. The color faded from dark blue at the waist to a silver ice where the skirt swept above the stone floor.

I gathered my mourning band and Castian's crescent moon pendant from the counter and put them on. I picked up the ribbons Samuel left me but decided to leave them out. After combing out the tangles, I French-braided my hair instead of my usual style and faced the mirror for one final look. After pinching my cheeks for color, I practically floated to the door.

The brothers Murray waited outside the chamber door, as Samuel said in his note. In the light of day, their similarity to Samuel lessened. What I had thought to be ebony hair in the bleached light of evening was, in fact, dark auburn. And, of course, Samuel's eyes were no longer the brown-black of his family, but the glittering opal of magic intervention.

Though I could not say for certain which was Deaglan and which Nolan, I bid them good morning and asked to be escorted to the small hall. The corridors of the building were wide and well-lit by electrical sconces. The windows rose toward the high ceilings, segmented by diamond-shaped leaded-glass. Stone and wood beam construction continued, giving off the opulence of a palace mixed with the same stable comfort I felt while in the old stone mill of our village.

"How old is the Silver Citadel?" I asked.

One of the brothers Murray swept a hand through the air, gesturing down the next shimmering silver corridor. "This way, if ye please. They're waiting on ye."

"They who?"

The taller one, Deaglan I felt sure, cast me an elitist sneer and opened a set of carved double doors exposing a grand dining room. As he ushered me inside, I marveled. If this was the small hall, how many could feast in the grand hall?

Two long wooden harvest tables ran end-to-end up the center of an intricate mosaic floor. Laden with gold trays and floral displays, I gauged the number of chairs and figured the room could sit more than a hundred diners.

An embroidered runner spanned the entire length of the abutted tables, dotted with centerpieces bursting several feet into the air. With brilliant, freshly cut flowers and colorful feathers they accented the velvet drapery and brocade tapestries hanging on the walls. The one long window wall looked out upon the vast green landscape with the standing stones just beyond.

As we entered the rectangular room, five men in matching knee-length, gray leather skirts and wine velvet vests fell silent. Standing rigid opposite the long window wall, they turned as one hostile force.

The hair rose on the nape of my neck.

Samuel was not among them.

Their huddle opened to the room, the five fanning out as they faced me. It was the male in front, pinning me with a sharp brown-black glare, which froze my breath in my lungs. Lithe and tall, with fine-drawn bones, the male could be no other than Samuel's sire. He held the same chiseled lines of face and jaw as his sons, with dark auburn hair tied back from his face in a leather thong.

There ended the similarity. He looked me over, a cruel tightness around his mouth and suppressed anger in his eyes. He eyed my dress, my hair and my curves. "Weel, if the lady Highborne does nae finally grace us with her presence."

I cast a glance over my shoulder. The exit was blocked. Was there no end to the Murray clan? "Where is Samuel?"

The elder Murray's smile grew. "Bound and beaten bloody, I should hope."

"Why would you say such a thing?"

He barked a laugh, his hand sliding to the hilt of the dagger sheathed on his hip. "Not that it's any of yer business, but the coward abandoned his duty and deserted his oath. Did ye know that?"

The other men clustered closer, exuding the scents of anger and mistrust.

Abandoned his duty? I frowned. "No one has sacrificed more in the name of duty than Samuel. In Castian's service, he has given up more than any lesser male could bear."

A low murmur of voices followed the shuffling of feet to stone floor but no others moved forward to speak.

"I beg to differ, Chuckie," the male said. "The lad turned from his place years ago. And when he finally showed his traitorous face, he brought with him a filthy Highborne."

"He brought me here for good reason."

"Aye, he said as much. Still, he knew the penance for his actions. Highbornes are not welcome here and no one leaves the Order. Not even spoiled lads who'd rather play at magic than serve the realm."

I rubbed at the pounding taking root in my head. Was this man even speaking about Samuel? My Samuel? "Your son serves the realm as a Talon enforcer and as an instructor of future warriors who will stand against the Scourge. He deserves your admiration, not disdain."

"He deserves the beating he got and more besides."

"You truly had him beaten?" I asked, though I feared I knew the answer. "Release him or at least take me to him."

The man stormed forward, pressing his face to mine. The heat of his sour breath tightened my stomach. His bushy rust eyebrows looked like fat, angry caterpillars arching on his brow. "Maybe I'd feel different if he sought out the council last night to set things right. Instead, the idiot roused the staff to prepare a room for the Queen's heir while he fussed with findin' a dress and pretty ribbons. Does that speak of his commitment to duty?"

The knot in my stomach squeezed tighter. Samuel had been incarcerated and beaten for putting my needs before his own. I whirled to go back the way I came. I would find Samuel myself and set things right, even if I had to shove my way past his entire family tree to do so.

Rough hands grabbed my shoulder and spun me.

Samuel's father locked on my upper arm. "Ah, Chuck, dinna leave just yet. We waited while ye had yer rest and prettied yerself up like a wee doll. Why such a rush to leave when ye've come so far in yer plans."

I blinked. "My plans? What plans?"

He glared at me. For the life of me, beyond a few physical features, I saw nothing of Samuel in this male. "Claiming to be the heir to the throne. Ye dinna think us so foolish we'd believe it, did ye? Is it the power ye want? The riches? Are yer people in league with Abaddon yet, or did ye just want to sit at the head of the Queen's table? Tell me, how'd ye come to wear the Queen's ring?" He gestured to the large blue diamond on my finger.

Confessing Abaddon placed the ring on me would only worsen my situation. My flesh flushed hot, building heat from the fire burning in my veins. I swallowed and cast a glance around the room.

"I lay no claim other than the truth. I am here to assume my duty to Castian and the Realm of the Fair. As Rheagan's heir, I have little say in the matter. You can argue my lineage and question my intentions but I am to be your Queen. And the first thing you shall do in my service is release Samuel."

Sulfurous anger rolled off my captor in a choking wave. Before I could react, he wrenched a fistful of my hair and pulled me against his chest. His fingers tightened, pulling hair from my scalp. "Highbornes make no demands under this roof. Yer traitorous race brought the near downfall to our realm. Do ye know how many graveyards are filled at the hands of the Queen's Noble Children?"

Tears burned behind my eyes, my heart racing in impotent rage. Samuel was in trouble. I was in trouble. And Samuel's father was the source of it all. I lived my entire life threatened by a vicious father and yet again, even as the Queen's heir, I remained helpless to aid either of us.

Castian's pendant grew warm against my chest and my hands tingled. Right. As Gemma said, I was the freakin' heir to the throne.

"Unhand me, Master Murray. No matter what you believe, I am not your enemy."

"Colum, stop," a voice said, ringing with authority. "The Order doesna hold wi' beatin' on a lass, even a Highborne. If we want the truth, we'd best get it from Samuel himself."

Rage flashed in the elder Murray's eyes and he shoved me.

Hurled off my feet, my cheek caught the edge of the wooden table and pain exploded behind my right eye. I twisted in my fall, my hip and elbow connecting hard with the mosaic floor before I could get my hands beneath me.

The double doors shattered open. A black swirling mass erupted through airborne splinters. Kobi's demon form materialized before me, black wings arched, eyes glowing scarlet. His long, spiked tail smacked against the stone floor as a demented growl ripped from his chest. "Back the fuck off, assholes."

The men of the Order scrambled, tripping over one another in their retreat.

Dazed, I rolled to hands and knees and fought to right myself. When I managed to stand, I made certain that I met the gaze of each of those males.

"You cowardly bastards," Kobi said, standing in his Talon leathers. "Samuel brought her here so you denizens of the high order could protect her. Are your fucking heads so far up your tight asses you'd seal your own fates by attacking her? Just because she's got a point to her ears?"

A weasel-faced male stepped forward from the back of the group. "And you know so much about what we do, you stand judge, demon?"

I smoothed a shaky hand down the front of my gown and took a tentative step closer to Kobi. Hot agony sluiced down my hip and into my leg, but I forced the next step without wincing. "Shall I search this castle chamber by chamber or is someone taking me to my *garda síochána?*"

The muffle of male voices grew more heated. Samuel's father stepped forward and Kobi drew his dagger.

His caterpillar brows creased. "*Garda síochána?* And what idiot would make Samuel yer guardian?"

I laid my hand against the crescent pendant heating my flesh. I wished Castian was there with me. Instantly, the air swirled again, this time filling the room with the scent of bergamot and mint.

"That idiot would be me." Castian's voice was a boom vibrating from every direction as he materialized at my side. Dressed in brown leather riding gear and an ice-blue cape, he brushed a gloved thumb over my bloodied cheek.

The air in the room crackled. In a move so fast it blurred, his hand lashed out. All five males flew backward, crashing into a wall or tapestry or cabinet.

The thuds echoed as each of them hung suspended like flies in an invisible web.

Castian spoke in a voice so calm it made the hair on my arms rise. "What idiot struck my niece? Who dishonors my family and makes an innocent woman bleed?"

The amused glint in Kobi's scarlet gaze struck fear in my heart. I swallowed. "I am fine, my Lord. It was an accident."

Castian cast me an emerald gaze and shook his head. "Even if I couldn't read thoughts, your glass face gives you away, young one. You're a terrible liar."

He laid his arm across my shoulder and gave me a gentle squeeze. "Go on with Kobi and find your guardian. These gentlemen and I need a private word about honor and what it means to obey their Queen. It's been lifetimes since the Order was put into active duty. They've grown fat and complacent."

CHAPTER TWENTY-FOUR

"And silver hair is the trait following the heir bloodline?" Deaglan escorted Kobi and me down to the dungeons. He stood with the same height and frame as Samuel and walked with much the same proud stride.

Despite my aching hip, our feet beat out a rhythmic echo on the stone flooring as we maneuvered the opulent halls. "From what I'm told, yes. My hair color is said to be a parting gift from Castian to his newborn niece as he sent my race into exile. Only he and the Aina Ohtar knew of Rheagan's child sired by her Highborne guard and longtime lover."

"Nay, not all the Aina Ohtar or Da and the others wouldna be in this mess now." He blew out a breath. "So, ye *are* the heir to the throne?"

"Bravo, asshole. Now you're getting it." Kobi rolled his eyes, taking my elbow as we followed Samuel's brother down a set of winding steps. The deeper we descended, the stronger the chill grew, until we stepped into a darkened corridor.

Stone pillars and arches supported the low ceiling. The rank bitterness of agony and fury burned my nostrils, and my blood heated. "What kind of defenders lock their own warriors in a dungeon to be brutalized?"

A painful pinch twisted Deaglan's face. "It seems harsh, aye, but ours is not a kind world and Samuel abandoned his calling long ago. You must understand, he knew the penance to be paid if he were ever to return."

Kobi cast me a solemn glance and shrugged. "I knew nothing about this, I swear."

"That never crossed my mind."

He frowned, his piercings glinting in the low, lantern light of the dungeon.

Deaglan instructed a guard to unlock the door to one of the iron cell doors and I pushed past. Stripped to the waist and shackled to the stone wall, wrist and ankle, Samuel's head lifted and lolled. The only color in his ashen, battered face was the flush of his sweat dampened cheeks and the bluish hue of swollen eyelids.

"Sweet Shalana," I said, rushing forward. "Look at you."

"Pass." Samuel croaked, his mouth lifting at the corners. "Yer a far better view. Nice dress."

His gaze narrowed on the gash pulsing on my cheek. "What happened to yer face, Luv?"

"What? You look like a pulped plum and are concerned about one mark on my cheek?"

He stiffened as the guard worked to unlock his shackles. "Aye, I am. What happened?"

"I stumbled into the edge of the dining table."

A garbled curse filled the dingy cell. "Ye stumbled, eh? Ye carry yerself with the grace and balance of a wee hummingbird and ye think me so daft as to believe that?"

As Samuel's wrists and ankles were freed, Deaglan scrambled to catch his brother's weight.

I traced the swelling on his chafed and welted wrists. The restraints had dug in, leaving angry raw gashes. "Believe what you wish, I answered truthfully."

He nodded. "All right, Luv, who helped ye stumble?"

Kobi chuckled and swept in to support Samuel's other side. "I wouldn't worry about the nick on her cheek, Merlin. Castian is upstairs taking it as a personal affront to his house. The five families of the sacred order will be lucky to survive."

I brushed my thumb over the blood-crusted gash on Samuel's side. "It seems the morning has been challenging all around. Come. Back to our room to clean these wounds."

"Our room?" Deaglan said, his expression forbidding.

Pressing the back of my hand against the hot sheen of Samuel's forehead, I sighed. I was far too furious to explain my personal arrangements to people who could do this to one of their own. I lifted my chin and locked gazes with the male. "Yes. Our room."

"Stupid male," I said, as Deaglan and Kobi lowered Samuel into the bath. I shut off the flow of water and poured in the milky remedy his youngest brother, Chad, brought from the healer to fight infection. I slipped two pain tablets into his mouth. "If you knew they would string you up and beat you, why in the two realms would you bring us here?"

"What were my choices?" He winced as the water licked the wound in his side, glaring out the slit of his swollen eyes. The tub, too short for his long legs, forced him to bend his knees to settle his feet against the bottom. "Haven is the safest alternative and even there Abaddon grabbed ye and evil souls tried to take ye over. Until the mess with Abaddon is settled and ye take yer place on the throne, ye need to stay safe."

"Safe? Your sire practically knocked me . . ." I bit my tongue and whirled toward the door.

"What's that ye say?"

Deaglan and Kobi made a hasty retreat. Cowards.

When it was just we two, I closed us in, pausing with my forehead on the wooden panel of the door. Even with my back to Samuel, I felt the heat of his stare before I turned.

He lifted a finger and pointed to my cheekbone. "My Da did that? He raised a hand to yer beautiful face?"

Occupying myself behind the linen cabinet door, I gathered clean face cloths and towels. "No. I *did* stumble and catch my cheek on the table."

"But ye had help, aye?"

I dropped the larger towels down beside the leg of the bathing basin and brushed a smaller cloth along the bruising scrape on his shoulder. Fathers were tricky. They held the power to build their children up to conquer the world or tear them down moment by hurtful moment until they doubted everything about their worth.

Galan protected me from ours the best he could. It grew plainer by the moment Samuel lost that protective barrier when his mother died.

The sleeve of my dress skimmed the water's surface and I pulled it back. "The past is behind us. Fash not. Focus on what comes next."

Unfastening my gown, I strode to the dressing stand and slipped it off my shoulders.

A low chuckle rumbled behind me. "And what have ye got in mind? I'm afraid I'm not in much of a shape to get naked with ye at the moment but I appreciate the sights."

I eased the padded hanger under the shoulders of the gown and hung it where I found it earlier. Then I wrapped a towel around myself and knelt beside the tub. "Are you making fun of me?"

"Never. Ye take my breath away."

I smiled. "As the only clean outfit I possess, I think it best not to douse my dress while I bathe you."

His lips twitched up at the sides. "Elven logic at its best."

Ignoring the flutter in my stomach, I reclaimed the cloth and blotted the bloody trickle running down his chin. The sheer orderliness of each punishing mark made me sick. A split lip, blackened eyes, reddened ribs, bruised arms, and ankles and wrists welted and bloody.

"Why did you do it?" I asked. I dipped the pink-stained cloth into the milky water, squeezed it and continued to probe and tend to the injury. "Daft as you are for offering yourself up to be beaten, I realize you did it for me. But why?"

He gave me a one-sided grin. "I'm not so bad off. Sore, but not really damaged. I'll be all right in a day or two."

One by one, I cleaned and cared for each cut, gouge, scrape and bruise. I washed his side as carefully as I could. Still, as the cloth scraped the scabbing of dried blood, droplets of fresh scarlet welled around the edges of the wound.

I apologized if it hurt him, but he never made a move nor a sound if it did.

"How much did yer brother tell ye about the Order?"

I thought back to the dark times of the past summer and wished, yet again, we had stayed in bed this morning. "Galan said the Aina Ohtar were Rheagan's Holy Warriors, a secret society formed to protect her before the exile but they grew into what we now consider the Scourge."

Samuel let his eyes ease closed. "Partly right. They are the Holy Warriors formed before the exile, but they were formed to protect the throne of the realm, not Rheagan herself. When Castian realized what his sister was up to, he tried to correct what had been set in motion."

"But the Oracles in Toronto said—"

"I ken what they said. I was there that afternoon." He laid quiet for so long, I wondered if he had drifted off to sleep. When he spoke again, the edge to his voice had calmed. "The Oracles dinnae get the facts just right. When Rheagan was exiled, a group of men broke off from the sect with plans to release her from her sentence. They used the name of the Aina Ohtar in their cause, but had no right to it."

"How is it you know more than the Oracles?"

He laughed. The movement caused little ripples of water to expand out from his chest. "The Murray's are one of the five founding families of the original organization. It has been our duty to safeguard the crown of the realm for millennia."

"Is that what you meant when you spoke of your father's and brothers' station?"

"Aye, that's what I meant."

"And you chose a different path."

He looked at me with a sad smile. "Aye, to my Da's disappointment,

I have much more of me Mam in me than he'd like. When she died, I lost the taste for this life of waiting and watching. I struck out on my own. Castian guided me to Reign and the Talon and you know the rest."

Leaving the gash to clot, I stroked the cloth across the tight plains of his chest. Samuel had sworn to protect me even before he knew me. Had he known I was the heir when he saved me from Abaddon? Had it been his duty all along to be my guardian and protector?

I circled the cloth around the gathered tip of his nipple.

"No damage there, duck, but I applaud yer thoroughness." He brushed a knuckle over his smile and chuckled. It was a deep, infectious sound until he winced. I waited for him to settle and realized he lay there studying me. He touched a fingertip to the flush warming my ears.

When I made to straighten, he caught my wrist. "Don't stop, please. I was teasing. Yer touch is the only pleasure I've had since the start of this chaotic mess almost a year ago."

"For me too." I found an unharmed spot on his cheek and gave him a gentle kiss. Almost a year ago—when he lost Jade and his heart was broken.

"Then why do ye look so sad?"

Wringing out the cloth over his chest, I watched the water trickle down the ridges of his abdominals. "It is nothing."

Samuel cocked a brow. "Lovers tell each other what weighs on them. Trust me with yer thoughts, *mo chridhe*."

Breathing in his rising anxiety I exhaled, not sure how to phrase things without raising his ire.

His jaw clenched as his opal gaze locked on me. "Is it Kobi? Have ye something to tell me about the demon? About him kissing ye the other night? He's held ye in his arms and the boils my blood, but if he's puttin the moves on ye—"

"Kobi is a friend." I squeezed out the cloth. "I hold no designs on him and told him so, quite plainly, that night. He saved my life and I healed him in return. Nothing more." I leaned over the tub and kissed his scraped cheek. "Only one male makes moth wings flutter in my chest."

His eyes danced with mischief. "Nice to hear."

I kissed him again, this time a gentle touch on his lips, letting more of my affection cross between us.

His smirk grew more crooked than usual behind his swollen lip. "Yer tryin to distract me, Luv. What had ye looking so downtrodden a moment ago?"

Swallowing past the lump in my throat, I relented. "I was thinking of Jade . . . moreover, your love for her. Jade is dynamic and an independent warrior. She is both magical and a teacher like you. You two had so much in common. So many bonds to share."

"Aye, we got on well on a lot of levels. Why is it a bother to ye now?"

"I am none of those things. While I know you moved past the intensity of your desire for her, I worry I can never fill that place in your heart. It is nonsensical because I have no right to stake a claim given my situation but wish I could. Or I wish I thought I could. If I could. Does that make any sense?"

Breathless, I dried my hands against the towel I wore and waited for his pique to rise.

"Aye, I see." He shifted in the water, raising his hand to scratch through the hair on his chest. "When we fought the other day and ye kicked me from yer room for misjudging ye, it felt like ye'd stolen my breath. It surprised me how much it hurt, to have caused yer pain and confusion. Then ye tried to end yer life."

He gestured to his injuries, his eyes growing glassy. "These bloody wounds are nothing to the agony of what that did to me, Lia. Not even close."

The rasp of his words tightened my throat. "Our quarrel left me bereft. It stirred up my disappointment with Galan too, and then Zophia showed me what happened. I realized you were in those caverns and witnessed what was done to me—"

"I swear I got ye out as soon as possible."

I shook my head. "I have no doubt about that. The things you endured and sacrificed to be accepted into Abaddon's circle . . . I owe you everything."

He placed a wet hand over his heart. "It ripped my guts out that ye felt so alone that ending things seemed a better option than coming to me. Ye see, that's where ye stole my heart, even before I knew ye'd done it. Do ye see?"

I shook my head.

"Jade never needed me, duck. Aye, we share a lot in common, but I'm a man who needs his woman to need him. I want to protect ye. I want to cuddle ye into my lap if tears threaten to take ye. I want to slay yer dragons and keep ye safe, so I know I've done my job as yer man. I never had that with Jade. That's how ye healed my heart to whole again, *mo chridhe*, by being exactly who ye are."

"A rabbit?" Tears of frustration brimmed my eyes and warmed my cheeks.

"Excuse me?"

"When I was young, Galan and I explored the canopy of the rainforest. He taught me of the world, numerations, myths, and the laws of the creatures of Shalana. One of the things we often discussed was that in the presence of wolves one is either a fox or a rabbit."

"And which do ye fancy him?"

"Oh, Galan is a fox. Almost effortlessly, he maneuvered within the insults and cruelties of my father, avoiding confrontation most of the time. He has a quick wit, a sly inner strength, and knows when to turn tail and when to bare teeth. I, however, have always been a rabbit."

"I don't agree."

"But I am. You see, it is the natural order for predators to devour the weak and timid. A rabbit retreats into her burrow to avoid the jaws of the wolf but sooner or later she is caught and preyed upon. It is the law of the natural world. It happened with Abaddon and my entire life before."

He shook his head and water droplets sprayed free from his shaggy black hair. "The mistake ye made was imagining yer father as the wolf when there are creatures far more dangerous and vile.

Brought up that way, ye couldna comprehend true evil. When it came lookin' for ye, ye had no way to protect yourself."

"Because I am a rabbit."

Samuel gathered my hands in his. "What happened was not yer fault. I'll tell ye that until I'm blue in the face if ye need to hear it. No matter how angry ye are at yourself or how ashamed, sometimes evil is too powerful to fight."

The pain in his gaze made me realize the wounds of Abaddon and the Scourge ran deep for both of us. "When ye haven't the strength to hold yerself up, let me keep watch for the wolves while ye lick yer wounds. And if yer heart shatters, let it shatter on me and I'll help pick up the pieces."

"But that is my point. I wish to slay my own dragons, to stand on my own, and fight my own battles."

"And ye will, sometimes. Other times ye'll need help. I like to think we can stand together. I'll catch ye when ye fall. And then, when I'm bleedin'," he gestured to me tending to his injuries, "ye'll maybe take the time to ease my suffering."

Oh, how I wished we could stand together. Forever.

When tears threatened, he reached behind my head and pulled my mouth to his. He had the most luscious lips, sweet silk, tugging me closer.

He groaned deep in his throat and leaned back against the rim of the basin, pulling me in on top of him. A swell of wet heat saturated the towel I wore as bathwater rose and splashed to the floor. I laughed and he repositioned me, sweeping his tongue against my lips.

Despite his split lip, kissing Samuel was delicious.

Tightening his embrace, he gave and demanded in that meeting of mouths. I ran my hands gently up his battered ribs, feeling all the heavy bones beneath his skin. A stinging pleasure went off deep inside me, hungering for more of him.

We went for a long while, his hands roaming over my towel-covered back, smoothing my hair, cupping the curve of my backside, neither of us inclined to stop.

Too soon, a shiver wracked its way up my spine.

"Damn, yer frozen. The bath has gone cold." Samuel pulled back, his eyes hidden beneath his bruises, his lips pink and swollen, but not from his beating. He rubbed his palms down the goose bumps on my arms and frowned. "Up ye get and shed that wet towel. I dinnae save yer life to have ye fall to pneumonia."

Getting out of the tub without hurting him was considerably more trouble than getting pulled in. After some awkward grappling and giggling on both sides, I was once again standing on the wet bathroom floor. I unwrapped the sopping towel, rang it over the vanity drain and dropped it into the sink with a heavy flop. I snatched several fresh towels from the linen cabinet, wrapped myself in one and shook out the other for Samuel.

"All right, your turn."

Samuel arched a brow, a strange look on his face. "Give me a few minutes to get myself outta this tub on my own. Go on, now. How much do ye wanna bet there's a lunch tray and some clothes set out for us in the bedroom?"

My stomach growled at the thought. With all the excitement, it had been a full twenty-four hours since the last time we ate. "Can I at least help you up?"

He shook his head and his smile grew. "Away ye go. I'm good. Just need a minute of privacy if ye don't mind."

"All right." I set the towel on the edge of the vanity, mussed his damp hair and headed for the door. "Call if you need me."

CHAPTER TWENTY-FIVE

*S*amuel was correct about the food and clothes, though judging by what was left, the skirts were for him and the dresses for me. I laughed and exchanged my towel for a camel-colored sheath dress with a high neck and long sleeves. I pulled on warm ivory stockings and slipped my feet into a lovely pair of brown leather boots left by the door. Standing before the mirror I stared at myself.

I had never worn something so fitted. The cut of the dress highlighted the volume of my breasts, my slender waist and pretty much every female curve I possessed.

Galan would hate it. I loved it.

No more *Lia girl* or *little one*. This dress made it clear I was no longer a youth.

I broke a warm pastry in half and moaned at the sweet succulence. "Samuel, you must needs hurry or I am liable to eat everything myself."

A deep-throated laugh rumbled in the bathroom. "Eat 'til ye burst, Luv. It's been too long since ye filled yer belly. Ye must be famished."

He shuffled out of the bathroom, a towel loosely wrapped around his hips and fisted in his hand.

Yes. *Famished.*

The gash on his side looked better with the blood and filth cleaned away but there were still a dozen bruises appearing and pooling dark at an alarming rate.

"How long until your injuries heal?"

Samuel chuckled, not at all fooled by the reason for my question. "A few days at least, I'm afraid."

Turning to the bed, I gestured for him to sit on the edge and handed him one of the other pastries. "Let me bind your ribs and help you dress."

After retrieving the medical supplies, I surveyed his ribs. I judged them to be intact but tender and bruised. "When shall I stand as queen?"

He hissed as I wound the strips of cloth around his chest, but soon enough they were tied and I eased his arms into a crisp, white dress shirt. "An hour? I expect the usual suspects are gatherin' as we speak."

"What? Now?"

Samuel nodded. "Better to move on it and foil any plan Abaddon and Rheagan have brewing. It will strengthen yer case in the Fae courts too, I expect. The Fates wouldna think twice about screwin' ye over as a regular Highborne citizen but they might think twice before pissing off Queen Lia, Ruler of the Realm of the Fair."

I opened my mouth to say something, but nothing productive came to mind.

"I may still have to smooth a few things out with the Order but consider yerself as good as coronated."

Not wanting to think about being coronated yet, I focused on the first part of his sentence. "Why should you smooth things over with them? They chained you to a wall and—"

Two fingers pressed to my lips. "Dinnae think too harshly of the Order. Rheagan and your ancestors almost wiped out the races living in this part of the realm. Hatred runs deep and Celts are stubborn as rocks. The last thing anyone expected was for me to appear a decade after I abandoned my position, with a Highborne at my side, declaring her to be queen."

I tossed the medical supplies back into the basket. "They despise me. What about that will change?"

"They dinnae know you."

I glared at him. "You despised me and my family for almost a year. Mayhap the Talon should be the ones to protect the throne."

He scowled back, shuffling over to his wardrobe, his hand pressed against his ribs as he walked. "Aye, I did but that wasna all my fault. Yer brother had a hand in it too. Like it or no, the Order is the protector of the throne. As long as Abaddon wants to take hold of it, these men will protect ye."

I straightened the bedding and yanked the golden coverlet back into place. "I have no interest in being protected by the people who tortured you."

"Well, birthright trumps yer interests on that score."

"And have I naught to say about this either? Is that it?"

He glanced over his shoulder and cocked a brow. "Not much I'm afraid."

I clenched my hands into fists. "You have no idea how infuriating it is to have no voice in your own future. To have the Fates decide who you are and where your life is headed, for the God of gods to tell you where your destiny lies regardless of any feeling you have to the contrary."

He dropped the towel and wrapped a plaid skirt around his waist. He glared over his shoulder, his lip curled. "No idea, eh? Did ye honestly just say that to me? I think I have a fair recollection of how that feels. I've had my guts ripped out by the Fates too, if ye remember."

The bitter mixture of fury and betrayal stung my sinuses. I swallowed and unclenched my fists. "Of course. Apologies."

Samuel continued to dress, first shoving his shirttails under the waistband of his skirt and then easing his arms into a leather vest as he cursed.

I gently hugged him from behind and laid my cheek against his back. "Forgive me, please. That was thoughtless."

After a moment, his shoulders relaxed. Turning in my arms, he kissed the top of my head and hugged me back. "Forgiven, lass. I'm sorry too."

My mind tumbled with all the things I had no control over while he struggled to finish dressing. His stockings and shoes presented a true challenge, unable to reach down with his ribs bound and bruised.

I knelt on the floor to aid him. "I cannot imagine anyone less suited to be Queen of a realm. The idea strikes me cold to my bones. I want you to know, I would be lost without your counsel. Verily, I hold no skills, no strengths for leading, no . . . anything."

He lifted me to stand before him and rose to his feet. Two fingers gently chucked my chin to meet his gaze. "Dinnae panic yet, Luv. There will be plenty of time for worrying later. For now, let's take things one disaster at a time. I'm sure the next will hit us soon enough."

He finished his outfit by buckling a small pouch and dagger across his hip. He was sheathing the blade when a soft knock drew our attention to the door.

"Come in," Samuel said. The door swung open and he cursed. "Aye, just as I predicted."

CHAPTER TWENTY-SIX

*G*alan stepped into our suite, dressed in formal pants and jacket, and set a suitcase and a large satchel on the floor. Tham came in behind him and they both stared at me standing beside the bed in my new outfit. I knew my brother well enough to read his displeasure but before he put it to voice he saw my cheek.

"Sweeting, what happened?" He strode to me and touched the gash. Both he and Tham glared at Samuel.

"What? Ye think I'd hit her, do ye?" Samuel's hand tightened around the hilt of his little dagger. "Ye condescending, piece of—"

I stepped between the three and stared Galan down. "Stop this. Samuel had nothing to do with it and you know it. Stop stirring up silt. The waters are plenty muddy and we have more important things to worry about."

Samuel turned back to the bed and picked up our two wet towels and shuffled into the bathroom to hang them.

"Wait," I said. "How are you here so quickly? It took us hours last night and you neither look weary from travel nor do you smell of horse."

Tham spun a dagger in the palm of his hand and winked. *Castian approved Julian's request to open a portal mirror on the grounds. Despite the Order objecting to magic on the premises, they relented and it was completed an hour ago.*

Samuel returned and looked like he had regained his composure. "So, I'm assuming that if yer here, Tham fetched ye and explained the situation.

Galan inclined his head and pointed to the satchel inside the door. "I brought the volumes of Highborne law and your notes from Reign's study, and Lia's personal items, yes. Though I am still at odds with her living here."

Samuel shrugged and held his hand out to me. I took my place at his side as he headed toward the door. "Good, thank you. And now that yer here, we should head down and get yer sister crowned Queen of the Realm. Follow me."

Samuel led us down and through the three upper levels of the elegant manse to a large set of double doors on the main floor. The wide archway curled between stone columns and held heavy, iron-studded doors.

I glanced up at the spiked metal portcullis suspended in its brackets above the entire opening. The tips, sharpened to pierce and impale, hung with threatening intent above those who passed beneath. "This entrance seems imposing."

Samuel glanced up, his kilt swishing as he moved. "Aye, the Queen's living and guest quarters are in the south wing and all the rooms related to realm business are in the north wing. These doors and gate separate the two and can be dropped and locked from either side if anything dangerous should happen in the course of yer duties."

My duties? That reality remained bizarre.

I spun the blue diamond on my finger. "And have these battlements needed to come down in the past?

Samuel raised a brow. "No, this Citadel was constructed long after the fall of Rheagan. The Order and their families use the buildings and grounds, but as the first to serve Castian and the Realm of the Fair from this location as Queen—you are the true and rightful owner of everything here."

Galan's silver brows arched so high I laughed. *Well, what does one say to that?* he asked into my mind.

I shook my head. *I have no idea . . . gratitude?*

As we breached the threshold and moved across the glass sheen of the granite floor, the heels of my new boots beat out a solid, sure-footed rhythm. It was a grave misrepresentation of my current condition. *Galan, did you feel this overwhelmed and under-qualified when Castian made you the Sentinel of Souls? Did you try to decline?*

He chuckled and hid his smile by scrubbing a hand over his mouth. *At least if not more, sweeting. Plus, it was the day after my mating and I found out my bride was Castian's biological daughter. Not where I thought life would take me.*

I slipped my hand in the crook of his elbow and pressed my good cheek against his arm. He smelled, as always, like sunshine and suede. I breathed his scent deep into my lungs. *Quite a pair are we not? So why us do you suppose?*

He barked a laugh. It rang through the corridor and eased the knotted ball twisting in my belly. *I have no idea, sister-mine, but this is Life's Journey after all. Why should only the males of our race endure an Ambar Lenn? In this realm, females have equal rights.*

Wonderful. *All the pomp and power I never wanted in a destiny I never asked for.*

He kissed the side of my head and squeezed me to his side.

The room Samuel took us to was located down the widest hall, in the center of the north wing, first floor. By the sounds of the voices rumbling up the art-adorned corridor to greet us, there were a dozen or more people in there.

Samuel nodded to the young male standing sentry outside the doorway and we entered. A massive rotunda the open space was decorated in charcoal gray and silver with pale blue, velvet drapes and a silver gilt dome high above.

The mumble of voices silenced as the people in the room became aware of our arrival. The faces of strangers far outweighed the faces I recognized. And while many of them seemed to share the local viewpoint of my utter filth, many more seemed politely curious.

I was curious too. I hadn't expected representatives from the other races of the realms, though it made sense that they would be there once I thought about it. There were Centaurs, Sprights, Weres, several races of Elves, Nimphs, Dwarves and Brownies. And those were only the ones I recognized.

"May I introduce my niece," Castian said, striding forward with a midnight blue robe draped over his arm. "Everyone welcome Lia Caleblasse, the rightful and future Queen of the Realm of the Fair."

The group pressed outward to the rounded walls opening the space. Galan and Samuel escorted me to the center of the room. Castian met me, swung the blue robe around my shoulders and clasped the ornate star brooch over my heart.

"It is not as heavy as I thought it would be," I said.

Castian smiled, his emerald eyes glittering like gems. "I promise you, neither is the position it signifies. You're gonna rock their stockings off."

Samuel snorted beside me and I tried not to laugh.

Castian leaned forward and pressed his lips to my forehead. The shock of his power was immediate. A surge of energy zinged through me. I clenched my fists and tried not to whimper. Only his hands under my elbows kept me on my feet. But as quickly as the electrocution began, it receded.

When he straightened, he cupped my face in his hands and gathered my tears with his thumbs. "All done, sweet one. Now you are truly ready to take on the realm. Come, there is much to be done."

The Queen's war room—*my* war room—sat through a hidden door in the back of the rounded throne room wall. A circular ebony table anchored the center of the room. Inlaid with a four-pointed star the tips of the star pointed to the four largest chairs. Fifteen gray upholstered chairs tucked under the table in even intervals around its edge. And where the sixteenth chair sat, the gray was replaced by an ebony, high-backed throne proportioned for a female.

It suited my tastes well.

Castian led me to the ebony throne and extended an elegant hand, gesturing for me to take my place. "We have many realm issues to address and questions to ask and answer. Let's get started."

Questions?

That was a gross understatement.

I strode to the main point of the table's design and settled into the cushioned throne as the males assembled. Castian sat opposite me while Samuel, Galan, Reign, Savage and Kobi stepped away to stand against the wall. Colum Murray, the four other men from the founding families and eight other Order men filled in the table.

I cast a wandering glance at the five males of the Order who had confronted me that morning in the small dining hall.

I raised my fingers to my sore cheek and realized each of five of them wore matching injuries. Apparently, Castian had settled the matter by mirroring the pain they inflicted on me. Samuel's father, though, looked worse. He wore the swollen bruise on his cheek like mine, but also bore the injuries he orchestrated for his son as well.

Hah. Served him right. I would bump his ribs in the hall if I could manage it. I cast a glance to Castian and sent him my gratitude. The smile he gave me was more radiant than the midday sun.

"So," Castian began, "this is your royal council, Lia. I believe you've met some of these gentlemen but the others should introduce themselves."

I held my hand up. "I'm sorry to interrupt, Sire, but these are the men chosen to advise me on the needs and status of the Realm of the Fair?"

Colum made a noise I had heard Samuel make many times when he was annoyed. "Aye, have ye got a problem with that?"

I nodded. "It seems to me that with the realm in such a state of upheaval, I would be better counseled by the race leaders so they could tell me what is happening in their communities. You and your men may know the laws of the regency but have any of you been off this property or involved in the day to day battles with the Scourge?"

"Our duty is to protect the throne?" Colum sputtered.

"The throne is more than a piece of furniture in a pretty silver palace. The throne represent a uniting leadership of all the races. The Realm of the Fair is under attack. We must come together as one people for the sake and safety of all."

Colum's face mottled a ruddy red color. "And ye think ye can change the way things are done because ye've been queen for all of ten minutes?"

"She absolutely can," Castian said, seemingly amused. "If this is not the council you imagined, what is, Lia?"

I looked at the angry and worried faces around the table and swallowed. "Mayhap Colum is right. I know little of what goes on—"

Castian shook his head. "Don't stop now. You're on a roll. What does your imagined council look like?"

I caught Samuel's gaze as I surveyed the room. He dipped his chin in an almost imperceptible nod. *Say it, Luv. Show them yer a fox. Yer choice. Yer life.*

I flattened my damp palms on the table and smiled. "With no offence meant to any of you fine men, I ask that you vacate all but one seat to the heads of the races. The Order shall retain one voice and one vote."

I swallowed again, my throat remaining dry. I wished I had something to drink. Instantly, a glass of wine appeared at my place. I sipped the burgundy liquid and nodded my thanks across the table to Castian.

After my second sip, I felt calmer. "Reign, as the Director of the Talon I want you at my table. Samuel, you are my guardian and my guide through this journey. Take a seat as well." The two nodded and pushed off the wall.

I looked to Deaglan standing guard at the door. "Please invite any leaders of the races to join us if they happen to be in attendance."

"All the races?" the weasel-faced man from the Order said. "That's almost thirty people."

"I am aware." I smiled as Samuel slipped into the seat to my right and Reign took the one to my left. "Reign, could you invite Bruin and Lexi to join us, please?"

"The council is fifteen. Fifteen of the senior Order." Colum said, his fists balled against the table.

"It was fifteen," I said. "Now it is more. And other than needing a larger table and more chairs, I fail to see the problem."

~

After the room shuffled and a half-dozen bewildered looking race leaders were brought into the room, I asked Reign to bring them up to speed. Samuel squeezed my knee under the table. It was meant as a show of approval, but the warmth of his touch called my desire forward unbidden.

I took another sip of wine, half hoping it would help me focus while the other half of me hoped he would inch up my dress and slide his hand between my thighs.

After Lexi and Bruin arrived, Reign described how Abaddon's forces had gained in strength and purpose, kidnapping me, releasing Rheagan's essence, and now escalating in violence. "As Queen, Lia will inspire a new order and unite the races of the realm. Our challenges lay in the fact that she has no experience in warfare and tactics. It falls to us to offer her counsel until she feels more confident."

Hah. He spoke as if that time might ever come.

"You lived among Abaddon and his men?" the weasel-faced male from the Order asked, looking disgusted.

Reign frowned. "She was taken, yes. Samuel infiltrated Abaddon's camp under the guise of a disgruntled Talon Enforcer to secure her and bring her back to safety."

"I found where Abaddon kept her and called for an extraction team." Samuel squeezed my thigh under the table once again and I eased open my knees.

"You?" his father said, the swelling in his lip making his sneer all the more twisted. "You retrieved the Queen's heir from within the walls of Abaddon's camp?"

"Aye, with the help of the Talon and her kin. What of it?"

"Ye shoulda called us in. Ye ken yer duty. The Aina Ohtar are sworn to protect—"

Hostility toward the man burned hot in my veins.

Castian pointed a finger. "Samuel knows his duty, Colum, and despite personal hardship, he served me, the Talon, and the Realm of the Fair. He did as ordered. To question him is to question me. Is that your intention?"

Colum glared at his son; the look, a silent promise of retribution. "No, milord."

"Right," Reign continued. "So, once Lia was reclaimed and safe at Haven, we hoped that would be the end of it."

"Until?" The Centaur leader asked.

"Until a few weeks ago when Abaddon laid a formal claim against Lia in the Fae courts. He claims her to be his wife from the time she spent in his compound. Since his act of force was thwarted, he means to take control of her through Highborne laws."

Colum cursed. *Ye gave Abaddon a foothold to the throne. How stupid are ye, ye fecking—*

I stood, my palms leaning heavy against the table. "I *gave* him nothing." The table looked startled. "If I lose my fight against Abaddon with the Fates, trouble shall knock on all our doors. If I win, there will be violent retaliation. You need to bite your tongue sir and learn to work together."

"Bite my tongue? I said nothing." *And I'll not fall to my knees for the likes of a madman's whore.*

"Be silent!" My entire body tingled. The moment froze in time, the energy inside me igniting my very cells—for what he said, for what he did to Samuel, for the smug arrogance in his leering male glances. "You will be silent or be gone from my sight."

Colum's mouth fell open as a queer look flashed across his face. Stumbling back, his hands gripped at his chest and he fell to the marble floor. Chaos ensued as chairs scraped floor and the Order men raced to his side. Reign rolled Colum to his back, opening the collar of his shirt. Samuel and Galan moved to stand at my sides.

In the next moment, Colum's reddened face fell lax. With one last shallow gasp, his eyes widened and then fell sightless.

Castian raised his hand and a glass of red wine appeared in his palm. He took a long swallow and glowered at the males of the Order. "Well, that was dramatic. Take his body out so we can continue with the meeting."

"Continue?" I said, my voice shaken. "Should we not . . . what about . . ."

"Death is nothing new, my dear. A man should consider his aging heart before getting so worked up. Still, no time for tears over a pompous tyrant. No offence to you, Samuel."

"None taken, Sire." Samuel's expressionless mask lent no indication of how he felt as his father's body was carried from the room.

My feelings were conflicted and I knew him less than a day. I lost my temper. And now, Samuel's father was dead . . . because of me.

Not because of you, sister-mine, Galan said, moving me back to the throne and taking a seat beside me. *The male let his anger and prejudice do him in. Not your fault. But Castian is right, there is much to discuss.*

The clarity of my brother's thoughts in my mind brought me back to Colum's insults. How did I hear Samuel's sire without him speaking aloud? His words rang in my mind with such a vile distaste, I had indeed wished him ill.

Before I could think further, Castian sat forward in his chair and grew serious. "Samuel, as oldest born of the Murray clan, you now assume your father's place as head of one of the founding families. Therefore, you are sworn to protect your Queen with your life and on your honor. Do you accept?"

Samuel blinked, his mouth dropping open. "I . . . uh, I am honored, Sire, but I cannot."

The other Order males gasped.

Samuel kept his gaze locked on the God of gods. "I will guard Lia, of course, with my life and on my honor. I will serve you and your realm, but to do that best, I must be free to leave these grounds, fight if I must—with both sword and magic—and put her before all else.

Even my own family oath. The honor of the Order should fall to Deaglan."

A hint of a smile graced Castian's face. "So be it. You can explain things to him once we're finished here. Carry on, Maximus. You were saying?"

CHAPTER TWENTY-SEVEN

"Keep yer guard up," Samuel called from the stone plinth he sat upon. Gathered in the open area behind the Queen's palace, a group of my protectors spent the better part of the next day drilling me in the damp shadows of the stone ruins. Kobi worked on the handling and wielding of weapons, Galan and Tham focused on using nature as a means of concealment, and now Savage was brutalizing me in the ways of hand-to-hand combat and defense.

"It is hard to keep my guard up," I said, grunting as Savage smacked my backside with a steel palm, "when I can no longer feel my arms." I turned and thrust forward, my wooden sword swatted to the side like a bothersome fly by my tattooed opponent.

"You're strangling the hilt," Kobi said from the sideline. "Relax your grip and attack like you mean it, Highborne. I tasted the wildcat you cage inside. Let her out to play."

I spun and threw the thing at his head.

True as an arrow, it soared through the air only to be evaded by an annoying demon. Kobi poofed to the side and plucked the projectile from the air, his chest bouncing with amusement. "There she is. Now this woman, we can work with, eh Sav?"

Savage swept my foot and I stumbled back and landed on my backside. Hard.

"All right," Samuel said, easing off his perch with one arm bound against his bruised ribs. He strode forward tall and strong, saluting Kobi with his middle finger as he passed. "That's enough for today, lads. Take the night off and we'll regroup in the morning after Lia eats and rests."

"What I need is to soak in a hot bath," I said, more curtly than I meant. "I expect tomorrow will fail to bring much improvement."

Galan poured something out of a tall Thermos and handed me the cup. "Then we shall practice each day until you feel confident to defend yourself."

I took a long swallow from the steaming cup and found there was quite a kick to the drink Galan gave me. Within moments it seeped a warm trail down my throat and pooled into my stomach. Enjoying the sensation, I tipped back the cup and drained it dry.

I accepted a refill as the air around us picked up with a succulent breeze. Zophia materialized in our midst.

The few times I had seen her, I marveled at her ethereal beauty: her long brunette hair, her flawless iridescent skin, her grace and natural resplendence. She was a goddess of the Veil. This evening, however, her look of distress had my stomach churning.

"When am I to appear?" I asked. I knew by the sadness in her gaze I assumed correctly.

"Tomorrow. Castian will Flash you and your party to stand before my sisters at dusk. Normally, we hold proceedings on the grounds of the palace, but Castian doesn't trust Abaddon to come Behind the Veil while Rheagan is spiriting around, so we will meet at Haven. Neutral ground, you could say."

"Advantage, home team," Kobi said, looking pleased.

I glanced at the quiet village of Lothendril. The stone houses with smoke puffing out their chimneys, the hills dotted with sheep grazing inside the labyrinth maze. Kobi, Savage, Galan and Tham all seemed anxious to leave.

But leaving meant my time with Samuel was over.

"It'll be all right, lass," he said, close to my ear. "I'll not let him have ye. He'll never win."

In truth, there was no stopping this. "Tomorrow night then," I ignored the heaving of my insides and bowed my head. "Gratitude for bringing the news yourself."

She managed a weak smile. "It is the least I can do after my last visit."

I downed the second glass of heated spirits and felt the jagged edge of my mood recede still further. "The past is over. Now, on to the future. We shall see you there."

Once again, the events of my life fell beyond my control. The thing I liked most about the idea of being the Queen was that in the past two days, I had an opinion and voice in things involving me and the safety of the realm.

Not with this.

Once Zophia vanished, I moved to Samuel, with as much confidence as I could muster. There was at least one thing I could do. Keeping a polite distance for the sake of my brother's sanity, I gestured to the two dozen stone houses in the distance. "Go spend some time with your family. They need you now and I am fine here surrounded by protectors."

His emotionless stare might have fooled the others, but I could read the tightness at the edge of his eyes. "The Murray clan dinnae need nor want me, duck. And you are far from fine. Do ye not think I know what it does to yer insides to be called before the Fates?"

"Lia is right," Galan said, joining us. "The four of us can stay with her for a few hours. You should be with your family. To mourn Colum's passing."

Samuel exhaled. "I dinnae mourn him, but ye might be right. I should pay my respects to my uncles and my siblings. I'll not be leaving Lia behind though, so ye might as well head home to Jade for tonight. We'll see ye at the tribunal tomorrow night."

Galan looked at me, visibly torn. "I shall stay if you need my support."

I shook my head, noticing how loose it felt on my shoulders.

"Samuel's right. Give Jade a hug from me and we shall see you tomorrow. All of you, go eat and enjoy yourselves. Tomorrow will be a long day and I am safe enough here."

Kobi and Savage looked to Samuel. "We'll head over to the town center around eight o'clock, lads. Yer time is yer own 'til then."

"Nice, fashionably late for a wake," Kobi said. "Do you have any female cousins to console? Sisters maybe?"

Samuel scowled. "Lia needs to soak in a bath and get some food in her stomach. My Da will be no less dead after dinner than he is now. And if either one of you lays a manly touch on any of my kin, I'll cast a spell to shrivel yer cocks so it's the last thing ye ever do."

When everyone left us, Samuel held out his elbow, ready to depart. Instead of accepting his gesture and leaving our practice area behind, I backed him against the stone plinth he had been sitting on earlier.

Checking that we were, indeed alone, I slid my hands under the hem of his kilt and over his muscled thighs. The dusk breeze brought the sweet spice of his arousal to me in an instant.

"What, here?" Samuel said, eyeing the clearing. "I'm not recovered by half, Luv, I'm sorry. I don't think I'll be much got to ye yet."

I pushed my hands higher, gathering the fabric and baring his flesh along my path. I nudged him backwards and he braced his weight on his palms behind him.

"You are very hard," I said, caressing a finger down the silky steel shaft I exposed.

"Aye," he choked, a smile curling at the edges of his mouth. "I could likely split marble."

"That must be uncomfortable."

"Lia, ye don't have to—"

His weak protestation cut off the moment I took him into my mouth. I licked the jewel of glistening moisture from his tip and smiled up at him. "I like the way your arousal tastes. A little bitter but a flavor that is uniquely you."

I stroked down his shaft as I sucked, teasing for more of a taste. He groaned, his hips flexing up to meet me. "Yer verra good at that. A natural, I'd say."

I flicked my tongue and teased the two orbs below. His gem pouch tightened beneath my touch and I dug my nails into his flesh. I was beginning to understand Samuel's body. Could command it to do as I bid.

"Christ, Lia, yer killin' me. I want to be inside ye. I bet yer slick and hot, throbbin' for some attention."

In truth, I was. "Nonsense, this is for you." An act of gratitude for all he had done and all I wish could be.

Ignoring the growing discomfort in my back and thighs from my position hovering over him, I assaulted him with my tongue, sucked hard while twisting and playing with his jewels.

The sounds and smells were primal, grounding, binding. They were us and we were them. I set every nuance of every detail of pleasuring Samuel to memory.

Micro-tremors wracked his body and he set his hand on the back of my head. Gripping my hair, he gave a gentle tug. "I'm going to come, Luv. Ye'll want some distance."

But I did *not* want distance. Not from Samuel. Not ever.

I remained focused, determined to share this with him, hungry for the taste of his bliss.

Samuel groaned and thrust deep into my mouth. His breathing caught as the first gush of moist heat hit my throat. It was bitter and thick but everything I wanted. I swallowed, greedy to take more from him.

Every way a female could take her male. And he was my male. Even though I could not keep him.

CHAPTER TWENTY-EIGHT

*T*he balance of life was a cruel, cruel thing. Lying awake, my mind stumbled over disjointed thoughts. The hearing with the Fates looming large later today, facing Abaddon knowing the truth of his claim, worrying over my impact as Queen of the Realm and saying goodbye to what I wanted with Samuel.

Samuel kicked next to me, trapped in a fitful state of rest. Ironic really. Across the courtyard, the Murray clan mourned the loss of their patriarch while I held Colum's oldest son in my arms. As much as I wanted to keep him, he was as lost to me as their sire to them.

Samuel grumbled something unintelligible, fighting his nocturnal battles. I brushed his rough chin. The gashes and swelling on his face had yet to recede enough to shave properly, so instead, he looked much the rugged warrior.

"Samuel, wake up."

Rousing from his slumber struggle, he blinked awake.

"Mornin', Luv. Everything all right?"

"Right as rain," I lied. I kissed him and snuggled closer. "Waking with you is my favorite part of the day."

He stretched, his skin glistening, the sheets slightly damp beneath him. "Aye, it does feel decadently domestic. If we could avoid the life and death struggles that generally come after we get outta bed, that would be even better."

"Agreed."

Reaching between us, he removed the elastic from my braid and freed my hair. I turned to give him greater access, relishing in the touch of his fingers combing along my scalp and through my locks.

"From the moment I first laid eyes on ye, I knew things would never be the same. Ye turned my life on it's head, Lia. And though ye don't see it yet, yer just as strong, brave and heroic as any of the women ye look up to."

I slid my arms around him and pulled him over me.

He winced a bit and caught his breath.

"Apologies. Are you terribly sore?" I lessened my hold, running my fingers over the scabs and bruises marring his back. "How I wish your injuries were healed so we could make love. I need you so desperately."

A dark masculine musk filled my sinuses and he lowered his lips to my neck. "What injuries? I'm good if you are." He moistened his swollen lips, his mouth just inches from mine.

"But you are recovering."

"I'm plenty healed up."

It was impossible to say who lunged first, but in one sweeping move our lips fused, Samuel's arms grappled around me. The sculptured muscles of his chest pressed against the wild beat of my heart. As he licked his way into my mouth, I tried to remember to be gentle.

I encouraged him to roll upon me but as he had done each time we joined, he resisted and found another position.

"Samuel," I said, breaking from his kiss. "Why will you not lay over me? I want the weight of you upon me, the thrust of your strength behind you. Is there something I am doing or not doing? I hope you would tell me if I am not—"

He silenced my words with his kiss. "Yer perfect, Luv. I just . . . it's only." He pulled back to consider his words, sadness clouding his expression. "I dinnae want to trigger any thoughts of what came before. I want ye to see and feel me inside ye, not battle with the ghosts of grief for the other."

"My protector e'ermore." I pulled him over me and opened my legs to allow him space to settle. He accepted his weight on his elbows, his hips cradled between my thighs. "My precious male, there is no likeness to confuse. And as much as I appreciate your caution, you promised to take me rough so I would never forget how you crave me."

He chuckled, his laughter vibrating flesh to flesh with marvelous friction. "That was meant to be more threat than promise."

I gripped the muscled rounds of his backside and dug my nails into his flesh. "Dude, nice ass."

Samuel burst out laughing. The joyful abandon of the sound squeezed my heart but I refused to let the hopelessness of our situation ruin this moment.

We were together. For this moment, we were together.

"Samuel, mark me. Claim me. I never want to forget how you feel inside me." The rasp in my voice surprised me. I nuzzled his neck, his skin warm against my cheek. Running my nails up his sides, I circled his nipples. "I want more of you. More kissing, more of your hands on my flesh, more of you everywhere."

The succulence of Samuel's need charged the air. Desperate and wanton, lust overpowered his usual masculine musk. And it was all for me. My eyes rolled closed, my head swimming with the aphrodisiac.

Indescribably caught in my wizard's spell.

I arched against him. His hips eased forward, his erection inside me a welcome stretching of flesh. "Gods, I love the feel of you moving inside me."

"It's where I belong, *mo chridhe*. My home."

I sank deeper into the pillows, memorizing as many of the sensations as I could absorb. The sway and pump of his hips. The way he drew his tongue down the column of my neck. The thrill of his erection probing deep inside me. The erotic sounds he made when utterly consumed.

I committed every nuance to memory. For though we were the only two in the world at that moment, our time together was limited. I was Abaddon's mate.

Samuel stilled beside me. "Hey, where'd ye go?" Raising his fingers to my mouth, he shook his head. "Nevermind, dinnae answer that. Tonight, will come soon enough. Tuck yer Elven logic away and live in this moment."

My heart ached for this to last forever, to be the beginning of something magical and not the end. "Samuel, do something for me."

"Anything," he whispered against my neck. "Name it."

"Call me *Ryanne*. I wish for you to be the male to have my soul name. My mate of choice."

Samuel stilled. He had studied Highborne customs and laws for weeks. I hoped he understood what my request meant. It was the most precious gift I could give him.

"*Ryanne*," he said, his soft Scottish brogue rolling off the 'R' so it sounded like a caress. "An exquisite name, for my exquisite female. I'm honored, my beloved *Ryanne*."

The speaking of my name rang some invisible bell within me. A wave of heat burst through my cells. My body tensed, squeezing in sudden greediness. The pleasure obliterated my ability to think or feel anything beyond the blissful oblivion of losing myself to him. His hips pressed and retreated, the friction so intense it almost hurt to ride out my release.

As my senses returned, he kissed me long and slow. Brushing errant curls back from my face. "Gods I love how your body shudders for me. Are ye all right?"

Tears threatened to overtake me, but I fought to keep the moment light. "Mayhap slightly better than all right."

"Weel," he said, his brogue unnaturally thick, his smile cocky, "if ye only give me slightly better than all right, I better up my game. Plenty of room to improve."

I caressed the corded muscles of his back and urged him on. "Very well, show me what perfection feels like."

He bit his bottom lip and nodded. "Perfection is a tall order. Might take a lot of trying."

The entire realm fell away as the grind of his hips began in earnest. Nothing would ever feel this good again. I wanted Samuel's silky voice, his body, his heart. He filled me with both the most indescribable strength and the most desperate vulnerability. And I would be forced to give him up.

At dusk, I ran a hand down the smooth stone column in the ancient Fae ceremonial circle. Standing in the center of a wide forest clearing on the Haven Mountain, it reminded me of the celebration site back in my village. Shaped like a horseshoe with two concentric circles made up of standing stones, lintel stones and monoliths, it stood the stage for my downfall.

Secluded, secure and its existence known to only a few who grew up on the mountain, it was the place where Galan and Jade mated and Recognized.

I hoped it might hold good fortune for me as well.

The power of the Fae gods flowed in currents underneath the site. The Ley-lines were invisible and usually undetectable but no matter how distant my tie to Castian and his Pantheon, I felt their power.

How I wish I had the power to change what would happen next. How I wish Samuel and I had remained buried beneath the silken covers and ignored the world. The entire day, we had said little while at the same time saying everything necessary with a touch, a kiss, a gaze. We never strayed from one another, always within arm's reach, always within each other's gaze.

But now here we were.

And here things would change forever.

Reign would speak first. He would argue the morality of Abaddon claiming me and cite the facts that I had still been a youth at the time of my abduction. He would also point out that Highborne females chose their partners. It would not matter. The mating law was absolute. Abaddon held legal right to claim me and the Fates, being who they were, would choose the course which leveled the most destruction.

It was hopeless.

The sun warmed the sky in blazing pinks and purples yet I felt none of its splendor. My heart ached.

"Dinnae wind yerself up yet. There is time enough before the Fates arrive." Samuel joined me in my vigil, standing tall and handsome against the horizon. "Reign, Julian and Aust locked this place down tight. You'll be safe. I dinnae want ye worrying about that on top of anything else."

I drew what breath I could and smiled. "What would make me feel safest is falling into your arms and letting you banish my fears with your lips and your hips. I suppose that is out of the question?"

His smile melted me. "Yer brother will blow a gasket if he finds out we've been sleeping together."

"I think that fact alone would inspire you to accept."

We chuckled, our words reminiscent of the conversation when we first agreed to work together for Jade's sake.

"How far we've come, aye?" He moved behind me, setting his chin atop my head. "I dinnae regret a moment. No matter how brief our encounter, yer soul has marked mine for life. No one will ever—could ever—touch that."

The male knew what I needed to hear.

At the rustling of scrub, Samuel's grip tightened on my upper arms. My Highborne family emerged from the tree line and he loosened his hold. Galan, Iadon and Nyssa, Aust and Elora, and Tham and Cameron strode out as one. Their grace and strength in motion remained something humans could never match.

I forced myself to step away from the warmth of Samuel's body and jogged to my family. I hugged those who lived and nodded to the two spirits who joined them.

Elora took my hand in hers and Nyssa followed suit. Oh, how I missed these females since moving to the Dens and then to the Silver Citadel.

I squeezed their holds. "If a family is comprised of the people you love most, the gods blessed me beyond measure. Without your support, I would be far more lost than I am. I love you all."

"As we love you, sweeting," Elora said. "No matter what is said or decided today, we stand with you."

Though I wished that changed things, hearing the words still helped.

"The wolves are in place along the tree line," Aust said. "Hawks and osprey are sweeping the forest. Whatever happens, we are prepared."

I kissed his cheek. "I have no doubt. Please extend my gratitude to your creatures if I am unable."

Galan frowned and moved in to kiss my temple. "After the Fates dismiss Abaddon's claim, we shall thank Aust's creatures together. Mayhap with a celebration run. It has been ages since we took to the forest together."

I looked at what Iadon carried and smiled. "Is that it?"

"Crafted with all my love," Iadon said, dipping his chin and presenting me with a garment bag. "A queen must needs look the part. A queen taking on a realm in conflict such as this must needs be that much more prepared."

"I suppose it is time to prepare. Ladies, will you help me?"

A short while later, I stood before Elora and Nyssa, my heart racing. With my transformation complete, I was stricken with second thoughts. "Have I made a terrible error in judgment? Speak only truth, what do you think?"

"You are resplendent," Elora said. "A child no longer, you look every bit a female of power."

"I agree," Nyssa said, tilting her head this way and that as she shaped the last locks of my hair against my mid back. "If this were my first time meeting you, I would take you for a self-possessed, confident female to be reckoned with."

I adjusted the ice blue corset and marveled at Iadon's talent. "Do you think it wise to assume this persona now? Mayhap playing the innocent maiden might be wiser?"

"You are Queen of the Realm," Nyssa said. "Show the Fates that the innocent maiden of a year ago is gone. This is the female you are now."

I strode a small circuit in front of the wolves. Faolan pushed her head into my palm. I buried my fingers into the depths of her thick silver coat, her ebony ears peaked and pointing to the sky. "And what say you, my friends? Do you recognize me?"

The wolves sniffed the air but alluded to nothing.

Holy-fricken-shamoly, Gemma said, tromping silently through the brush to join us. *Nicely done, girlfriend. You'll either knock'em dead by heart attack or you can beat them with your dominatrix stick. Cool accessory.*

I pointed my scepter at her and grinned. Clasping the bronze grips, I swung it over my head. It spun like a helicopter blade within my hands, aerodynamics causing it to sing through the air. "Savage crafted and weighted it for me."

Stand back, Jackie Chan.

I laughed though I had no idea who that might be. "I failed miserably in all other weapons training. Wielding a staff seemed my only *almost* skill. There is much to learn yet I feel less vulnerable with it in my hand."

Then go with it. Ooo, I like these metal vines. Very Elfy.

Elfy? I turned the staff in the waning light so she could examine the intricate leaf and vine work. The detailing wound up the shaft, encircled the edges of the grips, and secured the crescent moon sigil at the top.

"By the gods," Samuel gasped, coming into the mix. He stopped dead when he saw my attire, a mix of emotions flashing across his face.

My ladies-in-waiting giggled and left us to ourselves.

I ran a hand down the flat of my bare stomach to the waistband of my form-fitting pants. "Do I look all right?"

He took in the midnight blue suede of my pants and long jacket, its high collar and my hair hanging unbound. His expression remained guarded until he eyed the corset. His brow pinched, his frown subtle but unmistakable.

I rubbed my chest, a little light-headed. "I . . . uh, wanted Castian's brand to show and learned this week that skirts were a detriment if one must needs defend oneself. I also wanted to rid myself of the image of a youth. I thought if I—"

"Ye steal my breath." The smile he gave me was far too private for the proximity of my family. "I'm just not accustomed to anyone else seeing ye look so . . ." His face screwed up and he sighed. "A lot of yer skin is showing and yer . . . um, attributes are quite pronounced without the layers of skirts and full bodice and such."

"You hate it."

"No, yer spectacular. It's just . . ." He whetted his lips. "Ye see, until now, I was the only one who had the pleasure of eyeing yer feminine form."

I looked down at myself. "Mayhap I should change back into what I wore earlier."

He shook his head, looking abashed. "Absolutely not. Never second guess yerself because of someone else, including me. It's my issue. I'll deal with it. Yer stunning. Other men are bound to notice it. How do ye feel? Ye've never worn pants, have ye?"

"No, and it is odd. Light. I feel rather naked actually."

He leaned close and smiled. "I've seen ye naked and this does nae come close to that beautiful sight. That much, at least, I can claim for myself, aye?"

"Aye," I said, waving away his laughter at my imitation of his accent. "Naked is yours and yours alone as long as I retain any say in the matter."

Samuel's laughter died. We both knew that choice would be taken from me very soon. "Come, Luv, I want to see yer brother's face when he sees ye like this. I bet he turns seven shades of red, right to the tips of his ears."

By the time the sun sank toward the horizon, the tightening in my chest had increased to the point of near suffocation. The certainty of impending doom choked me as I fought to hold my control. The boon to Elven logic was that I could see the truth. What would be would be. It was in the hands of the gods and there was little to be done except wait. My anxiety had yet to face that truth.

With Faolan at my side, I made one last circuit of the standing stones. Rounding the far monolith I called upon Mika's Earth Mother and asked for her guidance. It seemed fitting to enlist all the help I could get.

I stopped when Faolan's shoulders tensed and her lupine gaze swung to the altar stone.

Castian and the Fates arrived.

Samuel and Galan both glanced to me and I nodded. It was time to accept fate's journey. And I would. Whatever came.

"How you holding up, Miss Caleblasse?" The velvet voice carried from the trees as a young male eased into my path. It took me a moment to recognize the handsome blond from Jade's class, the one who got Samuel and I started off the first day with his question.

"Tanner, is it?"

He nodded and stopped before me. "I wanted to catch you before the proceedings to wish you luck."

Odd that he knew about the hearing, let alone the location it was being held. Still, it was a kind thought. "Gratitude, though with the Fates' arrival, I must needs go."

He shook his head and his feathered hair fell back into place as if trained for a lifetime to do so. "In a minute. I need to speak to you. It will only take a sec."

After a glance past my shoulder, he stepped closer. "I wanted to speak to you for some time, but the Professor was always hovering. Then you stopped coming to class altogether."

I drew a deep breath. Just the smell of male attraction. During past lectures, I caught him looking at me more than once. "Yes, well, life's journey has taken Professor Murray and me in unexpected directions."

"Are you and the Professor . . ." Tanner waggled his brow.

The impertinence of the question warmed my ears. "Samuel is a dear friend who watches over me."

"Because he's your *garda síochána?*"

I balked and froze. The scent of male attraction remained but that was all the air held. No woody growth of the trees, no cool richness of the earth, not even the scent of Faolan's coat or the newly tanned suede of my outfit. Why? What was happening? Was it magic?

"Samuel is a friend," I repeated with what I hoped was an easy smile. I gripped my scepter tighter. "And speaking of him, it is quite rude of me to keep him waiting and the others waiting. If you would excuse me."

Tanner gripped my arm and took two quick steps forcing us from direct view of the clearing. With the rough bark of an ancient oak at my back, he raised his other arm so I was trapped within the cage of his body.

I raised my chin and steadied my footing. "I shall ask you this only once, sir, step back and let me pass. Whatever you are playing at it is unwelcome. I have had enough."

"Have you now?" His tight smile erased all traces of the handsome male I thought him to be. He dropped his gaze and stared boldly at the heave of my chest. A rush of male lust filled the air, the scent familiar and unwanted. "But, I haven't had enough. Not nearly enough."

When his gaze rose and his dark eyes met mine, magic tingled in my nose and the illusion dissolved. The pale complexion of a twenty-something boy morphed into a muscled, olive-skinned male. And there, his face inches from mine, stood Abaddon.

I swung my arm but he knocked the scepter to the forest floor as if it were nothing more than a twig. I pressed my hands against his chest. "Release me this instant or I shall scream and draw half of Talon's army here to aid me."

Abaddon tilted his head and laughed. The eerie sound sent a sickening wave twisting through my belly. "Scream away, we are veiled from prying ears." He leaned closer and my head pressed hard against the tree. His mouth brushed my cheek and his breath warmed my ear. "One moment is all I need to tell you what's about to happen. Then we'll go meet with the Fates hand in hand."

Now it was my turn to laugh. "I shall never go anywhere with you peaceably."

"I fucked you fair and square. You and I both know that makes you mine. Sooner or later, you'll come to heel. I'm looking forward to you putting up a fight."

Heat expanded in my chest and burned through my veins. "You are delusional."

"Am I? You think you can stand up to the big, bad wolf, little girl? I assure you, you'll lose if you try."

"Yet even if you win, you lose. My body is warded against possession or anyone displacing my soul, I claimed my duty as Queen, and Castian, the Talon, and the true Order of Aina Ohtar support me. If you thought me an easy path to reinstate Rheagan, think again."

Abaddon's lip twitched as he stared at the crescent moon tattoo on my heaving flesh.

"Yes, Castian ensured no one will ever use my body to take control of the realm. It is within his right to protect me from his Pantheon and the evils of his sister. I shall never be the vessel for Rheagan's resurrection."

He squeezed my breast and thrust hard against my pelvic bone. "Well, would you look at that, my little mate found her mettle. And where did this fleeting vein of strength come from, I wonder?"

A deafening crack exploded above us. A thousand sparks of blue magic rained over an invisible shield. Abaddon smirked as another flash of blue lightning struck.

"You underestimate him, you know? Samuel is more of a male, warrior and wizard than you could ever be."

Abaddon's gaze narrowed and the rising violence in his glare froze in my chest. "Impossible. The Celt couldn't have fucked you. Highborne laws are absolute."

I smiled and locked gazes with the monster in him. "A fact that shall set me free."

His nostril's flared as he inhaled. "A bluff and not a very convincing one at that."

With everything in me, I committed to my words. "You know the law but there is a spirit of the law you missed. Mating a Highborne is the claiming and pleasuring of a female after her age of eligibility. To be drugged and violated to the most intimate depths held no pleasure. Add to that, you took my body months before I was an adult and your claim is moot. I reject what was done to me by force and the Fates will find it as vile as everyone else."

Outside the bubble of my prison, Samuel mouthed a string of crazed oaths, his diamond eyes glowing with feral fury. The air inside our bubble began to change. Nash and the Asian Enforcer joined the magical assault on whatever field Abaddon erected.

It felt as if the invisible shield was weakening.

"If you wish to argue Highborne law, I welcome it. I admit that I have been mated most thoroughly—just not by you."

Abaddon whirled and exploded in a surge of dark sorcery.

The containment field erupted and the three wizards flew backward through the air. The blast of tainted air knocked me off my feet and tossed me to the scrub. My head cracked against the ground. The forest spun.

I let my head hang as the wolves closed ranks. Faolan nuzzled my neck and forced me to lift my gaze. Roars, snarls and screams erupted.

I gripped my staff and staggered to my feet.

Abaddon threw Samuel against a tree and the two fought in a strangled battle. A dagger flashed silver in the starlight. A strange heat burned across my skin.

A warning that something was about to . . .

The explosion shook the entire ruin site.

As I steadied my footing, Hell vomited Scourge in every direction.

Gunfire and magic bolts careened through the air. Savage and Cowboy all but dragged the Fates and the other females into the dense forest cover.

"Haven's under attack!" someone yelled.

Another explosion knocked me to my knees.

Rough hands jerked me from the ground. A Scourge Raider dragged me to my feet and threw me into the flow of the other attackers.

I swung my staff with all my might and caught him in the ear with a blunt blow. He listed to the side, a chunk of his putrid face dropping to the forest floor. I stumbled away and the wolves enveloped him.

"I've got ye, lass." The words lifted my spirits but when I turned, it wasn't Samuel who flanked me.

"Deaglan, help your brother."

The Celt shook his head as a half-dozen kilted males surrounded me. "After yer safe. Let's go."

Another explosion rocked the night. It threw up flames and destruction all around us. Hitting the ground, I smothered my cry as a sharp, fire raked across my hip. My exposed flesh fell victim to shards of debris.

Samuel cried out and doubled over. Abaddon's dagger sprayed an arc of blood as he withdrew and struck again.

"Samuel!" I screamed.

Rising to my feet, I harpooned my scepter through the air. I willed its flight to be true. Energy crackled around me as I envisioned Abaddon falling. The staff soared as if guided by the gods. A dull thud. Abaddon faltered, my wooden staff impaling his back.

I broke from my protectors and raced to close the distance. The same feral fury I saw in Samuel only moments ago now raged in me. My words put him in danger. My comments set this madman after him. I would kill this evil spawn for hurting him—even if it meant my own life.

Before I reached them, Abaddon Flashed and my scepter fell to the forest floor. I dropped to my knees next to Samuel's motionless body. Blood covered the ground.

He bled from his chest. His arms. His groin.

Tears spilled as my breathing hitched. His lean form sprawled and contorted on the forest floor broke my heart. For once, I reacted to the injuries without the malaise I suffered so many times in the clinic.

"Samuel," I said, fighting dizziness as I tore his shirt and pressed on his wounds. "Samuel, I am here. Stay with me. Aid is on the way. Please, stay with me."

CHAPTER TWENTY-NINE

"*O*pen yer eyes, lass."

Whatever the dream I dreamt, I wished it would last an eternity. Samuel's voice rang with all the love and serenity it always held when he whispered to me in private. If I woke, he may be dead. And if not dead, I would have to face losing him because of Abaddon.

"That's it, Luv. Come back to me."

Warm fingers traced a tender circle on my cheek. My eyes flickered open and there he was, his ebony hair flopping in front of his swirling opal eyes.

"You need a haircut, Professor Murray."

He laughed and kissed my nose. "Maybe so. I've been a wee bit busy lately."

My lips quivered. "I thought I lost you. There was so much blood. Abaddon . . . he . . . you were so still—" The pale green walls of Jade's clinic blurred. "I thought Abaddon killed you. It was my fault you were hurt . . . *are* hurt."

He pulled me closer, the two of us tucked into of one of the recovery beds. "Hush now. Here I am, living, breathing and loving ye as much as ever. The rest will sort itself out."

I shifted to my side and both of us winced.

"Careful, duck, yer stitched up. Ye took quite a blow yerself and lost a fair bit of blood. With Jade's powers bound, there's no magical healing this time around, I'm afraid. We'll have to mend the old-fashioned way."

If mending meant days of lounging in bed until he was well again, I welcomed old-fashioned. Where I remained clothed with gauze covering my throbbing hip, his body was bare, wrapped with intersecting bandages across his chest, around his arms and . . .

I lifted the sheet and his dressings blurred behind my tears. "I told him we were lovers—boasted about it—of course he struck out at you. What did he . . . are you . . . what has he done to you?"

"I'll survive," Samuel said, tugging the sheet from my hand to cover himself. "My machismo might be damaged but Jade thinks the surgery went as well as can be expected."

"What does that mean?"

"It means, the lads will make me the butt of their jokes for a good long while but things will function normally once my injuries heal. The only thing Jade's unsure of is if I'll be able to father weens. It's a wait-and-see-how-I-heal kinda thing now. Nothing I have nae been through before."

My breathing hitched on a sob, my words caught in my throat. This was my fault. Punishment for taking a lover after being bound to another.

"No, it's not," Zophia said, shuffling into our room. The Fate projected the same ethereal beauty as always but the opalescence of her skin was off. "This was Abaddon's doing and the blame sits squarely on his shoulders."

"You are hurt too."

She smiled. "A bit crushed beneath a well-meaning Talon Enforcer. Not to worry. I will heal the moment I return Behind the Veil but wanted to let you know the outcome of the hearing."

I looked from her to Samuel and back. "How long was I asleep?"

Zophia chuckled but stopped, bracing a hand against her ribs. "In truth, there was no hearing. My sisters are fickle, selfish and often manipulative, but they weren't in much of a mood to play games today. Officially, they cited the fact that Castian had given a formal warning to Abaddon that if he acted against you before the completion of the hearing, the claim would be nullified."

"And unofficially?"

She shrugged. "I pointed out your secret lover is Jade's ex and the man your brother despises most in the two realms. Add to that, he is a renowned wizard when your people and his both strictly forbid magic. And his family despise Highbornes and aren't fond of Samuel either. I convinced them the drama of watching it all play out would be far more entertaining than overseeing a hearing."

"So," Samuel chuckled. "Our messed-up lives are more amusing to them than giving Abaddon a foothold in his quest for Rheagan."

Before I could respond, Galan strode into the room carrying a platter of Elora's cupcakes. Each threw off magical fireworks, filling the air with the scent of bergamot and spelling out, *Congratulations*. My brother took a knee beside the recovery bed and the rest of our Highborne and Haven family filed in behind him.

"There she is," Cowboy said, winking as he sauntered inside the door. "We signed you up for javelin throw at the next Academy Games. Nice arm, Queenie."

"It was quite a throw," Reign said. "Seasoned warriors lose their nerve when facing such evil. It took true courage, Lia."

I laughed. "I peed a little."

Samuel chuckled. "In the face of being terrified, ye found yer strength. A true fox if ever there was one, right Galan?"

Galan nodded. "And Bree and Julian now have blood and tissue samples to work with. The Talon may have new insight into Abaddon and how to defeat him, sweeting."

"And something else to celebrate," Kobi said, grabbing a cupcake and licking off the icing. "After years of trying, Merlin finally got Jade to fondle his junk."

The room burst out in laughter and I stared at them. How could they think Samuel's injuries funny?

"Oh my god," Cowboy said, "he actually gave his left nut to save Lia."

"Hey, be nice," Jade said, shaking her head. "He's only got one ball and you're busting it"

"Stop," Bruin added, wiping his eyes. "Can't you see he's getting testis?"

"Yeah, yeah, yuck it up, arseholes." Samuel rolled his eyes and handed me one of the cupcakes, leaning close. "Ignore them, Luv. They'll run out of steam at some point. So, back to the topic of yer choice being returned to ye. Any thoughts about that ye'd like to share?"

I took a bite of lemon-elderberry ambrosia and nodded. "Samuel and I mated," I announced. "He is the male I chose and is a lover more virile and generous than any female could dream to have as her own."

Samuel's cheeks flushed pink. "I . . . uh, meant share with me but that's that I suppose."

The room fell silent as all eyes fell on Galan.

Samuel cleared his throat and met my brother's glare. "I suppose ye have something ye'd like to say to me, aye?"

Galan straightened to his full height and Jade took his hand. "Verily, I do. Mayhap in a few days when you have recovered enough to stand before me. There is no honor in beating on a male when he is stitched and suffering."

"Okaaaay," Jade said, turning toward the door. "Enough excitement for one day, am I right? "Let's give these two a little alone time to rest and recover, shall we?"

I woke sometime later with the feeling of being watched.

"How fare thee, little one?" Cameron asked. He sat in a plastic chair in the corner of our recovery room.

"Exhausted. Anxious. Relieved to be finished with the proceedings. Terrified about what has yet to come."

Samuel mumbled in his sleep beside me and I waited until the slow rise and fall of his chest resumed.

"Apologies, Cameron," I said, quieter this time. "I have no right to complain to you of all people. Are you well?"

Aust's sire laughed, a deep rich tenor I loved. "Aside from being dead and watching my son and my mate suffer for it, I suppose I am well enough."

I sat up and folded the coverlet against my lap. "Would you like me to tell them something? A message from you might ease them?"

He shook his head. "No. Let them think me gone so they can begin anew. Elora is a beautiful female with a heart so large and gentle, if she knew I watched over her, she would never allow herself to love again."

"She mourns you to the depths of her soul."

"Because of that, I ask a favor of you—as a male and a mate."

"Of course. If I am able, consider them granted."

He swept a hand across his waist and bowed. "The patriarch of the mountain here. He is a male of worth, yes?"

"Reign," I said, thinking of the huge warrior. Whether in a suit of silk or leather, the male stood an intimidating force. "He is a great male, warrior, leader and father, yes."

"He is attracted to my Elora. I follow him through his day and he dotes on her and creates opportunities to meet her by chance in the halls of Jade's manse."

"Elora is a treasure of a female. There are likely a great many males who adore her."

"He is the one," Cameron said. "I have loved Elora for near two centuries and though she holds polite affection for him, her loyalty to me restricts her from considering him as a suitor."

"And what are you asking of me?"

Cameron shrugged. "If the opportunity presents itself, nudge her forward. Let her know I would want her to love again, to have a male care for her, love her and protect her from life's evils. If Aust is troubled, reassure him as well. As I am, I can no longer be that for them."

I blinked back the sting of my eyes and tried to swallow past the lump in my throat. "You are a true male of worth, Cameron. I, of course, shall do as you wish. I have a favor to ask of you as well."

His head canted, a wistful smile sparkling in his eyes. "Oh? And what may I do for you, sweeting?"

"I would like you to hold position in my court. A great many disgruntled souls roam the realm. Soldiers. Farmers. Males of worth from many races who have been cut down by the evil of the Scourge. I wish to unite them. If Abaddon and Rheagan plan to use the undead as a weapon, I say we rally an army to meet them head on."

The idea seemed to take him by surprise.

"If spirits are held here by vengeance or a need to watch over their families," I continued, "why not allow those brave souls to join the fight.

"Agreed, thy will be done."

Staring at the ceiling of the recovery room the next morning, I thought about the past weeks and months while the gray of a new day burned off the night. It tangled my mind how life twisted in agonizing ways and then blessed one to soar anew to great heights. Was it a balance? Was it fate versus free will? Was there any true control or must we always wait to see what unfolds?

Gemma, Tham and Cameron . . . all good people building productive lives killed before their time. Abaddon, Rheagan and the Scourge Raiders cared nothing about who they killed or what damage they caused. The killing must stop. Lost lives honored somehow.

"Why the long face, Luv?"

I brightened and eased to my side, careful not to jostle our injuries. "Just thinking about life and death in a realm so twisted by conflict."

"Ah right, good, nothing too heavy for first thing in the morning,"

I giggled and kissed him. "I'm going to ask Gemma to come live with us at the Silver Citadel if that is all right with you. She cannot communicate with the world here at Haven. She has been locked in silence too long."

"And she has the hots for a certain Highborne ghost who will be with us. Are ye sure yer not matchmaking?"

I shrugged. "Mayhap a little. I think everyone deserves to find happiness in the end."

He eased me closer to his side and stroked a strong hand over my belly and across my breast. "And speaking of happy endings . . ."

I pulled back. "Jade was clear we were not to engage in anything sexual until your wounds heal and all the swelling subsides."

"Weel," he said, drawing out the word, his brogue thick, "that might take days or maybe weeks. I cannae wait to lay my hands on ye. I've suffered enough."

He gave my nipple a gentle twist and then rubbed the peak as it rose to his call. My back arched and I was lost to his touch and the glorious scent of his attraction.

"I'm not suggesting any acrobatics but my hands and my mouth work just fine. Let me pleasure ye for a bit. It would do us both good."

My knees fell open as his hand skimmed down my belly and between my legs. I was powerless against him and he knew it. "Mayhap we should ask Jade first. Surely, intimacy on any level shall stir things best left unstirred."

His fingers met a warm rush of wet and he shook his head. "Touching ye eases my suffering far more than doctoring. Trust me, *mo chridhe*. I promise I'll be fine and swear I'll tell ye if I'm not."

My breathing quickened, my pulse kicking up a fuss. I thought about Cameron's favor for the woman he loved. The woman he would never pleasure again. "For you then," I said, turning to take his mouth with mine. "To ease what aches."

He chuckled close to my ear, his thumb beginning a torturous rhythm of rubbing me as the scent of sex filled my senses. "For me, then. *Amin mela lle,* my sweet *Ryanne.*"

My eyes rolled closed as he spoke to my soul. Until now, we never exchanged the words, our futures so uncertain. And though they were just words, something inside me awoke—empowered and strengthened.

How did any female survive loving a male this much?

"Aye, Samuel, I love you too."

AFTERWORD

THANK YOU FOR READING

I sincerely hope you enjoyed *Blind Spirit*, book four in the Scourge Survivor series. If you'd like to be kept in the loop on my release dates and receive my newsletter, subscribe here: Newsletter

If you'd like to know more about my other series, drop by my website at: www.jlmadore.com

If you'd like to read an excerpt from book 5 in the Scourge Survivor Series, *Fate's Journey*, scroll to the next pages or find it on Amazon here: Fate's Journey

May the Fates be kind,
JL Madore

ALSO BY JL MADORE

Find Me:

Social Media – Facebook, Twitter, Instagram

Web page – www.jlmadore.com

Email – jlmadorewrites@gmail.com

Reader Group – JL Series Updates

JL's Reverse Harem Titles

Guardians of the Fae Realms

Guardians of the Phoenix – Calli's Harem

Book 1 – Rise of the Phoenix

Book 2 – Wolf's Soul

Book 3 – Bear's Strength

Book 4 – Hawk's Heart

Book 5 – Jaguar's Passion

Darkness Calls – Keyla's harem

Book 6 – Dark Curse

Book 7 – Dark Soul

Book 8 – Dark Crown

Guardians of the Crown – Honor's Harem

Book 9 – Honor Restored

Book 10 – Honor Guards

Book 11 – Honor Bound

Book 12 – Honor Empowered

Rise of the Amberloq – Lark's Harem

Book 13 – Find the Fallen

Book 14 – Rise from Ruin

Book 15 – Trust and Triumph

Exemplar Hall – Jesse's Harem

Book 1 – Captured by the Magi

Book 2 – Jesse and the Magi Vault

Book 3 – The Makings of a Magi Knight

Book 4 – Clash with the Magi Council

Book 5 – The Unstoppable Storme

JL's More Traditional M/F, M/M, or Menage

The Watchers of the Gray Series (Paranormal)

Watchers of the Gray Boxset – Complete Series

Book 1 – Watcher Untethered – Zander

Book 2 – Watcher Redeemed – Kyrian

Book 3 – Watcher Reborn – Danel

Book 4 – Watcher Divided – Phoenix

Book 5 – Watcher United – Seth

Book 6 – Watcher Compelled – Bo

Book 7 – Watcher Unfeigned – Brennus

Book 8 – Watcher Exposed – Taharqa

The Scourge Survivor Series (Fantasy)

Scourge Survivor Series Boxset - Complete Series

Book 1 – Blaze Ignites

Book 2 – Ursa Unearthed

Book 3 – Torrent of Tears

Book 4 – Blind Spirit

Book 5 – Fate's Journey

Book 6 – Savage Love – epilogue novella

Aliens of Atlantis Series (Sci-Fi)

Book 1 – Taryn's Tiderider

Book 2 – Kai's Captive

Book 3 – Alyandra's Shadow

www.ingramcontent.com/pod-product-compliance
Lightning Source LLC
Chambersburg PA
CBHW020616260626
47157CB00003B/1035